HANGING FROM

THE

HIGH WIRE

BY BRIDGET STRAUB

This book is dedicated to every parent who has ever felt lost and overwhelmed.

You are not alone. It happens to the best of us.

CHAPTER 1

I could taste the ocean on his skin as I kissed his neck, the sun baking into my back, mixing with the heat of our entangled bodies... then I woke up.

"No, no, no!" I groaned, as Gavin walked out of the bathroom buttoning his dress shirt, and the baby screamed in the background.

"Someone's calling you," Gav pointed out, continuing through our room and out to the hallway, where I heard our four year old Meg, greeting him.

I was exhausted. Three kids in four years were too many. I waited to hear Jack, our resident wild man, but if he was awake, his baby brother Nick was out screaming him. Nick was also getting closer. Gavin returned, holding him at an arms distance as he wiggled and hollered.

"He's soiled himself," he frowned, attempting to hand him to me.

I twisted away from both of them, got up, and headed for the bathroom, calling back that Nick was his child, too, and he could change him, himself. I took my time in the bathroom and at the last minute, despite (or perhaps because) of Nick's continued wailing, I chose to take a shower. He was nearly five months old, and I feared I could count on one hand how many showers I'd had since his arrival. Well, maybe two hands, but still, I needed a shower and decided if not then, when?

The warm water washed over me like a tranquil waterfall, and I was just beginning to dissolve back into my dream, the one where I actually liked Gavin, when he barged in, pulled back the shower curtain, and with Nick poorly diapered in one hand, and Jack and Meg on either side of him, looked at me with outrage in his eyes.

"What in God's name do you think you are doing?" he demanded, as the kids also looked baffled.

It should have been funny. I told myself to laugh, but instead I was furious.

"Get out of here!" I yelled.

"I've a meeting in ten minutes!" he said, all stupidly British, while puffing his chest out like some over inflated cartoon body builder.

You see, while I was drowning in children, hormones, and housework, he still found the time to get to the gym four or five nights a week.

"Get out of here or so help me God, I will leave your sorry ass!" I threatened, (with what could only be considered by him as my crass American attitude.)

"Right," he said, with his typical disdain, "of course you would choose today to go insane. Come along," he told Meg and Jack.

Again, just the way he said it should have been enough to break the tension and make me laugh, but instead I sat in the tub bawling my eyes out, as the water that had started out feeling so good, now spit at me, and told me I was a terrible mother, and an even worse wife.

As the minutes passed, I alternated between self-loathing and blaming Gavin for everything. This was all his fault. I'd been perfectly happy to just be married for a while, and to concentrate on our careers before having kids. When Meg had come along that was enough for me, but no, he had to have another. He 'd promised we'd be able to hire a nanny, and that we'd still make time for ourselves. Guess what happened the one time we did that. Exactly, along came Nick, and as luck would have it, with him came Gavin's termination from the literary/talent agency he'd worked at, for the past nine years. Why? Because he was always so sure he could do things his way, and that he knew better than his bosses.

Any dreams I'd had of writing went right out the window, and he was now scrambling to run his own agency. There was never money for anything, most especially a nanny. As for time alone, he'd barely managed to show up at the hospital for Nick's birth. Even then he'd brought his mom and the kids with him. At this point I still hadn't found the time to ask him why.

I'm not sure how much time passed as I sat weeping in the tub, but after what felt like several minutes, Gavin returned with only Nick who was now hungrily sucking down a bottle of formula. Finding me hugging my knees in the tub, there was a lot of impatient sighing before Gavin cleared his throat and spoke.

"Look, I know you're having a bit of a collapse, and I'm sorry, truly, but I have to be going. Our livelihood depends on it, now doesn't it? I need to secure this client, Kelly. You're going to have to pull yourself together, and with some haste I'm afraid. I've called round to find someone to help you, but no one's available, are they?"

I looked up at him, a naked, drowned rat with red rimmed eyes, and wondered how much more of this either one of us could take. I could see him weighing his options as he considered taking an even sterner position, or softening his tone. He wisely chose the latter. Offering his hand, he helped me out of the tub, reached around, and turned off the water.

"I'll do my best to get back at a decent hour," he said, handing me my plush, albeit stale breast milk smelling, terry cloth robe, which hung from the hook on the back of the bathroom door.

I sniffled as I wrapped it around the body that was no longer my own. After three pregnancies, there were scars and extra pounds that I wanted no part of. There were also the swollen breasts that leaked in a fit of jealousy that Nick was nearby, but choosing to drink from a bottle instead of them. Of course as soon as Gavin handed him to me, he abandoned the bottle for my chest. Gavin smiled at the sight of him greedily feeding off of me like a crazed little vampire from one of the horror novels my sister, Colleen, had managed to publish, and sell hundreds of thousands of copies.

"See there, now that's better, isn't it?" he said, kissing the top of my head and walking away.

My tears burned the corners of my eyes as I did my best to remind myself that I loved this baby attached to my body. I couldn't silence the voices that told me I was one step closer to losing it, though. I didn't know what that meant, how it would all implode, but like a building being loaded with sticks of dynamite, implosion was clearly on the horizon.

I moved through the day in a numbed out depression, dressing kids, dropping Meg at preschool, and avoiding the school's director who was due to remind me that we were late with this month's payment. I took Jack and Nick to the park, hopeful that I could tire them out and be treated to an extended naptime, but it wasn't in the cards. Nick fell asleep in the car on the way home, and by the time I'd fed Jack lunch, Meg was being dropped off, and Nick was waking up.

My brother Devon called around three from New York, where he had moved six months earlier to write a tongue in cheek, political column for a new cutting edge online paper. Like the rest of my family, he was burning up the literary/journalistic world.

"So it's official, huh?" he asked.

"What?"

"Colleen and Keith."

Colleen and Keith what?" I asked impatiently, wondering what my sister and her perfect, pretty suntanned, and successful Hollywood wunderkind boyfriend had done now.

"Their engagement."

"They are engaged?"

"Colleen hasn't told you? He proposed to her at the WGA Awards last weekend."

"Oh, for fucksake, please don't tell me he won an award for that screenplay of his."

"Two."

I heard a blood vessel pop in my head as I clenched my teeth, and pictured a rove stick of dynamite going off on its own. I was the writer. I had always been the writer. I was the one meant to have a brilliant career, not everyone else.

"I can't believe she hasn't told you," Devon continued on. "I just assumed the two of you would be knee deep in wedding preparations. It was all over the internet this week. How have you missed it?"

"I don't have time to go on the internet these days."

"Oh," he said, sounding like the sensitive four year old I always picture him as. "So you haven't been reading my column?"

"I try Dev, it's just that since Nick came along, and Gavin has been all but absent setting up this agency of his, I can't even find time for a shower. I'll make a point of reading it tonight, I'm sorry, I promise I will," I scrambled, feeling guilty because he was always the first to read anything I wrote, even if I hadn't written anything worth reading in years.

"It's just that I value your feedback, and here I was thinking no word, was good word," he said.

"I'll read it tonight, I swear," I repeated as Jack rolled off the couch, biting his tongue and opening his mouth in a drooling, bloody wail. "You're alright," I said, reaching for him while telling Devon that I had to go. "Did you talk to Colleen, though?" I asked, hurt that she wouldn't have called me.

"She left me a message sarcastically thanking me for my congratulations, and saying I need to come home for the party."

"What party?"

"That's what I was calling to ask you. Is he okay, is that Jack?" he inquired as I did my best to swipe at the poor kid with a tissue before he bled on me.

"Yeah, I have to go. I love you. We should talk someday."

"Yeah," he agreed.

A few hours later, as I was cleaning up the dishes from the dinner Gavin had missed, it hit me that Gavin had to know. He reps writers. He spends half his life looking at computer screens. How could he have not heard about this?

He walked through the front door at seven thirty, and both Meg and Jack threw their arms around his legs, squealing in delight that he had returned. I didn't get it. I was the one there to feed them and soothe them all day, every day. I was the one who took them to the park, and who played with them, yet all he had to do was walk in the door to receive the reception of a teen idol.

"Why didn't you tell me my sister is engaged?" I demanded.

"I assumed she'd have told you."

"Well, she hasn't." I announced, walking away to pull pajamas from the dryer for the kids.

When I returned, I found everyone in the kitchen. Jack was in Gavin's arms and Meg was looking in the refrigerator for something to eat.

"It's too late to eat, put on your nightie," I told her, taking Jack.

"I'm looking for food for Daddy," she informed me.

"You didn't save me any dinner?" he asked me.

"There was no time to get to the grocery store today. We had hot dogs and mac n cheese, the box kind. You wouldn't have eaten it anyway."

He rolled his eyes as Meg suggested he could have cereal.

"No time? Really?" he questioned, now angry.

I knew that his next question would be what had I done all day, and warned him not to say it. He walked away in disgust while Meg suggested that perhaps we could go to the store the next day to get something he liked.

"Or," I said, "he could grow up and do the shopping himself once in a while."

Even at four, she laughed at the thought.

An hour later I was nursing Nick in the hope that he would fall asleep, while at the same time on my laptop, reading all about

12

the romantic, and seemingly spontaneous proposal Keith had choreographed as he'd accepted his award for original screenplay of a television comedy. Gavin was watching a basketball game while simultaneously texting and replying to emails on his phone. We were ignoring each other completely. I found it impossible not to wonder if five years from now Colleen and Keith would be sitting with the same distance between them. After all, Gavin used to light up my world, and he'd certainly led me to believe that I did the same for his. That night he just annoyed me.

CHAPTER 2

I decided I would wait to hear from Colleen rather than contact her myself. We were three years apart in age, but had been unusually close during our teen years. That had changed when she went away to college. Suddenly, she viewed me as an immature baby who didn't know what the real world was like. By Christmas of that first year, she was a completely different person, snobby and dismissive. When it came time for me to go to college, I purposely chose Brown over Yale, where she was finishing out her last year. Later, in our twenties, we were able to mend some fences, but recently I had begun to feel a divide again. I worried that it was due to her success, and my stalled career. I didn't want to be jealous of her, but it was almost impossible not to be. She had it all, or so it seemed.

The next morning Gavin announced that he would take Jack and Meg to breakfast for me so that I could do the grocery shopping. "Oh, lucky day," I thought. Nick had been unusually fussy during the night, and Meg complained that he'd disturbed her, while at the same time arguing with me over what she would wear to school that day. She wanted to dress in a skirt and boots, but I was afraid she'd slip in her boots when running around. Jack joined in on the complaining to say he was hungry, and wanted to eat before going to breakfast. When I said he could wait, he began melting down, and Gavin passed by asking why I had to be so difficult.

"Pack him a bag of cereal. He's only a baby, you know he can't wait." he said dismissively.

A lump rose in my throat as I slowly walked out to the kitchen, pulled down the box of Gorilla Crunch that was Jack's favorite, and tearfully poured some into a sandwich bag. I handed the bag to Jack who had followed me out, and he proceeded to drop it. The round balls of cereal bounced all across the kitchen floor as he said, "uh-oh!" Nick was in his swing in the family room and began crying, as Meg walked out in the boots I had told her not to put on, stepping on, and crunching the mess into an even bigger mess. Again Gavin passed by, this time on the phone. Pulling Meg away from the next piece of cereal she was about to stomp, and looking at her scoldingly, I heard him say into the phone, "No problem."

"Change of plans, sorry," he told me. "I've got to meet with Sirri Bingington. She's scouting agents."

"But you promised," I said, sounding like a desperate child.

"Don't be absurd. Do you know who she is? I have to go. Meg, help mummy clean up this mess, the baby needs to be fed."

"I can't do this!" I cried, getting up from the floor and walking directly out the front door.

"Kelly, what the hell is wrong with you?" Gavin asked, following me out.

"I can't do this. I can't be her. I'm not her. How can you not see that? I'm not her!" I yelled.

"What are you talking about? Sirri? Of course you're not her. Come back in the house, you aren't making any sense."

"I have to get out of here. I'm not a mother. I can't be a good mother."

He put his hands on my arms and looked at me sternly, the way I had seen him do with Meg and Jack a million times before when he felt they were acting out.

"Listen here, this is not a job you can walk away from. Your children need taking care of and you'll do what needs to be done because you are their mum."

"I can't," I cried, beginning to shake.

"Fuck," he mumbled, before pulling me into an embrace and kissing the top of my head. "Alright, now come on, we'll get help, alright? Just come back inside. They aren't safe in there alone, now are they? We'll get help," he repeated, leading me back inside where Nick was now screaming at a frenetic pace. "Go on then, Kel, you've got to feed him," he said, all but pushing me into the family room.

My milk let down instantly, so that I'd only be dripping all over myself if I refused. I carefully pulled Nick out of the swing, and let him latch on. He was angry, so he latched on, gulped, choked, screamed, latched on again, and repeated the sequence several times as Jack ran around in circles claiming to be Superman. I closed my eyes and wondered what was going to happen when I lost it for good.

I fell into a momentary fantasy, picturing myself on an island with a soccer ball as my best friend, like Tom Hank's character in *Cast Away,* and it seemed preferable to where I was. I reasoned that I could write my novel in the sand if need be, but at least I'd be able to think. I wouldn't smell of stale breast milk either. The sun would return my pasty skin to the golden brown it had been a long, long time ago, and my hair would be streaked with blonde highlights. I could go running every day and get my body back.

"Right," Gavin said full of false cheer, and snapping me out of my daydream. "I've arranged to drop Meg at Bob and Kate's. Kate will take her to school for you today, alright? And I've left a message with your Mum to see if she can't come in for a day or two so that you can catch up on some sleep. I've really got to be going. Just take some deep breaths, Sweetheart, and Jack's going to be a good little man today, aren't you?" he asked, patting him on the head.

"I'm Superman!" he announced again.

"Of course you are. You'll be mummy's superman. Come along Meg, give Mummy a kiss goodbye, we've got to be going. I can't miss this opportunity. Sirri Bingington is just the client we need to put us on the proverbial map, as they say."

They left, and the front door closing behind them echoed like the banging of a prison gate.

My mother lives two hours away in the little coastal town of La Jolla, California, where she and my father spend their days sitting out on their deck overlooking the Pacific Ocean, sipping pitchers of Sangria and lime, while working on my father's memoir. As a former editor at Simon and Schuster, my mother is overseeing this project personally. My father has traveled the world, both as a journalist, and in the past fifteen years, as a bestselling novelist, who has so far seen two of his books turned into films. To say I come from a literary family is an understatement.

To pretend that my mother was going to drop everything to come up and help with my kids, was nothing short of delusional on Gavin's part. She'd rarely bothered to take care of her own kids, so why would she take care of mine? The fact that she called later that afternoon could only be attributed to the wine, and her mad crush on Gavin.

"Sweetie, any word yet on Sirri Bingington? That would be a great match for Gav, don't you think?"

"I haven't heard from him. He leaves the house and doesn't let me know anything. For all I know he could be doing anything."

"Well with that sexy accent and charm, I'm sure he could, not that he would of course," she added hastily.

I groaned, and she told me I couldn't blame her for being aware of his appeal.

"It's so inappropriate, Mom."

"Only if I pursued him," she laughed.

"Really? You're saying that to me, your daughter?"

"Oh Kelly, what's wrong with appreciating the good taste of my daughters? Keith is a luscious specimen himself."

"Are you saying this in front of Dad?" I challenged.

"He's right here and couldn't care less, would you like to talk to him?"

"Please."

My Dad is just as irresponsible as my mom, and in fact, probably even more so, but somehow he is much less offensive.

"Hi kitten," he said taking the phone. "What's up? How's that novel of yours coming along?"

"Doesn't it bother you that Mom is lusting after my husband?'

"Not in the least, although I suspect it might bother him if he knew about it," he laughed, asking "does he know about it?"

"Who knows? Do I ever see him?"

"Well it's hard work building an agency."

"Built a lot of them, have you?"

"No, but I can imagine it's not easy. So how is your book coming along?" he asked again.

"I haven't written but two words since Nick was born, and you know it."

"What is it, a time thing, or writer's block?"

"What do you think?"

"Well, Honey, hire a nanny like we did."

"They expect to be paid, Dad."

"Not in the budget?"

"What budget?"

"You know I'd pay for it, but as I recall your husband doesn't accept offers of help too gracefully. In fact I believe it's one of the many things your mother admires about him."

"I'm losing my mind."

"Not you. You're my most brilliant child. You are going to write great things, you just have to make the time. You need to organize. Ask that foolish Brit if just this once I can't help you out. I really want to read what you have to say. You're my favorite writer, not that I wouldn't deny that to your brother and sister, speaking of which, great news about your sister, isn't it?"

"Fabulous. She hasn't even bothered to call me and tell me about it."

"Let me give you back to your mother. Love you."

I could practically see him tossing her the phone as though it suddenly had cooties. My Dad wants no part of mine and Colleen's discord. He likes to pretend that we are the perfect family, and that he has everything to do with that.

"What's the problem, still not writing?" my mom asked.

"I can't," I whined, as Meg and Jack began fighting over the play dough that I'd allowed them to play with against my better judgment. "Stop it, or I'm throwing it away," I threatened.

"But Mommy, he is trying to make me eat it," Meg complained.

"I have to go," I told my mom. "I'm guessing you weren't calling to say you are coming up to help with the kids," I sighed.

"You know I'm not good with kids, but we do miss them. Give them kisses from us, will you? But do hire a sitter for the party."

"What party?"

"The engagement party next weekend."

"I haven't been invited to any party. In fact Colleen hasn't even bothered to inform me she's engaged," I said, as Jack pushed Meg and yelled "Mine!" snatching the blue play dough. "I have to go," I repeated.

"I'll have Colleen call you with all the details," she said.

On the verge of losing it again, I decided I had to get out of the house for a while before starting dinner. I bundled Nick, putting him in the snuggly, and forced Jack into the stroller, while allowing Meg to take her scooter. We stepped out onto our small front porch and Jack told me he was cold, so I had to run back and grab his favorite blankie.

Figuring a short walk would at least break up the afternoon, we made it down the block and around the corner, before we ran into the local crazy. I shouldn't call him that, but I don't know his name. All I do know is that he has been a fixture in the neighborhood for longer than we have.

He's young, probably in his early twenties, and I've never been able to confirm whether or not he is really homeless, or if he just wanders the streets during the day. I never see him after dark, and although he is sometimes a little dirty, he has a variety of clothes. He looks to be in good physical condition, but he never looks us in the eye and will hide to avoid us, unless he is praying. More often than not he is knelt down on the sidewalk, saying a mumbled prayer, and rocking psychotically. It breaks my heart every time I see him. I look at Jack and it reminds me that this misplaced guy is somebody's little boy. That he was once a two year old with a favorite blankie, and it just makes me ache.

I hurried Meg around him and continued down the street, but I felt my eyes leaking as I did so, and it wasn't due to the cold air as I told Meg it was when she asked why I was crying. When we got back to the house I was more depressed than ever, and the message on the answering machine did nothing to cheer me up. It was from Colleen.

"God Kelly, I can't believe you are whining about my not calling you. I'm the one who should be complaining. Hello! I'm the one who's just gotten engaged, you know? You are supposed to call me. I'm a little busy anyway. I don't need Mom calling me in the middle of a book signing to guilt me. The party is next Friday night at the Beverly Wilshire Hotel, and definitely not for kids, but we do want Meg to be our flower girl of course. Oh, and it's formal so you are going to have to wear something good, okay? I trust you aren't pregnant again. No maternity clothes!"

And that was it, merely a mission statement. I momentarily thought to myself that she could go fuck herself, and that I wouldn't even attend the party, but I wasn't so crazy as to believe I could pull that off. Instead, I entertained fantasies of telling her she could only have Meg as her flower girl if she allowed Jack to be the ring bearer, and then he could toss the ring, and all hell would break loose.

Nick needed to be fed again, so I got Jack and Meg a snack, turned on Sesame Street, and silently rehashed every argument and hurt Colleen and I had been through over the years. I was just about caught up when Gavin came home and had a bouquet of flowers in his hand.

"Ask me how it went?" he beamed.

"How did it go?"

"Brilliantly, what's for dinner?" he asked, dropping the flowers on the breakfast bar.

I burst into tears because I'd forgotten to go shopping again.

CHAPTER 3

I have to give Gavin credit for knowing we were in trouble. The problem was, he had no idea what to do about it. He decided a good night's rest would take care of everything, and put me to bed. That night, for the first time in four years, he slept down in the nursery and dealt with his kids. Nick was willing to take a bottle in the middle of the night, but by morning he wanted to nurse, and according to Gavin, wasn't having any of this formula rubbish.

"You'll feed him now, won't you?" he asked, clearly praying that my head didn't begin spinning, or worse yet, that I'd start weeping again.

Gavin was raised to always be cheerful, and although he will tell you it was a ridiculous way to be expected to act during times of adversity, it is nonetheless what he is most comfortable with. I know this about him, and alternate between doing my best to comply, to challenging him to deal with my emotions. On this morning I wanted nothing more than to believe that a good night's sleep was all I had needed.

"Of course," I said, forcing myself to smile as I took our squalling son from him.

Nick latched on with such force that I instinctively let out a cry as I pulled him off my breast and nearly threw him across the bed.

"What are you doing?" Gavin demanded.

"He bit me," I wept.

"He hasn't any teeth Kelly, you're being ridiculous." he scoffed.

"I'm being ridiculous? I'm being ridiculous?" I yelled.

"Lower your voice. Do you want to petrify all three of the children?"

"Look at this?" I cried shoving my reddened breast under his nose.

He ran his hand through his hair before picking Nick up off the bed and trying to bounce him into some kind of submission. Nick was beside himself, and as I dropped my head to sob, I felt guilty for being both angry and scared of him.

"What am I to do, Kelly?" Gavin asked. "We can barely make the mortgage this month. I can't stay home, and we can't afford to hire someone to come in and help just yet. What am I to do?"

"I don't know," I cried.

"I can call Kate and ask her to take Meg again, but she can't be expected to care for Jack and Nick as well, now can she? For

God sake, Kelly," he said becoming overwhelmed by Nick's hysteria, and no doubt mine as well, "you have to feed him. Will you please feed him?"

I took Nick back and put my finger in his mouth trying to get him to latch on more carefully this time. Meg came to the door and hesitantly mentioned that she was hungry, and said she and Jack had finished the chocolate milk, which Gavin had apparently given them to buy their silence.

"Yes well, you'll just have to give us a few more minutes, won't you?" Gavin told her.

She turned and walked away looking dejected. Gavin paced around our bedroom trying to figure out what his next move should be, while Nick alternated between gulping greedily, to letting me know that he was still upset. I just kept thinking, "I can't do this anymore," and yet I knew I had no choice. I couldn't help but wonder what was wrong with me that I could want to give up on my own children.

"What is this really?' Gavin asked. "Do you think its chemicals and hormones?" he asked almost hopefully.

I shook my head.

"Then what? You don't love your children?" he asked accusingly.

I cried harder and Nick joined me.

"What then? Is it me? I've let you down? Well I'm sorry. We all make mistakes, don't we? I'm doing my best to remedy this, aren't I? What more do you want me to do? I'm working my arse off 24/7!"

"It's not you, it's me!" I wept.

"You what? If you want to write, bloody write!" he said angrily. "They take naps you know, and what about at night, huh? If you want this then you'll bloody well do it. I'm sick and tired of this nonsense. Your self-indulgence has got to stop. You are better than this."

"I don't have time to think! You don't understand. You've never understood. You haven't a clue what it takes to write a novel."

"Oh, haven't I? It takes determination and desire, and I'm beginning to think you have neither. I've been around writers my entire life. Believe me, I know what it takes."

"I'm so tired, and you think I can just give up sleep while still seeing to it that I have dinner on the table, and clean clothes for you and the kids, and then after getting the kids to bed you think I'd be able to write a single sentence that makes one bit of sense? You are fucking delusional."

"So instead what the hell are you doing? You're short changing us all, I'll tell you that."

"How many times can you make this about you?" I yelled.

"It's not about either one of us," he yelled back. "Christ, Kelly, it's about them," he said taking Nick and walking him, while holding him close and telling him it was okay and to calm down.

"I don't want to be a horrible mother," I cried.

He continued soothing Nick and as he began to settle, apologized.

"What are we doing? I know this isn't how you want it to be, Kel. I'm sorry. You're not a horrible mother."

"Then why can't I do this?"

"I don't know," he admitted.

"I need help."

"Yes, well I've just told you we can't afford help."

"So let my parents pay for it. I don't care anymore. What's more important to you, your kids or your pride?"

"Do what you want," he said, walking out while making it very clear that my choice would not be the same as his.

He returned two minutes later as I was trying to force myself out of bed.

"Kelly," he sighed. "Can't you please hang in here a little while longer? I'll help out more, I promise I will, alright? We can get you through this together, don't you think?"

"I don't know."

"Of course we can," he said, coming over and taking my hand to help me out of bed.

I stood up and he smiled.

"That's my girl. You'll be fine. You're a fantastic mother. Try to get a little rest when the kids have a lie down and I'll be home at a reasonable hour, alright? I love you," he threw in for good measure.

And so I began another day of disintegration.

CHAPTER 4

Sirri Bingington is the author of many books in the genre of romantic thrillers. She first received attention when she became involved with a well-known director who cheated on her with a well-known actress, and she chose to write about it, not once, but in an entire series referred to as the "Hollywood Chronicles". She was also taken to court for defamation of character by the aforementioned director, who lost his case, because after all, the whole world had read about what a scumbag he was, and he couldn't exactly deny anything she had written. Although at the time I had applauded Sirri for standing up to that arrogant jerk, it now came as no surprise that she would prove to be a lot of work.

She had told Gavin to send her the contract for representation, but then asked him to have dinner with her. I had dropped Meg at school, and then gone to the grocery store with both Jack and Nick, only to have my credit card denied. I'd been forced to go to the bank, get some cash, and return to do the shopping all over again, only on a tighter budget than I had originally planned. I'd spent the entire afternoon juggling the kids, laundry, vacuuming, and making Gavin a meal he might appreciate, only to have him call a half hour before it was ready, to say he wouldn't be home.

"That's great," I said, unable to keep my mouth shut.

"It can't be avoided," he told me.

"Well, I'm just glad that you didn't tell me before I'd had the pleasure of having our credit card denied in the grocery store."

"What?"

"And then I got to go to the bank before going back to the store. And then I came home to make you a dinner you wouldn't complain about, but shoo, that pressure is off now, isn't it?"

"How much were you buying?" he asked.

"Oh, my God! Really? Jesus, Gavin, have you any idea how humiliated I was?"

"Yes, yes, of course. I'll straighten it out. I'm sorry, but this deal is potentially huge. I can't blow this, can I?"

"No," I agreed.

"So I'll be home later," he sighed.

I hung up and swallowed hard, reminding myself that he was doing this for us, just as much, if not more, than for himself. This would be a great way of showing his previous agency that they'd underestimated him. He'd been a cocky asshole, but it wasn't complete ego on his part. He was good at his job, and had it not been such a prestigious establishment, several of his former clients, all writers, would have gone with him. The timing was all wrong was all, or so he had been told.

While attempting to compose myself, I vowed to be more understanding, trying to convince myself that we'd hit rock bottom, but now Sirri would pull us out. She was a name client, and once he had someone like her, others would certainly follow.

He didn't get home until close to eleven that night, and when he did, he reeked of cigarettes and wine, not to mention, perfume. He also had homework. She wanted him to give her a three year proposal, listing everything he could do for her that another agent couldn't. Then she wanted him to attend a party the next night.

"She wants to sleep with you!" I blurted out.

"Don't be ridiculous."

"Oh come on, dinners and parties? Is she dating you or working with you? I'll bet she didn't suggest you bring me along, did she? Does she know you're married?"

"You are letting your imagination get the better of you. Save it for your book," he said dismissively.

"She wants to sleep with you, and you are flattered by it. You probably want to sleep with her, too."

"Are you quite finished? What did you do this evening? Did you think to pick up a pen or go to the computer? Clearly your imagination is working," he said, with a fair degree of impatience.

"I'm not wrong," I said, as Jack began crying.

I walked out to deal with him, and when I came back to bed Gavin was snoring. When Nick woke up at three, Mr. "I'll Help

More", didn't budge. Apparently he'd had enough wine to sleep right through it, not that he didn't usually just roll over anyway.

The next day was no better than any of the rest, and I found myself missing my college roommate, and best friend, Corky. Corky, like me, was going to set the literary world on fire, and she is a wonderful writer, but two years into college she'd met a boy, Danny, who was an actor, and suddenly she'd wanted to be in the cast of every play he was in, and she still does. They are no longer a couple, but she was currently in the cast of a play he was starring in, loosely based on the life of Buddy Holly. They had been in Chicago for almost four months now. The show was a big hit, and there was talk of it going all the way to Broadway, although Corky said they'd probably fire everyone but Danny, and recast in New York. She was dreading the day she'd have to come back to Los Angeles, unemployed and alone. We'd mostly been communicating through emails and texts, because she had to save her voice for the eight performances they did each week.

Gavin was inadvertently responsible for her leaving in the first place. He'd introduced Corky to Scott, his closest friend, because he thought they'd make a great couple, and they had, until Scott decided things were moving too fast and he needed out of the relationship. Corky was still in love with him, and hadn't been able to stand sitting by the phone, waiting for him to come to his senses. Danny had told her to audition for the role of a back-up singer, and the rest was recent history.

When both boys actually took a nap at the same time, I set Meg up with a movie, and went back to my room to try calling

Corky. I wanted to ask if I was crazy to worry that Gav would ever have an affair, or be interested in Sirri. When her phone went straight to voice mail, I inexplicably began crying, but tried to speak at the same time. She picked up immediately.

"Kelly, what is it? What's wrong?" she asked, in an urgent whisper.

"I, I just need you," I sobbed, surprising even myself.

"Why, what's happened? Oh God, it's not one of the kids, is it?"

"I think I'm losing my mind. I can't do it anymore."

"Do what? Shit, Kel, I'm at the theatre, and I can't really talk right now, I'm supposed to be learning a new dance move. What's going on?"

"Nothing," I said, suddenly livid.

It was unfair and irrational, but I hung up and cursed her for being too busy to be my friend, and then threw a few pillows before deciding to take a bath.

I don't know why I did that. Again, it was irrational, but I felt entitled, and just went for it. Forty five minutes later, when Meg came back to tell me both boys were screaming, I was asleep in a tub of warm water. She also informed me the phone had rung about a hundred times. The phone rang a few more times over the remainder of the afternoon and evening, but I had decided I was in this alone, and didn't bother answering. Instead, I told Meg she could have whatever she wanted for dinner, and when she chose ice cream, Jack and I joined her.

Gavin came home at seven, wanting to know why I had refused to answer the phone all afternoon.

"What do you care? You never call anyway."

"I do actually, you see, this is why I know you haven't been answering. What am I to wear to this stupid party, that as it happens, you could have come to with me, if in fact we had a sitter, but of course we don't. Do tell me you picked up my shirts," he added, heading back to the bedroom, as Jack whined for him to look at his blankie cape.

I hadn't even bothered to drop his shirts to the cleaners, so picking them up was a moot point. Nick needed to be changed, so I grabbed a diaper and laid him on the floor. Gavin walked out with the shirt he wished to wear in his hand.

"You didn't even take them?"

I ignored him as Meg told him to guess what she'd gotten to have for dinner.

"I haven't time for guessing games, Meg."

"Guess!" she persisted.

"What am I to wear?" he demanded.

"Guess ice cream," she told him.

"Brilliant Kelly, so you've just quit then, is that it?" he asked.

I picked up Nick's wet diaper and threw it at him as I stood up and walked out the front door, this time having the good sense to grab my keys. I was in the car and backing out of the driveway before he could get to the porch and yell for me not to do this.

CHAPTER 5

I drove as fast and as far away as I could, coming up with all kinds of crazy plans as I did so. One minute I was going to drive up to San Francisco, and the next I was going to drive across the entire country for inspiration, and eventually to visit Devon. It wasn't until the gas light came on that I stopped to wonder how I would pay for any of this. I pulled over and searched the car for spare change, only finding a ten dollar bill. I wasn't sure that was even enough to get home. In a panic that I wouldn't find a gas station before stalling out, I began crying and hyperventilating all at once, and it slowly dawned on me that the implosion had begun.

I somehow made it to a gas station, but needed twenty minutes to pull myself together before going in to pay for what little gas I could afford. I then attempted to drive home, but ran out of gas two blocks away from the house. I managed to pull over enough to make it look as though I just didn't know how to park, and I sat there wondering what to do next. I knew I could walk home, but then what? Gavin and I were so out of sync by this time that I couldn't even gauge how he would react. He could be angry, concerned, or just pretend I'd now gotten this out of my system, and that nothing out of the ordinary had happened.

I felt paralyzed and sad. An hour passed before I was able to get out of the car and start walking. Normally I'd be scared to death walking down the dark street alone, so late at night, but the only fear I felt then was internal. I was dreading going back home and having to ask Gavin to forgive me for having run out on him. I felt guilty and inferior, and as if I didn't trust myself not to run again. I stood on the front porch for a good five minutes before trying the door that I knew would be locked. It was after midnight by now, but I could see that the light was on in the family room. I hesitantly put my key in the door and pushed it open, alerting Gavin that I was back.

"Bloody fuck, Kelly," Gavin said pulling me inside. "Where have you been? Are you alright?"

I just shook my head and he told me we'd get help.

"I'm so sorry," I sobbed, falling into his arms.

"We'll get help," he repeated, and we went to bed.

The warm southern California sun came streaming in through the window as I felt Gavin's lips on my shoulder. I looked back and saw that he had a devilish glint in his eye as his smile widened to reveal the fangs he was about to bite me with. I jolted awake, and opened my eyes to darkness. Gavin was asleep next to me, but I heard Nick beginning to stir in the next room, and my breasts ached with the need to feed him. When I got out of bed it was Gavin who jolted awake.

"Where are you going?" he asked.

"To Nick," I said.

A minute later, as I was feeding and rocking the baby, Gavin came and stood in the nursery doorway.

"Where did you go?" he asked softly.

"Nowhere, I just drove."

"What made you come back?"

"I don't know," I said, but looking up at him, I instantly regretted having answered that way.

He just nodded, and walked away, and I realized he'd wanted to hear that I'd come back for him and the kids, and not just because I had nowhere else to go.

I rocked Nick long after he had gone to sleep because I felt paralyzed again. By the time I went back to bed, Gavin was asleep, and I fell into another dream.

This time I was on an island with Corky, only she wouldn't speak to me. She was mad because we were on an episode of *Survivor* and she had sworn she'd never do reality TV. I kept trying to get her to lighten up, and to realize that if we won, she'd never have to work again, because Scott would be so impressed, he'd marry her on the spot. This brought a smile to her face.

"He would, wouldn't he?"

"You would be the awesomest woman in the world to him," I assured her.

We slapped high fives and began plotting our strategy, but then Gavin came stomping down the beach and threw a dirty diaper in my face. Corky was shocked.

"I had it coming," I sighed, as a horn sounded and we were told we'd been disqualified.

I awoke, and Gavin was already up and getting dressed. Jack came in missing his pajama bottoms, and pulling at his diaper, complained that it hurt. Sure enough he had a rash, so I forced myself to get up to get him some lotion along with a fresh diaper. Nick was the next to fuss, so I changed him too, and then I sat in the rocking chair nursing him and ignoring Jack's repeated requests that I feed him as well. Meg came in and asked if she could get some ice cream for breakfast.

"Of course not."

"Then what?"

"Then what? Then what? How should I know?" I snapped. "Get out of here and leave me alone. Go ask Daddy. Why do I have to do everything? Jesus, you all act as though you're as helpless as a baby. Are you a baby, Meg?" I taunted.

She burst into tears, and I realized how selfish and childish I was being.

"I'm sorry," I cried as she ran from the room.

"What you doing?" Jack whined.

"I never should have come back," I wept, as I heard Meg crying to Gavin that I was mean.

Jack eventually left as well, and I sat dripping tears onto Nick's face, as he objected and twisted to get a better position, wanting nothing more than to be allowed to enjoy his meal.

Gavin came back some time later, and seeing what a mess I was, announced that it had to be chemical.

"We'll find you a doctor, get you some medication, and you'll be feeling better in no time."

I wanted to believe him, but I knew it went much deeper than that, and so did he. When I didn't answer, he sighed.

"I don't know where else to start. Have you any better ideas? What would you have me do? Do you think I should just let you leave us then?"

I shook my head, and sighing again, he came over and touched Nick's face.

"You love them, don't you?" he quietly asked.

I nodded, and told him I loved him, too.

"Do you?" he asked. "Because I don't understand how you can want to leave us if you do."

"I'm not good at this. I'm hurting you, and them, and that's not what I want to do. Don't you get that?"

"What is there to be good at, Kel? You love them and feed them, and you be here for us. That's all we're asking, and if you love us as you say, then how hard should that be?"

"It's so hard, and I know it shouldn't be."

"It didn't use to be, did it?" he asked, but that was just it, it was, and it had been ever since we'd had kids, and I'd given up the things I did for me, in order to do everything for them.

CHAPTER 6

Colleen showed up, no advanced warning or anything. She just arrived as we were in the midst of this emotional discussion. Gavin took Nick and went out to answer the door, and hearing her, I snuck back to our room to wash my face, and to do my best to appear normal. A few minutes later, she came back to our room and hugged me, not saying a word. I was baffled. We stood there embracing for an uncomfortably long time, before she stepped back.

"What do you need?" she asked sympathetically.

I just stood there, staring down at my feet, not knowing how to answer.

"Come here," she said, taking my hand and sitting down on the bed.

I could hear Jack melting down about something in the other room, and looked toward the door, wondering how Gavin would handle whatever it was that was upsetting him.

"He can deal with it, Kelly. What's going on? Since when does he admit that you aren't in a good place?"

I began crying, and she said we needed to get out of there, and told me to get dressed while she went out to talk to Gavin. I didn't know what to make of this new, protective sister side of her, but I decided to go with it, and got dressed. She came back a few minutes later and asked where my car was. I explained about the night before, and she looked oddly proud.

"You walked out on him?" she smiled. "Ha! That must have blown his mind, the poor guy. No wonder he's being all forthcoming. Good for you, Kelly. It's about time. Come on, we're going shopping, my treat. You look good for someone having a breakdown," she added.

We walked out and Jack threw himself at my feet, weeping and begging for me to take him with us. I looked at Gavin and felt guilty, as he looked completely overwhelmed. I hesitated, but Colleen grabbed my arm, wishing Gavin good luck, before telling me to come on. Once out on the porch she called back, "Oh, Gavin, her car is over on Chester, she ran out of gas." Then she told me he'd be fine, and to come on.

She had a new, shiny silver Porsche parked in our driveway, that she unlocked with a wave of her key chain. The dark leather interior and wood paneled dashboard added nicely to the luxury of it all.

"Keith got this for me," she explained, adding, "It's a little flashy, I know, but it's so fun to drive that I can't give it back."

Again, I didn't know what to say to that, so I didn't say a thing.

"I have some Xanax if you want some," she offered, handing me her purse that I noticed was also a really soft leather, dyed a buttery yellow. "I'm not sure, though, maybe you shouldn't take it if you are still nursing the baby, are you?"

"Nick, yeah."

"I know his name, Kelly, God," she sighed, sounding more like the sister I was used to.

After a moment, though, she apologized.

"I'm fried too, I hate promoting the books. Can we be real for a minute? Paranormal fans are not normal," she laughed, "seriously demented and a little creepy. Not all of them, but you know."

I nodded, as her phone rang somewhere in her purse, but she didn't bother acknowledging it.

"Shouldn't you get that?" I inquired.

"Nope, I'm running away today, too. Relax and let the wind blow back your hair," she suggested, as she pulled onto the freeway and turned up the radio.

Needless to say, the car had a killer sound system.

I closed my eyes and wished we could just keep going, which for a long time we did. She said she'd discovered this great mall about an hour outside of town, in the middle of the meth capital of LA County. When I raised my brow, she told me Keith had been researching the area for something he'd been writing, and that they often took drives out to the middle of nowhere.

"It's inspirational, you should try it. Zylicol is really just Bakersfield," she said referring to the imaginary city in her books.

"Kids don't like long drives," I sighed.

"Yeah, I guess not, but you have to start writing. It's killing you not to, Kel. I can see it all over your face, and in your posture. You look beaten down."

"I am," I mumbled.

The mall was outdoors and beautiful, just as she had told me it would be. There were several fountains, a plethora of potted plants, and a variety of outdoor cafes. The weather was sunny and warm, with just the slightest breeze. Everything was perfect, and yet I was tired and guilt- ridden, on the verge of tears. I felt frumpy besides.

Colleen was slender and beautiful in a simple and effortless way. Her hair was the same honey blonde that mine was, but it was both longer, and had a better cut. Her skin was similar to mine, and yet she had the time to get the occasional tan, and her nails were professionally manicured. She was a half inch taller than me, and she also had on two inch heeled boots to give her some extra height. Lastly, she had better quality clothing, and could wear jewelry without worrying that someone might rip an earring through her ear lobe, or yank on her necklace. She was perfectly put together.

We wandered in and out of shops looking for engagement party dresses, and while she found several to choose from, I couldn't find anything in my size.

"You are being too picky," she insisted, handing me a turquoise green, low cut dress that I was sure would be too short.

I didn't feel like fighting, so I tried it on, disappointed that it was snug over my stomach, and as predicted, a little short. I walked out declaring it too small and she shook her head.

"Are you crazy? All you need are some Spanx, and a great pair of shoes."

"It's too short, and my boobs are about to spill out. The whole thing is too tight," I objected, pulling on it in an effort to breathe.

"You are wrong. I'm buying it for you. I'm telling you, when you see it all put together, you're going to feel sexy. You still have good legs. Gavin will be drooling. When's the last time you got all dressed up for him?"

"Our wedding," I muttered.

"Are the two of you even having sex?"

She shifted her weight and put her hand on her hip waiting for my answer.

"Don't be gross."

"Kelly! Since when is that gross?"

"Since I still need to lose the baby fat, and to get my shit together. I'm too tired to have sex."

She stared at me in stunned silence.

"No wonder you're depressed," she finally said. "God, this is worse than I thought. Gavin still wants to though, right?"

"You aren't grasping this whole reality. There is no time or energy for sex. He's working like mad, and I'm a frumpy, hormonal, lactating mess."

"Wow."

"Yeah, wow!" I agreed.

She told me to take the dress off while she processed what I had just told her, and that she'd be waiting for me at the register. I went back into the dressing room, sat on the bench and dropped my head in my hands, trying to process it myself.

Once Colleen had paid an obscene amount of money for the dress, she marched me over to a lingerie store where she insisted I not only get some Spanx, but also replace my nursing bra that she and the sale's assistant both declared to be hideous. I said I should call to check on the kids and Colleen said absolutely not, and that she had told Gavin we wouldn't be back until after dark. My mouth literally fell open.

"We have all day?"

"Of course we have all day."

"Gavin went for that?" I asked, suddenly feeling a love for him that I hadn't felt in a long time.

"I didn't offer him a choice, but sure, I guess in his own quiet way he did. I mean, he didn't stop us, did he?"

"I don't think I've ever had a whole day since Meg was born."

"Yeah, and then you think it's me ignoring you," she said shaking her head. "Let's get some lunch and figure out how we are going to change this."

"I could order a drink," I thought aloud.

"You could order two, you're not driving," she pointed out.

I felt almost dizzy, and definitely a little giddy.

CHAPTER 7

We chose a table out on the trellis covered patio of an Italian restaurant, next to the fountain, and while Colleen ordered a glass of wine, I asked for a vodka tonic. Then we oohed and awed over everything on the menu, while trying to make a decision as to what sounded best. In the end we decided that if I got the three cheese tortellini, she would order the parmesan chicken, and we'd both have a little of each. With that settled we sipped our drinks and listened to the comforting sound of the water trickling down the fountain. For the first time in what felt like forever, I relaxed.

"Tell me about your book," Colleen said after a few minutes.

"What book?"

"The book you want to write."

"There are a couple of them."

"So, tell me, what are they about?"

"One is loosely based on that summer when Dad was in Italy, and Mom decided to go surprise him, only I'd have to change it a lot to protect, well, myself," I laughed.

"Do you think he was fooling around with that journalist, really?" she asked, knowing exactly what I was alluding to.

"I don't know, and I'm not sure if in the book he would be or not. I kind of don't think it would be about a sexual betrayal as much as a betrayal of what the wife thought was unique between them, namely the intimacy and connection they had."

"That summer is the single most frightening thing about marrying Keith," she confessed. "I feel as if by agreeing to marry him, I have handed over the last part of my heart, the part that grew hard that summer. I swore I'd never allow myself to love anyone with complete abandon, because it gives them the power to bring you to your knees. I don't want to be that vulnerable. To be honest with you, I sometimes think that's why you and I fight as much as we do. They did a real number on me that summer," she smiled.

"Me too," I admitted.

We'd been eleven and fourteen at the time, and my dad was spending six weeks in Italy researching an article on the Italian government. My mother was all over the place that summer. Her moods changed so often that Colleen and I worried she was pregnant again. Devon was eight at the time. We'd been invited to the upstate New York home of an editor friend of my mother's, and were vacationing on a lake, while crushing on the sixteen-year-old boy who lived next door. Late one night, out of the blue, my mother announced that we were

49

leaving and going to Italy. In retrospect, it is not clear to me if my father was having an affair or not, but it is obvious that my mother thought he was.

When we arrived to surprise him, it was this journalist, Jessica, who was supposedly assisting him, that answered the door of his hotel suite. My Dad was caught off guard, although she and he were not alone. There were a whole group of expats playing a game of cards, but there was an electricity in the room that appeared to both amuse, and intrigue the others once we had arrived.

The next three weeks were nothing but misery. My mom pretended to like Jessica, who continued to assist my dad in his research, and Jessica pretended to like my mother, but it was clear that they were both in a constant battle for my dad's attention. There were muffled arguments almost every night, and when my dad was out working, my mom was wound so tight that if we so much as asked for a treat we were in for a lecture, and on occasion, the back of her hand. Not something she had ever done before. Of course up until then, we had generally been in the care of a nanny, but that was another strange thing about that summer, our nanny of the past five years had suddenly, and inexplicably, been fired.

"You don't think Dad and Elizabeth..." I started to ask.

"Eww, God no," Colleen laughed, before I could even complete the question. "She was fired because she told Mom that Dev was less than perfect. I heard the firing. Mom said she wouldn't have anyone watching us who was not going to celebrate our differences, but was instead trying to make us conform to what society purported to be normal. Dad backed her up on it too."

"Yeah, it was just a weird time I guess."

"What other book have you got percolating in that brain of yours?" Colleen asked.

"I want to write something about a group of friends coming of age, and the way in which childhood friendships change. You know, how the people you think you'll always be closest to, you end up drifting apart from, and sometimes the stronger connections are with those people you originally took for granted."

"I'd read that," she nodded. "Those could both be great books, Kelly. You have got to write them. Certainly you could work something out with Gavin. I mean why can't you say from eight until ten each night you are going to lock yourself in your room and write?"

"Other than the fact that sometimes he doesn't get home before eight, I don't know," I said, never having considered that I could do that. "I mean, half the time I'm falling asleep by nine, but maybe that could work. He says if I want to write, I will."

"Sure, so long as he takes a turn with the kids once in a while," she said.

"It would be nice to finally get these stories out."

"Of course it would. We are writers. This is what we do. We have stories to tell, and tell them we must. You can't ignore the gifts you have been given, and you are a great writer, we all know that."

'We do?" I asked.

"Yes," she said as our food arrived.

We took a moment to organize and divide up our meal, and then she began again.

"Of course in order to write, you have to live, too," she said.

"In what way?"

"In every way. How can you and Gavin not be having sex? Nick is five months old!"

"I know, but there's never time."

She looked at me in clear disbelief.

"I swear."

"Do you kiss? Please tell me you kiss."

"Sort of, sometimes," I shrugged, while franticly searching my mind for when the last time was that we had really kissed.

I couldn't remember.

Finding it alarmingly hopeless, I changed the subject and asked when she and Keith were planning to be married, and what kind of ceremony they were considering.

"He wants to get married up near Yosemite at this beautiful lodge that his aunt and uncle own. It's really spectacular up there, but I don't know," she frowned, "a location wedding could complicate things."

"Definitely," I agreed, immediately imagining trying to keep Meg and Jack from falling off a cliff, or into a rushing river.

"He wants to get married soon too, and that's another issue. I have some time before the final book in the series is released, and the promotion for this one is wrapping up, but he's working until May, which is when he wants to do this."

"May of this year? This is March. Have you any idea how impossible that would be?"

"Of course I do, but we want to honeymoon in Europe and he'll have to be back to work by July, so you know, I was thinking that if I made you and Dee Dee co-maids of honor, we might be able to pull it off, don't you think?"

Dee Dee was Colleen's best friend and a control freak. I just looked at her because she knew Dee Dee was not my favorite person, and even she had to laugh.

"I know, Keith gave me the same look. He's with you on this one, but I know it's too much to ask you to do alone, and Dee Dee may be a bitch, but she has great organizational skills and she loves me, so in this instance it could work, don't you think? I mean she's mellowed a lot in the last year, I promise. She's with this great guy, Roman, and he's been a good influence on her."

"There are just so many little details. May what?" I asked, ignoring the fact that I hated Dee Dee.

"May 19th. I wanted the next week for Memorial Day because I figured people wouldn't have to work, but obviously the lodge is booked then. The week before, though, will make it easier for people to find accommodations, because not only is there the lodge, but his aunt and uncle have a big house up there that they don't even use."

"Won't they be at the wedding?" I asked.

"Oh, right, but still, it'll work. We aren't going to have a huge wedding," she said. "It's either this or have it at Mom and Dad's overlooking the beach and all, but if you want to talk controlling, well, I think we both know how Mom can be," she shuddered.

"Bridal bouquets have roses Kelly! No daughter of mine is walking down the aisle with a handful of tulips. Are you going to wear wooden shoes?" I mimicked, remembering all too well the issues she had tried to control in my own wedding. Colleen laughed and we both agreed a Yosemite wedding would be preferable.

After lunch we shopped for shoes, and then went for a mani/pedi. It was after that, as we headed back to her car, that she suggested we stop at Dee Dee's before returning to my place, just so that she could prove to me that Dee Dee had changed. I really didn't want to, but she had me trapped. I knew getting together would be inevitable if I agreed to be a part of the wedding, and there was no way I was going to refuse to be in my sister's wedding, so I went along with her.

CHAPTER 8

On the way back into town Colleen filled me in on how Dee Dee
and Roman had met, explaining they'd each been on vacation
in Hawaii, with their respective families. They kept showing up
at all of the same places, got to talking, and discovered they
had much in common. For example, he'd just bought a house
and had no idea how to decorate it, as that had been his ex-
wife's job. Dee Dee is an interior designer. She had also been
through a divorce, and they lived in the same city. When they
returned to LA, she went to his house for a consultation, and
she'd been living there ever since. I had to admit the Dee Dee I
knew never would have moved so quickly.

It came as no surprise that the house was palatial, but it was
also located in the hills just above Studio City, where I lived. In
essence, she could gaze out her floor to ceiling windows and
look down on my neighborhood of considerably smaller homes.
Spanish in design, there was an abundance of charming
archways, both inside and out. We were greeted at the front
door by an over-zealous Labrador and Dee Dee, who did her
best to hold him back.

"Down, Killer," Colleen laughed, as Dee Dee called for Roman to come control his dog.

Roman was older than I expected. He had gray hair that curled a little at the edges where it was bordering on getting too long, and he had deep laugh lines around his liquid brown eyes. Dressed casually in expensive looking sweats and a thick sweater, his appearance screamed successful Hollywood producer, which is what Colleen had told me he was. In contrast, Dee Dee looked to have botoxed out any of the character lines she should have had by thirty seven, which like Colleen, was how old she was.

Roman apologized for the dog, and took him out to the backyard. Dee Dee told me I looked wonderful, but at the same time she exchanged a quick glance with Colleen that made it clear she didn't really believe it. Roman returned, and she formally introduced us.

"You're the one with all the babies, right?" he smiled. "Come in and sit down. Can I get you something to drink?" he offered, ushering us into their beautiful living room with the most spectacular views of the entire San Fernando Valley.

"I'm good, thanks," I said, as Colleen told Dee Dee she had to give me a tour of the house.

She proudly led us through room after room of beautiful windows, hardwood floors, and custom furnishings, the likes of which I could only dream of one day owning. It was as perfect a house as you could imagine, and yet it lacked any sign of living. There was no clutter, and nothing was out of place. It looked like a model home. Granted, the nicest one I had ever seen, but it made my chest hurt both because my breasts were reaching full and I needed to feed Nick, but also because as filled with beautiful things as it was, it felt empty.

We settled in the living room once the tour was complete, and Dee Dee said she had a ton of ideas for the wedding, bridal shower, rehearsal dinner, etc.

"I think we should go up to the lodge, just the three of us, either this week or next at the latest, so that we can scout locations and get a real visual picture of the layout," she suggested.

"Just for the day," Colleen told me.

"And I would leave the kids where?" I asked.

"A babysitter," Dee Dee said.

"We don't have a babysitter, and I'm still nursing."

"Just for the day," Colleen repeated.

"Colleen, I'd love to, I really would, but they have laws about these things. You can't leave them, even just for the day."

"We'll figure something out," Dee Dee said, waving me off. "What day works best for you?" she asked Colleen, throwing in that Thursdays were best for her.

Colleen pulled out her phone, searched her datebook, and announced that she could do this Thursday, but not the next.

"So we'll go this week. That's really best because this is going to be a mad rush. It's only a five to six hour drive," Dee Dee assured me, as if six hours in a car was somehow going to make this okay. I concluded she hadn't changed a bit.

For the next hour the two of them discussed dress shops, debated designers, made plans to go to florists and caterers, bakers and make-up artists, all the while excluding me as they pretended they were doing no such thing.

"Colleen, I really need to get home before my boobs explode," I interrupted.

She looked annoyed only for a second before agreeing that we could talk again the next day. We left, and I told her she had to know that there was no way I was going to be able to accompany her to all of these places.

"We can take the kids with us at least some of the time. I mean come on, what kid doesn't love a bakery, right?" she asked.

I nodded, and she pointed out that Meg was in preschool four mornings a week so sometimes it would just be two kids, and she was sure that between the three of us we could handle two kids.

"Maybe," I said.

"You need to get out, Kelly. You have to live, remember? This is going to be good for you. I know you think I don't have a clue what your life is like, but it doesn't take a rocket scientist to see that you need to shake things up."

I couldn't argue with that.

As soon as we drove into the driveway I could see Gavin through the front window walking Nick, and by the time we reached the porch, we could hear Nick's wailing. My milk let down and I groaned as it quickly soaked through the breast pads. Gavin's friend, Scott, was sitting on the couch with his feet up on the coffee table, and held a sleeping Jack in his lap.

"How could you not answer your phone?" Gavin angrily asked Colleen, as he all but threw Nick at me.

"I told you we'd be gone all day," she defended.

"Bloody irresponsible of both of you. I'm going to get your car," he announced, slamming out of the house.

I looked at Scott and Jack, and he told me Jack had cried for an hour and a half before falling asleep.

"And that one," he said referring to Nick, "well, he never stops does he?"

Colleen sat next to Scott and told him Jack might be a bit of a handful, but said he had to admit he looked pretty innocent now. She and Scott had known each other even before Gavin and I had first met. They were both at Yale together, and had shared several classes.

I walked back to the nursery to feed Nick, but was able to overhear their continued conversation once Nick stopped pulling away from my breast every five seconds to wail at me.

"So how nuts is she?" Scott asked.

"How nuts would you be living in this 24/7?" Colleen asked back.

"Hey, three hours has been more than I can take," he laughed.

"She has to write or she's going to kill herself."

"Seriously?"

"I would," she said.

"I know you would," he said, "but is she really that depressed? Gavin thinks it's at least partially chemical."

"So why the hell isn't he doing anything about it?"

"He's trying to figure it out."

"And maybe when she's dead he'll have his answer," she sighed.

"So tell him. Hell, tell her. Why isn't she doing anything about it?" he asked.

"Because she can't get out of the house. She says Gavin doesn't even get home until after eight, and they aren't even having sex. He's not cheating on her, is he?" she demanded, much to my disbelief.

"Are you crazier than her? He's working to pay for this house, and so that she can stay home and be miserable all day."

"Yeah well, would it kill him to make her feel attractive?"

"Are we really discussing this?" he asked, as I wondered the same.

"Yes Scott, we are. Are you having sex these days?"

"How did this become about me?" he laughed.

"Just are you or aren't you?"

"On occasion. Not as much as I'd like."

"Which makes my point. People need to connect."

"Okay."

I heard the front door open and they turned their attention to Gavin.

"Did you find it?" Scott asked.

"It's dead," he announced.

"I told you that this morning," Colleen said. "She ran out of gas."

"Yes, thank you, I know that. Now I've gotten some gas and need one of you to give me a lift back there so that I can drive it back here."

"You can't walk two blocks?" Colleen asked, as admittedly I thought the same.

He obviously turned to leave again because I heard Scott telling him to wait up, and Jack let out a cry as he must have been transferred to Colleen. The door closed and Jack cried for me.

"Mommy's here, don't cry Jackie," Colleen told him.

She brought him back to the nursery where he took one look at me feeding Nick and wept even louder.

CHAPTER 9

I didn't hear from Colleen the next day as she had promised I would, but Gavin heard from Sirri, who wanted to meet for drinks so that they could go over his proposal. He swore he wouldn't be gone for long, and then didn't return for over three hours. When he did however, it was with the signed contract in his hand.

"This will change everything," he told me. "Her new novel is nearly complete. This is the break we've been waiting for."

I wanted to be excited for him, for us, and yet I felt incredibly apprehensive.

"Well, say something," he sighed.

"It's great, congratulations," I said, forcing a smile and kissing him.

"Mommy," Meg called, with impeccable timing, "I can't get my blankets untangled."

I went in to untwist them and Gavin followed me, telling Meg that he was going to buy her a treat the next day for having been so good this weekend. Needless to say she wanted to know what kind of a treat, but he told her she'd just have to wait and see. We both said goodnight, and then I headed for our bedroom to get my laptop. Again he followed me and when he did, he closed the bedroom door.

"I was going to try to write," I said.

"They are all three in bed at once," he smiled, unbuttoning his shirt, "and we've got something to celebrate."

"Oh God," I accidentally groaned aloud.

"It's been a long time, Kelly," he said, sitting on the bed to take off his shoes.

"Gav, it's not that I don't want to," I lied, "it's just that I'm not on the pill right now, and I don't know that we have anything else."

"Don't worry," he said, reaching into his pocket and pulling out a pack of condoms. "I thought of that too."

"Oh, good," I said, not at all convincingly.

"Oh stop, come over here," he said, offering his hand.

I stood in front of him and he held both of my hands in his, looking up at me.

"You used to like this," he reminded me.

"I know, but I was fifteen pounds lighter and awake back then."

"Oh I'll wake you up," he grinned, pulling me onto the bed.

"And the fifteen pounds?" I thought to myself, "How are you going to erase those?"

I insisted that he turn out the light, but that made for a lot of fumbling when it came to opening the condoms. Still he managed, all the while telling me it was silly to feel insecure in front of him, and that I was beautiful to him, and always would be.

I tried to let it go, to get out of my head, and not to listen for the kids, but I couldn't do it. I was sure I heard Nick beginning to stir, and I wound up faking it just to hurry things along. Then, of course, I felt both guilty, and a little angry that Gavin chose to believe my performance. Two or three years earlier, he'd have seen right through it and been appalled. Now he just finished up, told me he loved me, and rolled away from me mumbling something about getting some sleep because he had to be up early.

It was 9:25pm.

I lay awake listening for Nick who now seemed settled. I considered getting up to write, or taking a bath, deciding on the latter, with the reasoning that I could sort through ideas for my book while I relaxed. As soon as I put one foot on the floor, Gavin objected.

"Stay," he moaned, pulling me back. "Just sleep Kel, you'll be tired tomorrow if you don't."

"Right, because that's all this is," I sighed, knowing that nothing had changed.

The entire weekend had come and gone and I'd never found the time or the nerve to tell him that I was a writer and had to be allowed to write, and that that meant he had to step up. I wanted to tell him he had to give me time for myself and my needs. Instead I went to sleep and got up with the baby in the middle of the night, and again at six a.m. with Jack when he had a coughing fit and told me his throat hurt.

Gavin was up and out of the house by seven, and I was left with a cranky, coughing, stuffy nosed two year old who wanted nothing more than my undivided attention. Unfortunately, his baby brother wanted the same, and his older sister had needs of her own. Dee Dee called around noon to suggest we get together to discuss Colleen's bridal shower.

"I can't go anywhere today, Jack is sick," I informed her.

"We don't have any time. I mean I'm thinking late April, aren't you?"

"Aren't I what?"

"Thinking late April for her shower."

"Sure, if that's what she wants, I guess," I said, as Jack coughed in my face and whined that he wanted juice.

"He doesn't sound good. Have you taken him to the doctor?" she asked.

"No, he just does this. It'll be croup tonight, and we'll have to steam him. It's a whole cycle," I sighed.

"Alright, tomorrow then. I'll pick you up around ten," she said, hanging up before I could object.

For the rest of the day I was walking a tight rope, doing my best not to be overwhelmed by Jack and Nick, and their need to physically be on me all day long. Every time I put one of them down, they would cry. Nick slept on occasion, but Jack would only sleep on me. Meg was incredibly patient and sympathetic to the fact that Jack wasn't feeling well. She'd seen him like this enough times in the past to understand that he was truly miserable. Plus she was anxiously waiting to see what treat her daddy was going to bring her.

When he called around three just to check in, I was surprised. I also reminded him of his promise, and told him how good Meg was continuing to be.

"Right, I'd forgotten that. What should I get her?"

"P-O-L-L-Y P-O-C-K-E-T-S," I spelled out."

"Yes, excellent, I'll stop at Target on my way home. Do you need anything else?'

"There's not going to be a real dinner because I can't get the boys off of me long enough to throw anything together," I warned.

"I'll pick up a pizza."

"Thank you," I said, suddenly fighting back tears.

When Gavin and I first got together, I did all of the stupid things girls do in front of guys when they want to be thought of as perfect. Among other things, I never ate too much in front of him, in fear of his thinking I was a pig. That is, until the night we went for pizza. That night all pretenses were tossed aside as

I devoured piece after piece, all but moaning as I did so. From that point forward he used to appear with a pizza any time we'd had a disagreement, and he'd sometimes bring one as a treat simply because he knew how much I loved a good deep dish, cheesy pizza. His saying he'd bring one home that night meant a lot.

CHAPTER 10

The next morning I had forgotten about Dee Dee and her plan to meet. I was all but walking into walls after a night of walking the floor with Jack, keeping him as upright as possible, and trying to help him breathe his way through another bout of croup. Gavin had fed Nick for me at his usual 3:00 a.m. waking, but Jack wanted me and only me, so Gavin had gone back to bed as soon as the baby was down again. I had spent hours steaming Jack in the guest bathroom, sitting on the edge of the tub, nodding off and jerking awake.

Seeing that I was barely functioning at breakfast, Gavin arranged for our neighbor Kate to drive Meg to school again, and asked if I didn't think I should be taking Jack in to see the doctor. I knew the routine by now. That would only prove to cost us money we didn't have because our co-pay was high.

"They'll only tell me to do what I'm doing," I sighed.

He nodded, and said he had to be going, but hoped I'd get to sleep when the boys slept. Then he and Meg cheerfully left to walk over to Kate and Bob's.

Kate and Bob live directly across the street from us, and I swear it is just naturally lighter on that side of the street. Not only does the sun appear to shine more brightly, but the people on that side of the street are unusually upbeat. Gavin jokes that he both loves and detests them for it. Bob is a firefighter, and Kate is a stay at home mom to Bea, seven and Griffin, four. Kate worked as a preschool teacher before having kids, but is now content to stay home and "be there" for her kids. Their house is always clean, and their garden is the first to bloom each spring.

Jack and I watched Sesame St. and sat in a vegetative state until Nick tired of the baby swing I'd put him in. He grew increasingly fussy, but it was too early to feed him again and Jack wanted me to put Nick down, so he kept climbing on me, and trying to push his brother out of his way.

"You cannot do that!" I scolded.

Being as tired as I was, Jack fell to pieces and I felt myself on the verge of doing the same. I wanted nothing more than to curl up and have a good cry, but then I heard the doorbell. I must have looked as bad as I felt, with my hair uncombed, dressed in only my robe, and Nick squalling in my arms. I opened the door wondering who was going to try and sell me what. Dee Dee looked positively startled. I was automatically embarrassed.

"Kelly?" she asked, as if somehow she wasn't sure.

"This isn't a good time," I said, as Jack ran to the door still crying and coughing, his nose beginning to run.

"Obviously," she said, pushing past me to come inside.

"Shit," I cursed as a tear escaped my eye.

"Give me the baby. Is this Nick or Jack?" she asked, taking him from me.

"Nick," I answered, swiping at my cheek.

"What's the matter, Nick?" she asked cuddling him like a pro.

I was shocked. Jack threw himself at me, so I picked him up and told him to calm down, before apologizing to Dee Dee for how messy the house was.

"Is he okay?" she asked, looking at Jack as he continued to bark like a sad sea lion.

"Yes and no," I sighed. "He will be in another day or two. It's croup. He gets it every couple of months."

"Why?" she asked.

"I wish I knew," I said, inexplicably bursting into tears.

Mostly it was exhaustion, but it was also the overwhelming realization that I didn't know why he kept getting it, and I hated how miserable it made him. Suddenly I was overcome with love and sympathy for him, and wanted nothing more than to be able to make him feel better.

"Oh Kelly," Dee Dee said hugging me, "Honey, he'll be okay."

"I'm a mess," I confessed.

"Of course you are. Your baby's sick," she sympathized. "What can I do to help?" she asked.

My mouth nearly fell open. I wondered if I had somehow lost my mind, because this was so far from the bossy, self-obsessed girl I knew, that I figured I had to be imagining this. Not only that, but Nick was now contentedly resting on her shoulder.

"I'm going to take him outside for a minute," I sniffled, referring to Jack, explaining that sometimes fresh air made him stop choking.

"Sure, we're good," she smiled, giving Nick a squeeze.

Jack and I sat out on the bench we had in our hideously neglected back yard. Before Gavin had lost his job we'd been able to afford a gardener, but it had been months since then, and although Gavin and I had reasoned that we should be able to handle our small yard on our own, we hadn't. Slowly, Jack calmed down and as he did so, his coughing began to subside.

"Who that lady is?" he asked, as I was still wondering the same.

"Dee Dee, she's Colleen's friend."

"Colleen is here?"

"Nope."

"I tursty," he announced, actually getting off of me to go inside and further investigate the stranger in our house.

Dee Dee was sitting on the family room sofa, next to a forgotten burp cloth, surrounded by discarded toys, sippy cups, and a basket of unfolded laundry, making silly noises that had Nick breaking into a smile.

"Aw, feeling better?" she asked Jack.

He hid behind my leg, but then peeked around to say hi.

"Colleen's on her way over, so we can either just talk here or do this tomorrow. Whatever you want," she informed me.

"Colleen," Jack repeated happily.

"We can try to talk here, I guess." I agreed.

To be honest, at that point there was a part of me that never wanted her to leave.

I got Jack some juice and quickly tried to pile the breakfast dishes, and put away a few toys. Dee Dee told me not to worry about the mess and asked where Meg was. Just as I was telling her that she'd be back around lunch time, the phone rang and it was Corky.

"Why haven't you called me back?" she demanded.

I just looked at the phone, thinking, "Are you kidding me?"

"Kel, Gavin says you're a mess."

"When did you talk to Gavin?"

"I called him yesterday because I was worried you were mad at me."

"I am mad at you," I said.

"I tried calling back a couple of times, but I couldn't get into a lengthy discussion in the midst of rehearsals. Come on, you have to understand that."

"Yeah."

"So why are you shutting me out?"

"Because you aren't here, why do you think? I really can't talk right now," I said, as Jack pulled on my robe and whined to be picked up again.

"Is that Jack? Let me talk to him," she insisted.

"It's Corky," I explained, holding the phone to his ear.

"Who it is?" he questioned, as I saw Colleen on approach.

I walked to the front door to let her in and she shook her head when she saw me.

"Oh Kel, did our day do nothing?"

"Did you seriously think it would?" I asked, taking the phone back from Jack and telling Corky I couldn't talk, but that I missed her even if we did never get to talk.

"Well, fear not because I got my walking papers. We're closing in a week."

"Really?' I asked, trying not to sound too happy, but secretly delighted.

"Yes," she sighed.

"So you'll be coming home?"

"I don't have a home anymore, remember? I gave up my apartment. Why in hell did I give up my apartment?" she groaned.

"Because you hated it, but you can stay here until you find a place," I offered.

"Isn't Nick in my room?" she asked.

"We'll figure something out."

"Okay, but we should talk. I'm going to call you tonight, okay?"

"Sure," I said, so relieved that she was coming home that I felt, at least momentarily, a thousand times better.

CHAPTER 11

Jack was no better on the second night, and having listened to him bark endlessly, Gavin insisted I call the doctor the next day to make an appointment. I explained to the nurse what was going on and she told me what I already knew, which was that it generally lasted three nights. She said if it hadn't cleared up in the next few days to call back, but that there wasn't anything they could do, and that I knew the drill. I hung up and cried, while Gavin said we needed a new doctor.

Once again he paced around the room, running his hands through his hair, trying to decide what to do about the fact that now neither Jack nor I was functioning.

"What about online, have you looked up homeopathic treatments for this?" he asked, grabbing my laptop and beginning to search.

He went from site to site, becoming increasingly annoyed with the lack of options, rolling his eyes, and telling me that it said to comfort the child.

"There's some bloody brilliant advice. All better now, aren't we?"

His phone rang and when I heard him saying he had a family emergency and would have to cancel, I was relieved that he knew better than to leave me alone with this. He hung up and I tearfully thanked him. He hugged me but Jack objected, as he was in my arms and between us. Gavin went back to looking for solutions online, and pointed out that one said we could give him some Tylenol for fever.

"He doesn't have a fever," I pointed out.

"Yes, but perhaps it would relax him into sleep," he suggested.

"Do you want some medicine, Jack?" I asked.

He shook his head no.

"You don't ask him, Kelly, for goodness sake. It'll make you feel better Jack" he insisted.

Jack squirmed, cried, and choked as Gavin did his best to force him to take some, and we both wound up wearing more of it than what actually got into his mouth.

"Right, this is ridiculous, come here Jackie," Gavin insisted, prying him off of me. "You have to get some sleep now, Kelly. Go on then, put on some headphones while I walk him to sleep. Meg can stay home and be my helper this morning. She fed Nick a bottle the other day, did she tell you?"

Jack screamed and barked, reaching for me as Gavin pushed me towards our bed, assuring me that Jack would stop once I was out of sight.

I wasn't instantly able to sleep, but as Jack finally did settle a bit, I drifted off and didn't wake up for several hours. When I did wake up it was to the sound of Colleen laughing. I looked at the clock and saw that it said 3:07p.m. I had been sleeping for almost five hours.

I quickly ran to the bathroom, and then went out to find Colleen and Meg in the guest bathroom playing with face paint. Nick was on the floor in his bouncer seat with a yellow flower painted on his cheek.

"Mommy, look it what Colleen can do!" Meg exclaimed excitedly, as Colleen was painting a giraffe on her face.

"Wow. What are you doing here? Where's Gavin?"

"He had a meeting. Go get dressed, we're going to go out to get something to eat as soon as Jack wakes up," Colleen told me.

"How long has he been sleeping?"

"A few hours I guess, I don't know, I've been here for over two."

I walked back to his room and found him in his crib, passed out on his back, propped up on a couple of pillows. I shook my head, wondering what Gavin had been thinking in putting a bunch of pillows in a baby's bed, while at the same time being a little impressed that it had managed to quiet his cough enough to let him get the sleep he so clearly needed. I hesitated to leave him that way, but not wanting to disturb him, I walked back to Colleen and Meg.

"Have you been checking him?" I inquired.

"No, I didn't want to disturb him, plus I've been watching these two. I figured I should leave well enough alone."

"Gavin has put a bunch of pillows in his bed. He could have suffocated."

"Yikes, I trust he hasn't though."

"It's not a good idea, but he's still out and on his back. Can you just check him every couple of minutes while I take a shower?"

"Sure, but hurry, we're hungry."

Although Colleen and I sometimes rub each other the wrong way, she loves my kids and they love her. For that I am grateful. I just wish she'd pay attention to them more often. On my way to the shower the phone rang, so I picked it up in the bedroom.

"Hey, Kelly," Devon casually asked, "Is it true you are having some kind of mental collapse?"

"Who told you that?"

"Mom says Gavin raised his voice to her, and was very rude, so now she's offended and telling me I should be forewarned."

"Wait, what? What do you mean he raised his voice? When, what did he say?"

"This morning, and he told her you were too fragile to be left with a sick child or something, I'm not sure. He seems to have her confused with someone capable of pulling their head out of their ass. Who is sick, Jack again?"

"Seriously, he told her I'm fragile?"

"I believe he did. Are you?"

"I might be. And her solution was to call you?"

"Apparently."

"Good grief Dev, I'm surrounded by idiots," I muttered, thinking first Gavin insults my mother, and then he puts his son in a crib with a bunch of pillows and goes to work, not even bothering to mention that he's done so.

"That's universal; there are a lot of idiots on this coast, too. So have you got a shrink? I know a good one." he said.

"Who? Although it doesn't matter because our insurance won't cover it."

"Remember that girl, Carina, that I saw a couple of years ago? When we broke up, I went to her mom, who is a really cool woman. She specializes in screwed up adults whose parents as she said, had the best of intentions, and then messed their kids up royally. I could call her and see if she'd give you a deal," he offered.

"You went to your girlfriend's mother?"

"Yeah, she was awesome, and she's close by besides."

"Don't. We really can't afford it," I told him.

"Are you sure?"

"Positive."

"Okay," he sighed. "I'll see you this weekend then I guess."

"I can't wait," I told him.

We said goodbye and I started out to ask Colleen what she knew about Gavin insulting our mom, but was waylaid by Jack who called to me in a hoarse voice. I went in to get him and he handed me one of the pillows and threw the other on the ground, thinking it was funny. I was relieved to see that although he looked a mess, he obviously felt better. Hearing him, Meg ran in to show him the giraffe Colleen had finished, and to ask him if he wanted to go get a treat at a restaurant. I did not relish the idea of going to a restaurant with three little kids.

I convinced Colleen that we should just walk down to a sandwich shop that had a few tables outside in a courtyard where Meg and Jack could at least move around a little without bothering anyone. First of course, I had to feed Nick who was now fussy, and I still hadn't managed to get dressed. By the time we got out of the house, it was definitely dinner we were going to eat. I waited until the kids were settled with their food to ask what she knew about Gavin calling our mother.

"He's been family for how long?" she laughed.

"Eight years, well, six that we've been married," I answered.

"He can't fathom how a mother could ignore her child's need of her."

"Dev says she told him he was rude to her and raised his voice."

"He's worried Kelly, we all are. You hear such horrible things about people and the things they do when they are pushed too far."

"Who is we all? Clearly not Mom," I laughed.

"Oh she probably is in her own weird way. Corky, Gavin, me, and even Dee Dee is all, oh and Keith sends his love."

"Dee Dee has changed, you are right," I admitted.

"Right? I told you. Roman has been great for her."

I nodded, and told her about the shrink Devon had told me about. We both laughed at the fact that only Dev could break up with a girl, and then go into therapy with her mother.

"I told Gavin this afternoon that he has to let you write. I can't believe you haven't even told him what we worked out. Every night, you have got to write something, every night. I don't care if it's just a description of the room," she said firmly. "And I've told Scott to tell him, you have to have sex, so for God sake shave your legs."

I spit my coffee across the table.

CHAPTER 12

Gavin was home when we got back, but only long enough to check in and say that he had to run out again, because one of his lesser known writers was doing a reading at a bookstore in Santa Monica, and had asked that he be there for moral support. The writer was panicked that no one would show up even though they had done their best to promote it. It was a panic both Colleen and I could relate to, having been in that situation ourselves.

Although my first book, a collection of short stories, had been critically acclaimed, it had not received the promotion I'd have liked. We had also attended many of our father's readings. In fact, it was at a reading of my Dad's where Colleen and I had first met Gavin.

Every year the LA Times sponsors a book festival, and eight years earlier, my father had been one of the featured authors. Colleen and I were milling around when Scott whistled across the room with such ear splitting volume that everyone within

30 miles turned to look. I was shocked when Colleen let out a squeal, grabbed my arm, and dragged me across the floor, announcing that it was Scott from Yale.

Up to that point, all I knew about Scott from Yale was that she'd had a mad crush on him for two years, finally gone out with him for a few weeks, and then they'd broken up amicably. As far as I knew, she hadn't seen or heard from him in years, and now he had suddenly reappeared. The two of them had a grand old reunion while Gavin and I stood awkwardly by, waiting to be introduced. Scott explained that he had been interning, and eventually writing for a magazine in London for the past five years. He said he had just relocated to L.A., dragging his friend, Gavin, back with him. Gavin, he told us, worked for a very high profile agency representing some of the finest writers in the world. And then and only then, did he think to introduce him to us.

I was instantly attracted to Gavin's sleepy bedroom eyes, and his rich, dark brown hair that appeared to have a mind of its own, as it waved and kinked into the occasional ringlet. He also had a shy smile that made him irresistible, so when he spoke with a soft British accent, it was icing on the cake.

Scott suggested we all have dinner, and after my Dad's reading, we met them at a nearby restaurant. I wanted to engage Gavin in conversation and did my best to draw him out, but after a while I gave up. He was so quiet that I assumed he had no interest in me, and went home disappointed. Three days later he invited me to a party he had to attend at the home of one of his clients. He explained that he had been quiet that first night because he'd been so taken by the view. I accused him of handing me a line, but he swore he was sincere. From that night on, things progressed quickly, and within a couple of months he was all but living at my place.

"Gavin, Gavin, Gavin," Colleen said shaking her head. "Did you hear nothing I said earlier?"

"Did you hear nothing I said?" he asked back. "We have bills to pay, and I've commitments I've made in order to enable me to pay those bills. I'm sorry Kel," he said turning to me, "but it can't be avoided. You understand, right?"

"Sure," I sighed.

"I have to leave, too," Colleen said, kissing my cheek. "Tomorrow, Gwen's Bridal, at eleven, don't be late."

I'd forgotten that I'd said I'd meet her and Dee Dee there on Wednesday. Somehow it had felt further away at the time I had agreed. Within a matter of seconds I was on my own again, in the house with three tired and cranky kids. Nick was in desperate need of a bath, Jack was beginning to cough, and Meg was getting whiny. She said she wanted to go to the bride store with us.

"You'll be at school," I reminded her.

"No," she pouted, "I want to go with you and Colleen."

"It'll be boring, Meg."

"No!" she insisted loudly.

"Don't yell at me Meg," I said, instantly angry.

"I'm not going to school tomorrow. I don't have to!"

"You do have to, and if you yell again you'll be in bed."

"No!" she yelled.

And so it began. What should have been nothing more than a tired preschooler acting out, became a full on battle that left us both in tears, and me hiding in the bathroom for ten minutes because I wanted to hit her so badly that I didn't trust myself not to. I eventually went out and apologized, agreeing she could come with us, because I felt so guilty.

Gavin got home at 10:30 p.m. and found me sitting on the sofa in the family room, numbing myself with the bottle of wine we had been saving for a special occasion. I was on my second glass.

"Kel?" he asked tentatively, "is everything okay?"

"I almost hit her," I mumbled.

"Who?" he asked, taking off his coat and going to the kitchen to get a glass.

"Meg," I said, holding out my glass for a refill as he grabbed the bottle to fill his own.

He just nodded, and looked towards the doorway as Jack began coughing and choking.

"Did you give him some pillows?" he asked.

"You can't put pillows in a crib. He's a baby. He could suffocate."

"He's suffocating now," he insisted, emptying the bottle into my glass, and going in to prop him up.

I didn't stop him even though I thought I should. Instead I drank my wine and worried that something bad was going to happen. That sooner or later I was going to pay a horrible price for being such a bad mother. Gavin returned a few minutes later, sat next to me, and drank his wine, not saying anything. When he'd finished he got up, corked the empty bottle, took my hand, and said we should sleep.

It was another sleepless night however, as we juggled both Jack's croup and Nick's need to be fed, as well as him being disturbed by Jack's barking and crying. Finally at 5:30 a.m. the house quieted, and we all slept until the phone rang at eight thirty. It was Sirri wanting to take an emergency meeting.

CHAPTER 13

"What kind of emergency meeting? What does that even mean?" Dee Dee asked as we sat in the bridal shop waiting for Colleen to emerge in the Vera Wang gown she'd gone to try on.

"I have no idea," I yawned.

I was nursing Nick, as I seemed to be doing constantly, and while Meg was obediently sitting on a big round ottoman that she liked, Jack was threatening to run through a rack of dresses.

"Jack, get back here," I said, as he took off.

He didn't listen, of course, and instead dove in, much to the horror of one of the bridal consultants. Dee Dee pulled him out as I apologized, and he collapsed to the floor refusing to cooperate.

"I knew this was a bad idea," I moaned.

"I'm being good Mommy," Meg volunteered.

"I know, thanks," I said, interrupting Nick's feeding to deal with Jack who was quickly going from meltdown to ballistic.

Nick didn't appreciate the disruption, and went the route of "if you can't beat 'em, join 'em." I took them out to the parking lot, doing my best to reason with Jack, as Nick kicked and raged in my arms. It wasn't good. Jack squirmed to get away from me, and succeeded just as a car pulled in too quickly. I screamed, sure that he was going to be hit. In that moment I knew my worst fears were going to come true.

The brakes screeched and the horn honked, as I grabbed Jack and pulled him back just in time, but it was so frightening that I lost it. I cursed at the driver that this wasn't the fucking autobahn, as he told me to hold on to my kid, placing the blame on me, while demanding to know what kind of a mother I was.

Having heard the screeching tires and yelling, Colleen and Dee Dee ran out, Colleen in this stunning gown, just as I physically collapsed to the ground, crying uncontrollably. Dee Dee took Nick from me, and everything spun out of control.

The implosion took place, but in a weird way I missed it. I've been told that Colleen did her best to help me up off the ground, but then seeing that the driver was still complaining to Dee Dee, I ran at him and tried to hit him, before literally passing out.

I have vague flashes of being loaded into an ambulance, and of being in the emergency room. I know I was asked a lot of questions, but I couldn't tell you how I answered, if in fact I answered at all. It's all a blur. All I know is that it felt like forever before Gavin was brought in to talk to me. I remember him asking me if I wanted to stay there, and him saying that they were threatening to put me on a 72hr. hold if I didn't agree to see a shrink.

"I'm so sorry," I told him, knowing that we couldn't afford this, and that he had to be disappointed in me.

"What does that mean, Kelly, you do want to stay?" he asked, on the verge of panic.

I shook my head no, and he looked relieved. Taking a deep breath, he told me I had to tell them that, and I had to cooperate. I wasn't aware that I hadn't been. A doctor came in and asked me if I had thoughts of suicide, and as soon as I said no, I was released. After that I remember Gavin never once stopped talking the entire way home.

He told me that Colleen had already found me a doctor who could help sort me out, and that he didn't know how we were going to pay for this, but that it didn't matter. He said the important thing was that we were going to get me the help I needed in dealing with the kids so that I could write, because he knew how creative I was, and of course I needed to pursue the things that made me happy. My creativity, he said, was what had drawn him to me in the first place, and it was a shame that I wasn't being allowed to pursue that. He just wanted me to be happy. If I was happy, he'd be happy, and if we were both happy, well then it only stood to reason that the children would be happy as well. Everything was going to be just fine. I had no reason to worry about this unfortunate incident, because it was simply that, an unfortunate incident that had occurred due to a lack of sleep and some nasty post natal hormones. I'd be feeling better in no time, he was sure of it. On and on he anxiously chattered right up until we pulled into the driveway.

Somehow, walking back into the house felt surreal. Colleen was there, as was Keith. They each hugged me, and Colleen told me to get some sleep, and that they were going to take Jack and Meg to their house for the night, so that I'd only have to deal with Nick, who would hopefully be up just once during the night.

The kids were watching a Winnie the Pooh Bear movie in the family room, and if they were aware that anything was out of the ordinary, they chose to ignore it. I went back to my room and didn't even bother to get undressed. I crawled under the covers and fell fast asleep, not moving until Gavin brought me Nick at 3:30 in the morning, asking if I wanted to nurse him, or if he should try to get him to take a bottle.

I nursed him, and sat in the dark wondering what would happen next. I was in a daze, and it was hard to imagine that all that had gone on that day was real. I couldn't help wondering if that was as bad as things would get, or if there was more to come.

Nick drifted off in my arms, and I held him a few minutes longer, remembering that at least Colleen and Dee Dee should be going up to the lodge the next day. Suddenly, driving up there sounded like a fine idea. I pictured myself sitting next to the Merced River, which ran past the lodge, allowing the sun to kiss my skin. It seemed as though up there I might be able to breathe deeply enough to truly catch my breath, and stop the unraveling.

Gavin rolled over and asked what I was doing, pointing out the obvious, that I should be sleeping.

"Do you want me to put him down?" he whispered.

"No," I said, getting up to do it myself.

I came back to bed and curled into myself, hugging my pillow, listening to Gavin's even breathing, but I couldn't fall back to sleep no matter how many times I tried to clear my mind to do so. For the rest of the night I merely stare, as shadows from the gently swaying tree just outside our bedroom window danced on the wall.

Nick woke at 6:45a.m. and I quickly went to him in an effort to allow Gavin more sleep. I could only imagine how much he didn't want to face another day of crazy. Gavin's father is a famous London playwright, with a reputation as a man of many demons. Long since divorced from Claire, Gavin's mum, he has a tendency to ring us up about twice a year to voice his regret that he and Gavin aren't closer. He blames Claire, and insists that she has poisoned Gavin against him, which to some extent I think she probably has, but she couldn't have done so if he hadn't handed her so much ammunition. He is known for his indiscreet affairs with young girls, and public drunkenness. Gavin and his Mum have definitely seen their share of crazy. The sad part is, that when he is sober and lucid, Gavin's dad is every bit as charming as Gavin himself. I know that buried deep, there is a great man.

I fed Nick and tried picking up the house a little, before Gavin woke up. He came out just after eight and asked how I was feeling.

"I don't know what happened yesterday. I don't know what's wrong with me." I said, feeling guilty for putting him through what I knew was such an uncomfortable and stressful situation.

He nodded, and told me I should go get ready for the appointment Colleen had made for me. I agreed and walked away, dreading what was to come.

CHAPTER 14

We had no choice but to take Nick with us, which was immediately frowned upon. As soon as we walked into the waiting room we were met by the polite smile of the receptionist who assured us the pediatrician's office was down the hallway. It was embarrassing, but I explained that I was the one with the appointment, and that we hadn't been able to get a sitter.

"Oh, well alright," we were told, but the underlying message was that assumptions were already being made.

I was handed a pile of papers so thick it rivaled *War & Peace*, and told to fill them out, but to give thoughtful answers. Then Gavin was handed an equal pile of insurance forms and told I'd also have to complete those once I was done with the psychological questionnaire. It was overwhelming, and I wasn't sure how to reply to any of the questions. Gavin kept telling me to just circle the answer that seemed the closest to how I was feeling and so I did my best to find the answer that reflected that. The receptionist kept checking to see if I was done, saying the doctor needed to review my answers before talking to me.

The pressure was tremendous, and I finally began just circling random answers. I handed them in, and then walked Nick who was getting bored and fussy, while Gavin did his best to fill out both the medical and insurance questions.

It began to feel as though hours were passing before I was taken back and actually introduced to the doctor, a man in his late forties, with salt and pepper hair, and a slight gap in his teeth. He was dressed in a designer suit, and said he was Dr. Sollaman, but I could call him by his first name, Robert, if I'd prefer.

His office was huge, with a couch and two chairs off to the side, while at the far end of the room was a large desk, and another two chairs in front of that. He motioned for me to have a seat as he walked around to his desk and quickly glanced through all of the papers we'd filled out. Then he sat back and gave me an appraising look, before leaning forward, resting his chin on his hands, and asking me what had brought me to his office.

"I'm, well, I guess I'm not handling my everyday life very well right now. It's been stressful, especially since the birth of our last child."

"Children require an adjustment," he said, but then he didn't say anything more, which left an awkward silence.

"Okay, yes, well um, my husband also lost his job, and I'm a writer, and I haven't been able to write…"

"It says here you are a stay at home mom, not a writer," he interrupted.

"Because I never have time to write."

"I'm confused. How can you be a writer if you don't have time to write?" he asked.

"That's the point, isn't it? I need to write, to express myself, but I can't even think straight I'm so busy tending to our kids and…"

"You have confused thoughts?"

"Sure, I mean it's overwhelming…"

"The confusion?"

"And the kids, and the lack of money to do anything, and…"

"What is it you want to do?"

"Write! I told you, I want to write."

"Write what?"

"Alphabetical lists," I sarcastically told him. "Are you kidding me right now?" I asked, quickly beginning to suspect that this was a huge waste of time.

"Kelly, do you mind if I call you Kelly?"

"It's my name," I said choking back tears of frustration.

"Kelly, you seem very quick to anger. Has this always been a problem?"

I shook my head, and he suggested we start again, repeating the question, "What is it you wish to write?"

"Novels, I'm a novelist."

"So you've written novels before?"

"Not exactly. I've written short stories mostly, and I've been published in the past in numerous magazines, but I've yet to complete a novel."

"Let's try to remain focused on what you actually have done then, shall we? Tell me about your day yesterday. What went on there?"

I ran through as much of it as I could remember, and he sat taking notes. Then he asked Gavin to join us. He explained that he needed Gavin to verify some of the things I'd told him, as well as the answers I'd put down on the questionnaire. When he read back some of my answers, taken out of context, it made me sound insane. I kept trying to jump in and explain, but was accused of doing the twisting that he himself was doing.

At the end of our appointment we were told I was suffering a nervous breakdown, probably due at least in part, to a previously undiagnosed bipolar condition, brought to the surface due to the exhaustion, and stress of the past year. He suggested that I have a complete blood work up, along with a physical, before starting on a trial dose of lithium and an antidepressant he was going to prescribe, both of which he felt I needed to begin taking immediately.

On our way out he added that there was to be no more nursing either, because the drugs could crossover to the baby, and besides, in my current state, it was just too draining on every level. We were ushered out of his office, because he had another patient, but told to pay at the desk, and to schedule a weekly appointment to track my progress.

As soon as we were out in the hallway I burst into tears, told Gavin I was never going back, and demanded to know where Colleen had found this crackpot. He urged me to calm down.

"I didn't say those things," I cried, desperate to make him see that I wasn't that crazy. "He twisted everything. I'm not bipolar Gavin, you know that. You know me."

"Let's talk in the car. Kelly, stop now," he said, looking around, obviously concerned that someone would hear us. The fact that he was obviously embarrassed to be seen with me right now was crushing.

I did my best to reign myself in, and followed him to the car, wanting nothing more than to disappear. By the time he had strapped Nick into his seat and come around to the driver's side of the car, I was too depressed to speak. I felt as though I had somehow done this to myself. As if this was my punishment for being a bad mother, a lousy wife, and a hopeless writer. Gavin got in the car, rested his head on the seat back, and took a deep breath before speaking.

"He comes highly recommended. Some actress from one of the shows Keith writes for said he was invaluable to her after the birth of her second child. I don't know, Kelly, he sighed. "Bipolar seems a bit of a stretch to me too, but then I've had a tendency to ignore all that has been happening, haven't I? You certainly do seem moody."

I didn't say anything. I couldn't even look at him. I just curled up in my seat, closed my eyes and cried. Flustered, he drove to Colleen's, where I refused to get out of the car.

"This is going fantastically well," he muttered, slamming the door as he got out of the car to go get Meg and Jack.

It startled Nick, who'd been sleeping, and soon his wailing filled the car.

I attempted to twist in my seat and get by with just patting his chunky little leg, but he wasn't having it. He wanted out of his seat, and of course having been told to stop nursing him, I wanted nothing more than to do just that. Drying my eyes, I took a moment to blow my nose, and then got out of the car, went around to the backseat, pulled Nick out of his seat, and walked across the street to a nearby bench in the park across from Colleen's condo.

Nick settled almost instantly, and after a quick drink, gave me a big smile as he reached his hand to my mouth, starting to giggle when I gently nibbled on his fingers. The sun felt warm and comforting as it burned into my clothing, and for a moment I couldn't imagine how I could be anything but happy. For just a moment there was no one else in the world other than the two of us, and I loved that baby with all my heart. I was grateful to have him, and knew how blessed I was, but I knew we couldn't stay there forever, and as if to underline that thought, a cloud passed in front of the sun, leaving us shadowed and cold.

I looked over to Colleen's and saw Gavin on approach, alone. He'd spotted us from Colleen's bay window I imagined, and when he reached us, instead of saying anything he just sat down, put his arm around me, and leaned his head against mine. Nick hollered his approval as this was a rare occurrence indeed. He was not used to getting attention from the both of us at the same time. Handing him to Gavin, I closed my shirt while Nick excitedly waved his hands and babbled some kind of welcome.

"I don't want to make a mess of things any more so than I already have, Kel," Gavin sighed, allowing Nick to stand and bounce on his lap as he spoke. "I don't know what's going on. Colleen agrees with you that you aren't bipolar, and in stepping back, of course it sounds ridiculous, but that was some crazy shit that guy read back to me, and yesterday was frightening, and most frightening of all is how unhappy you are. I'm scared, Kelly. I'm scared you are going to walk away from us and not come back. I don't want that to happen. That would break my heart if that happened, do you understand that?"

I nodded, fighting a losing battle against the flood of tears that rolled down my cheeks.

"This is what I am thinking" he continued. "For less money than it will take us to chase after a diagnosis none of us believes in, we could hire someone to come in and watch the kids for a little while. You and Colleen can go up to that lodge she wants to go check out, or whatever it is she's talking about, and you could get some much needed rest. Perhaps nursing this one is taking it out of you as that chap said, and it's not as though he can't take a bottle, is it, Nick?" he asked, nuzzling his cheek.

Nick squirmed and smiled, reaching back to me. I sat him on my lap and leaned into Gavin, a million thoughts, questions and concerns swimming through my head. I was torn between the same fears he had, as well as relieved to hear that it would bother him if I left. At times it was hard to believe that he and the kids (especially the kids) wouldn't be better off without me.

A cool breeze blew, and squeezing my shoulder, Gavin suggested that we should move inside.

"The kids want to show you the tent Keith has set up for them in the living room. There's been none of that two chairs and a blanket rubbish we've been known to do. He has a full on tent erected, as if they were in the woods somewhere."

We slowly made our way across the street, and when we got upstairs, Meg loudly and enthusiastically showed me the tent. I asked Jack if he'd slept in it too, and he threw himself on the floor, kicking and screaming. Colleen insisted that he'd been a sweetheart up until then, but now he was angry, and not about to fail in letting me know.

CHAPTER 15

With the engagement party scheduled for Saturday, it was agreed we would contact a nanny agency (of which there are dozens in Los Angeles) that afternoon, and hopefully have a temporary nanny by the next day. Colleen said that way the kids could get used to her with me there, and then she, Dee Dee, and I, could drive up to the lodge on Sunday.

We were sent résumés and security checks on three nannies willing to take a temporary position. Of the three, Hilary stood out as the best. She was forty five, had two college aged children, and had been married for twenty four years. Gavin thought she sounded very stable.

During the remainder of the day, Jack's croup seemed better. At bedtime he threw a tantrum about having to sleep in his crib instead of a tent, but when he finally exhausted himself, he actually slept through the night. I checked on him both when I went to bed, and again when I got up with Nick in the middle of the night, and although he had a slight rasp to his breathing, he appeared to have turned the corner and be through this latest bout.

Hilary arrived the next morning at 7:30 am, as Gavin had arranged when he'd spoken to her the night before. I was relieved to see that she looked normal. All night I had been waking up imagining the worst, but she was dressed in a pair of Calvin Klein jeans, a casual navy blue t-shirt, no doubt from the Gap, and a pair of sneakers. She had shoulder length brown hair, smiling eyes, and best of all, an extra fifteen or twenty pounds on her that added softness, and an air of unpretentiousness to her.

Jack hid behind my leg, and Meg refused to speak, but Nick cautiously allowed her to carry him as I showed her around the house, apologizing for how messy it was, even though I had of course spent the day before giving it a through scrubbing. With only 1500 square feet in its entirety, it didn't take long to give her the tour.

Back in the family room I was unsure what to do next, and looked to Gavin who was still sitting at the kitchen table, eating his breakfast and scrolling articles online. I cleared my throat to get his attention, but he took no notice.

"Gavin," I said.

He held up his hand to indicate that he had to finish what he was doing before he could acknowledge me. Hilary asked Meg if she was in school and she nodded. The silence was killing me. I picked up Jack and told him to stop hiding, assuring him that Hilary was nice and not about to bite him.

"What a perfectly awful image to put in his head," Gavin announced. "Hilary is here to play with you and show you a good time, Jackie," he said, as I thought to myself that he was making her out to sound like more of a hooker than a nanny.

Jack buried his head in my chest and whined, while Meg, as uncomfortable as I was with the awkwardness, asked if it was time to go to school. It wasn't.

"Why don't you show Hilary your rocking horse, Jack?" I suggested trying to put him down.

He burst into tears, and on the verge of doing the same, I relented. I sat with him on the couch and promised I wouldn't put him down until he was ready. Of course as soon as I said it, Nick decided he needed me as well, and all but leapt out of Hilary's arms. Jack pushed him, and they both cried as Gavin stood up, looked at me and sighed, making me feel inept.

"You mustn't let them do this. You may not push," he scolded Jack. "My wife is exhausted and not herself right now," he explained, suggesting Meg find a book that Hilary could read to her and Jack.

Meg hesitated but then ran over to the book shelf and began asking Jack what story he wanted to hear. He continued to bury his head in my lap and weep. Gavin took Nick and placed him in the baby swing, assuring Hilary that he'd settle in a few minutes. I knew he wouldn't, but didn't bother saying it. Gavin kissed Meg and told her to be good, saying I'd walk her over to Kate's later because she was going to take her to school again.

"I want Mommy or you to take me to school," she whined.

"Not today. Mummy shouldn't be driving, and I've a meeting."

"She could drive."

"End of discussion, Meg," he said firmly, as he came over, and resting his hand on Jack's head, leaned down to kiss the top of my head. "Get some rest," he instructed, and then he left.

I swallowed hard, wanting to run after him because for whatever reason, I was feeling just as scared and uncertain as the kids, even though Hilary seemed perfectly fine. Once Gavin was gone, Jack sat up on my lap, and taking my face in his hands, announced that he wanted to go bye bye.

Hilary was able to win over Meg fairly quickly, but Jack was not about to have anything to do with her. Nick alternated between flirting with her, to suddenly falling to pieces. When it came time to walk Meg over to Kate's, I sent her with Hilary on the theory that I could watch them through the front window, and the fact that I didn't want to do it myself. I wasn't sure how much Gavin had been telling Kate about my sanity, and I didn't really want to know.

Gavin called around noon to see how it was going, and I asked him to come home. When he dared to ask why, I got angry and hung up on him. When he called back, I didn't bother to pick up. A few minutes later Scott showed up, took me out to the backyard, and demanded to know what was going on, because Gavin was in a meeting and had called him, asking him to come check on us.

"I hate him!" I wept, like the two year old I spent every day with. The two year old I had just put down for a nap, and whom I could see standing in his crib, crying for me to come back.

"Kelly, he put everyone off yesterday. He can't just stop working. Clients don't like agents who do nothing."

"And I've never asked him to come home, ever! I'm not okay, and he doesn't even care," I sobbed.

"Shit," he said. "Where the hell is Corky? She's the one who should be here for you."

"You chased her away!" I yelled.

"What? Are you fucking kidding me? Is that what she told you?"

"You and your stupid commitment issues. Who the hell are you waiting for?"

"Her! I was waiting for her. Just because I didn't want to get married, that didn't mean I didn't want her. Jesus Christ. Really? She told you she left because of me?"

"She's in love with you."

"She has a pretty stupid way of showing it."

"So do you!"

"I can't believe she told you that," he said, as Jack let out a particularly blood curdling scream.

"Just tell Gavin thanks a lot!" I said, stomping back into the house.

I informed Hilary that I was going to take Jack into my room to lay down with him, and told her to ignore the idiot talking to himself in the backyard.

Jack and I slept for close to two hours, and when we awoke we heard Devon out in the backyard playing with Meg. We got up and went out to say hello, and Dev hugged us tightly as Meg told me he had been pushing her on the swing up to the sky. Jack of course burrowed into me again, unsure about Devon as well, because he hadn't seen him for six months, a huge time span for a two year old.

"How are you doing?" Devon asked, with concern.

"Not great."

"Nick is beautiful. His pictures haven't done him justice, and you," he said ruffling Jack's hair, "look at you all grown up and hiding."

"He doesn't like new people," Meg announced.

"I'm not new people!" Devon objected.

"He doesn't remember you."

"He should."

"How are you? When did you get in?" I asked.

"I'm worried about my sister, and I got in just a little while ago. I met Colleen for lunch and then came here. The shrink called you bipolar?"

"He's a quack."

"Go see the ducks?" Jack asked.

"Not today," I told him, and he dropped his head back down onto my shoulder.

"You need to talk to Estelle, Carina's mom," Devon insisted.

"I need to get myself together," I sighed.

Then I changed the subject, grilling him about his life in New York, and teasingly asked if he had a girlfriend whose mother he wasn't seeing.

"Sort of," he smiled, "although I have to admit, I have met her mom and I liked her."

"You have issues."

"Like you and Colleen don't."

"At least we don't go around crushing on our spouse's mothers."

"I'm not crushing on Estelle. I'm just telling you she could help you."

"Ha! Nobody can help me but me. That's being made very clear, but I don't want to talk about it anymore," I said, taking Jack over to the swings.

Devon stayed for a little over an hour and then had to go meet some of his L.A. friends for drinks. I did my best to pry the kids off of me throughout the rest of the afternoon as Hilary continued to work on winning them over. I liked that she wasn't overly pushy and suggested we all make some cookies as a special treat. Jack loved getting to hand me things, and allowed Hilary to lift him onto the counter so that he could see. Nick was also warming to her.

Gavin came in just before six, and dropped a manuscript on the counter, before giving me an angry glance that I was sure no one but me saw. He smiled at everyone else, oozing charm as he asked Hilary how her first day had gone, and arranging for her to come back the next night so that we could attend Colleen and Keith's engagement party.

CHAPTER 16

"I don't care, do I?" Gavin hissed in fury.

We were in our bedroom, and he'd just slammed the door behind us as all three kids were in bed, but hardly asleep yet. He couldn't wait to let me have it, as he had clearly been fuming ever since Scott had felt the need to tell him what I had said.

"I needed you! I was scared, and you were too fucking busy!" I cried.

"Working, Kelly, I was working. And why was I working? Oh right, for you! So that you can have a bloody nanny. She expects to be paid. Has that escaped you?"

"I needed help," I yelled. "I needed to know that I'm okay, but I'm not, and you aren't going to be here for me to reassure me, are you? So now I know. Now I know I'm on my own and you don't fucking care, deal with it."

I reached for the door, but he grabbed my arm and pulled me back, staring intensely as he did so. For a long moment we just stood there challenging each other.

"What the hell do you mean you were scared? Scared of what? What is going on in that mind of yours?" he asked.

I just blubbered, and he pulled me into the very embrace I had so desperately needed when I'd asked him to come home in the first place.

"We're all scared, Kelly. Do you think I'm not scared? Do you think the past six months have been easy for me? Do you think I haven't seen this coming? But what is one to do? I have to keep moving forward and trying to fix things. That's what we do, isn't it? We keep our head up and bluff our way through until things get better, and they will, I promise you that, alright? Look at me," he insisted, lifting my head so that our eyes met. "They will."

I really studied his face to see if he believed it, or if it was just more bluffing.

"Okay," I said, deciding to go with him on this.

"Okay," he nodded. "Now go take a bath, relax for a while, and work on your opening line. You'll be expected to make a toast at the party, don't you think?"

"Oh God no," I groaned.

He patted my behind, something he hadn't done in months, and told me to go on, while he joked that he was going to go beat all three of our children, all of whom were crying.

"Spare the little guy. He can't help himself," I mumbled, and he turned and smiled at me.

"That's my girl. You see, you really do love us," he said opening the door.

I knew he meant it to be comforting, but all I could think was what kind of a monster had I become that he would have to question that?

I listened as he went out and told Meg he'd expected better from her, cringing as he did so. I knew how much he loved her, but sometimes I feared his expectations of her were set impossibly high. Right or wrong, I blamed it on his British upbringing and the fact that he was an only child. I suspected his mother had confided in him far more than she should have when he was small. He counted on Meg to be his helper and the mature one, but she was only four and barely that.

Sinking into the bath, drowning any outside noise by turning the faucet full force, I closed my eyes and fell asleep. I was startled awake when I slid under the overflowing tide and sat up sputtering and choking on swallowed water. I was so disoriented that it took me a moment to realize what had happened, and to reach for the faucet.

There was water everywhere, the bath mat soaked through, and the flow heading for the door, ready to soak our bedroom as well. Cursing, I got out of the tub just as Gavin walked in and did a double take.

"What have you done?" he shrieked.

"I fell asleep and nearly drowned," I said, becoming aware of my aching, swollen breasts. "I need to feed Nick."

"You can't," he said tossing me a towel, while throwing another on the floor. "This is going to soak into the wood and begin to smell," he muttered.

"It hurts, look at me, Christ. I have to."

"It'll pass, it always does, and clearly that doctor was spot on when it comes to your being exhausted."

"It passes because you wean slowly. You don't just quit."

"Well, you have to, don't you? Just pump them, or whatever it is others do," he said, with a fair degree of exasperation.

"It hurts," I complained again.

"For God's sake, Kelly, if you aren't going to help clean up the mess you've made, at least get out of the way." he insisted, trying to pick up the bath mat and squeeze it out over the tub.

I walked away, and he called out to me that Nick had just drunk an entire bottle and wasn't going to be hungry anyway. I threw on a nightgown and marched down to the nursery just the same, but seeing Nick sleeping soundly, knees tucked under him, his butt in the air, I couldn't justify disturbing him. Instead I went to the guest bathroom and did my best to coax the milk from my breasts. Any other time I'd be dripping all over the place, but of course now that I needed my milk to let down, I couldn't squeeze out a single drop. Gavin found me twenty minutes later, sitting on the toilet seat, crying.

"Come here, how difficult can this be, really?" he sighed.

Gently taking one of my breasts in his hands, with confidence and a firm grasp, he began milking me like the cow I felt I was at that moment. While I sobbed and was humiliated, he told me to relax, and much to my horror, became aroused.

"Are you insane?" I wept, as he leaned into me and whispered that it was kind of sexy.

"I'm quite certain we both are by this point," he laughed, "but if you'd just relax Kel, you might actually derive some pleasure from it."

"You are milking me like a fucking cow!"

"Play whatever role you like, but it's working for me," he said, lifting my nightgown.

I was not only shocked, but then even more stunned when it began working for me as well. It was as though I had nothing left to lose, so why not surrender to a desire so primal that it could no longer be denied? Besides, I knew Colleen would enjoy the story.

When Nick woke for his middle of the night feeding I automatically began to get up, but Gavin threw his arm over me and mumbled that he had this. Then he continued to sleep. After a moment or two I attempted to move his arm and he suddenly sat up, once again assuring me that he'd go. Nick grew increasingly frantic as Gavin wiped the sleep from his eyes, and yet made no move to get him. I was feeling the need to nurse and got out of bed.

"No, no, sleep. I'm sorry, I'm going," Gavin promised, meeting me at the door.

I went back to bed and listened as Nick continued to cry and Gavin did his best to talk him out of it. My milk let down and I ran to the kitchen to try and express some into a bottle for him, but of course I couldn't get much and wound up frustrated and annoyed again. Gavin came out with Nick to get him a bottle and asked what I was doing. I explained and he commended me on a noble effort, but complained that now Nick wanted me instead of a bottle. I took Nick from him intending to just hold him while Gavin got the formula, but Nick did everything in his power to help himself to my chest.

"I'll just let him have a sip while you mix his bottle," I reasoned.

"That's not a good idea. He's not going to want this now," he sighed.

"He will, I've got an idea," I said, allowing Nick to latch on. "I'll annoy him by switching sides back and forth and he'll be fed up and go for the bottle."

"No he won't, that's ridiculous."

"Trust me," I persisted, interrupting the poor baby, who had just settled.

I let him take a little from the other side and then handed him to Gavin, suggesting he go back to the nursery and rock him as he fed him. Nick was at first confused, and then just angry. I went back to bed, lying awake for the next forty minutes as Gavin struggled to get him to take the bottle, but then got angry and put Nick back into his crib to cry it out. Knowing that I was still awake, he announced that Nick was getting too big for a middle of the night feeding, and that he shouldn't be allowed to have them anymore, anyway.

Meg came in to see why we were ignoring the baby, and before I could get her back to bed, Jack was calling as well. Gavin screamed into his pillow, and then got up for a second try with Nick. In the end, all three kids wound up in our bed, and it was not a restful night.

CHAPTER 17

On our way to the hotel where Colleen and Keith's engagement party was to take place, I suddenly remembered that I'd never confronted Gavin about yelling at my mother, if in fact he really had. I was uncomfortably stuffed into the dress that Colleen had insisted on buying me, and as she had predicted, Gavin had told me I looked hot. I envied him his well-fitting suit. He looked cool and relaxed, one hand on the wheel, and the other resting against his window, as we made our way through the Saturday night traffic. Twisting in my seat, my curiosity got the better of me.

"Gav, is it true you yelled at my mother?" I inquired, as casually as possible.

"Who told you that?"

"I can't remember," I lied, not wanting to indict Devon.

"We may have had words," he mumbled.

"Rude words?"

"I merely expressed an opinion that perhaps in retrospect I should have kept to myself, but I was quite honestly stunned that she could remain as aloof as she has. I still am."

"So is this going to be awkward?"

"Not after a few glasses of champagne," he said.

"What did you say?" I pressed.

"I don't remember," he lied, with a smile that said we were even.

"Alright, fine, but you'll apologize, right?"

He glanced at me but didn't answer.

"She is who she is, Gavin. She's not going to change."

"Meaning what, Luv? She's free and clear of any responsibility?"

"Responsibility for what?"

"You are her daughter, Kelly. She's your mum. It's not something that comes with an expiration date, now is it? If your child needs you, it's your duty to do anything you can to help them. Have you any idea how many times my own mum has offered to get on a plane and come over here to help out? I'd have taken her up on it too, if I'd not known it would drive you batty."

"I love your mom, I do, but I just feel the need to entertain her when she's here."

"I know she can be difficult. It's fine," he assured me.

"I suspect all parents are difficult, but she means well."

"Who are we discussing now, my mum or yours?"

"Mine."

Again he didn't answer and I fell silent. I couldn't help but think responsibility was an interesting choice of word. To me, my parents had done their best to raise us, and now that we were adults, it made sense that they would be more interested in their own lives rather than ours. I wished I had the kind of mother that could ride in, entertain my kids and give me the occasional pat on the back, but the reality was, that didn't interest her. What interested her was who Gavin was representing, and what I had written. As soon as we'd begun having kids and I'd stopped writing, her interest had doubled down on Colleen and Devon. She loved our kids, but I knew they demanded a kind of attention that she didn't have the patience to give. Should any of them choose to write however, then she would be fascinated.

The room the party was being held in was bathed in golden light, and lavishly decorated with beautiful flowers and tables off to the side of the dance floor. There was a DJ blasting songs from bands like Maroon Five, Foo Fighters and The Black Eyed Peas, and the celebration was well under way by the time we arrived. Gavin took my hand and directed me straight to the bar, where the drinks were on the house. He ordered a whiskey sour and a Vodka tonic for me.

"Lets enjoy ourselves, shall we?" he smiled. "Two drinks and we hit the dance floor. We won't speak to anyone."

"Tempting," I admitted, as he took his first gulp of the drink just handed to him.

"Go on then, drink up."

"Gav," I laughed.

"There you are! I thought you were standing us up," Colleen said, from behind me.

I turned to see her looking stunning in a tight, low cut black dress that accentuated all of her finest attributes. Her hair was curled into soft ringlets and her smoky eye shadow made her eyes look huge. Keith was hanging on her, and looking every bit as pretty in his designer suit. They made a picture perfect couple.

"I was just about to call and see if you were alright," Colleen continued.

"Congratulations," Gavin said, kissing her cheek and adding that she looked fantastic.

"What do you think of the dress I made Kelly get?" she asked proudly.

"Sensational," he smiled, lifting his glass to her, and finishing the rest of his drink without taking a breath. Then he told me to drink up, ordered us each another, and asked Keith and Colleen if they wanted anything. Keith put in their order while Colleen gave me a look of "what's up with him?" I shrugged and downed my first drink as quickly as I could.

"You both might want to pace yourselves," Colleen cautioned. "There's going to be champagne in a while, you know."

"Excellent, we're going to dance," Gavin announced handing me my second drink as I was already beginning to feel the first.

He dragged me out to the floor with a seductive smile. As he put his hands on my hips and told me to drink up, I felt a spark between us that had been missing for too long. I swallowed my drink in a rush, handed it off to a passing waiter, and falling against Gavin, my head swimming, told him I loved him. He kissed me, and as our lips parted I couldn't help but laugh. The DJ played *Moves Like Jagger,* and when Gavin began doing the Mick Jagger impersonation that he generally saved for private showings, I not only knew the alcohol was hitting him harder than usual, but I nearly wet myself laughing.

I was, of course, not the only one enjoying his performance, and while a few family members looked on with concern, most of the room broke into spontaneous applause as the song ended. Gavin gave a bow, and then moved back over to the bar to order us another round. Hugging me as we waited, he told me it had been far too long since I had really laughed.

"I'm sorry things have been so difficult of late," he said softly.

"Don't make me cry," I said, dropping my head to his chest.

"To us," he said a moment later, clanking glasses. "You're a gem, Kel."

I nearly spit my drink because it struck me as such a funny, yet odd toast. He smiled, looking genuinely relaxed for the first time in over a year, and suggested we dance again. We were interrupted when Keith's brother, Erik, grabbed a microphone and began making a toast to the future bride and groom, just as waiters began circling the floor, handing out champagne.

Erik was followed by Keith's father, and then Dee Dee appeared at my arm and told me we were next.

"You go, I'm drunk," I laughed.

"Me too, come on," she said, pulling me away from Gavin.

Taking the mic from Keith's dad, she said as co-maids of honor she was going to leave the toast to me, since she was not capable of putting words together in the manor for which our family was known.

"You're good," I said, but she forced the mic into my hand and left me with no choice. "Okay then," I giggled, "well you are all in for a treat because I can barely speak, let alone weave words together," I said swaying a little, "but I'll do my best. Keith and Colleen, you are both beautiful people. I mean seriously, somewhat disarmingly beautiful people. You are that way on the inside too though, and I am so glad you have found each other because you are meant to be together. It's evident in everything from how you hang on each other, to how you finish each other's sentences. There will come a day, probably not too long from now, when that will just become infuriating," I laughed. "Marriage is hard, but there are moments when you look at your chosen one and nothing else matters. Moments that are sometimes few and far between, but when it happens you are struck like someone opening a door to a hurricane. It'll slam you with the same love you were overwhelmed by when you first realized that this was real and different than any love you have ever felt before. I hope those moments are plentiful and sustain you for the rest of your lives."

I raised my glass, swallowed the rest of my champagne, and then sat down and cried in one of those overwhelming moments of my own. Devon took the mic from me, and mumbled for me to get up. I was so drunk that I couldn't get my legs to work, but Gavin swooped in, lifted me, and told Dev that he had me. I looked over at Colleen to see if she was as disgusted as I would have been had she gotten sloppy at my party, but she was looking at Devon who began another toast.

"Let's go, can we just go?" I asked Gavin.

He laughed, and walking me away from everyone, said no we could not.

"I've drunk more than you. We are in need of some serious sobering up. Let's get a room and have sex," he grinned.

"Like you could," I laughed.

"You know better than to challenge me," he mumbled, burying his head into my chest.

"Hey, drunk lovers," Scott laughed, seemingly appearing out of nowhere, "separate."

"Why?" Gavin slurred, and again I doubled over in laughter.

Scott told us to follow him, and took us to the hotel restaurant where he ordered us coffee. Gavin told him that although his friendship was deeply appreciated, he had been about to get lucky. Scott suggested that neither one of us would have been lucky in that scenario.

CHAPTER 18

Once we had begun to sober up, we debated going back to the party to apologize, but Gavin felt it would be best to let Scott pass on our apologies and to call it a night. I knew it was my parents he was avoiding, and considered pushing it, but then I decided he was right, better we should leave well enough alone.

That night when Nick woke up for his middle of the night feeding it wasn't only my breasts that were aching. Much to my astonishment, Gavin got up and went out to deal with him. I fell back asleep and didn't wake up again until the phone rang at just after eight the next morning. Opening my eyes, I discovered I was alone, and a little nauseous. There was a momentary panic as I hadn't been sick to my stomach since my last pregnancy, but then it came back to me all that I'd drunk, and it made perfect sense. I rolled onto my stomach but quickly realized my breasts were so engorged that they were hard as rocks. I sat up thinking I would try a hot shower because that had occasionally worked when my milk had first come in, but then Gavin came in carrying Nick, followed by Meg and Jack.

"That was Colleen. She's on her way here to pick you up," he informed me.

"I don't want you to go," Meg whined.

"Where am I going?" I asked, unable to suppress a disgusting burp.

"To the lodge," Gavin said, as Jack laughed and tried to burp as well. "Stop that. Mummy was being rude," Gavin said disapprovingly.

"Don't you feel sick?" I asked.

"I'm certainly not relishing the idea of being left alone all day."

"I need some relief," I said reaching for Nick.

"I don't know that you should do that," Gavin objected, as I tried to get Nick to latch on.

Unfortunately my breasts were so full that he couldn't really get it to work, and as luck would have it, he wasn't all that interested.

"It's for the best," Gavin insisted.

I took a shower but got little relief there, and before I knew it Colleen was pounding on the bathroom door, telling me to hurry up. I walked out to the family room a few minutes later expecting to find Colleen, and instead found Keith, Devon, and my parents all being entertained by Meg. She was telling a story about her school and how she was allowed to water all of the plants. Colleen was in the kitchen with Gavin, and Jack, who was looking nervous and shy.

"Are we having an intervention?" I asked. "Because seriously, I don't generally drink as much as I did last night."

"Zero tolerance policy, Kel," Devon laughed.

"We thought we could all go to breakfast," my dad announced.

The very idea made my stomach turn, but my mother stood up and said she'd suggested they just have us meet them at the hotel, but Devon wanted the House of Pancakes.

"It's delicious and kid friendly besides," he told me.

I looked at Gavin and he said he really needed to do some reading. He had Sirri Bingington's new novel, and she was anxiously awaiting his praise.

"A brief respite before you leave me to go up to the lodge would be fantastic. Nick is due a nap soon, so I could keep him," he offered.

"Sure, okay," I agreed, even though I didn't want any part of this.

Devon said he'd ride with me and the kids, and spent the entire time telling me about how he had talked to Estelle, Carina's mother. He said he'd told her what that quack had said about my being bipolar and she had told him she was sure she could help me, and would be happy to meet.

"I have to fly out tonight, but I'm going to leave you her number and you should call her."

"We'll see," I said, refusing to promise.

Breakfast became a bit of a circus as Jack got over his shyness, and both he and Meg tried to focus attention on themselves. It wasn't until we were saying goodbye that my mom and I acknowledged that anything was out of the ordinary.

"You know how much I love you," she said giving me a hug.

"Sure."

"I'm rooting for you always."

"I know you are."

"I'm sorry this is a tough time for both you and Gavin. I wish you only the best. I know he doesn't understand that, but you do, right?"

"Of course, and I'm sorry if he was rude Mom. He's just stressed out right now."

"I understand that. You tell him I love him and that this will all blow over. Sirri Bingington is going to bring him more clients. You mark my words."

"I'll tell him," I said, as Colleen told us to say goodbye already because we still had a six hour drive ahead of us.

It was agreed that she was going to drop Keith off, and then swing by the house to pick me up, before going to Dee Dee's where we would drive up to the lodge in her Range Rover. Devon told me again to call Estelle, and then left with my parents.

On the way home Meg campaigned to be allowed to go with us, while Jack told me not to go bye bye.

"Mommy stay home me!" he insisted.

"I can't," I told him.

By the time we got to the house, Meg was in tears and angrily told me I was mean. Gavin was sitting on the couch in the living room looking miserable.

"What's wrong?"

"It's crap"

"What's crap?"

"Sirri's book. It's unmitigated crap."

"Are you sure? Maybe it's just not your cup of tea. I mean she doesn't write for guys so..." I fizzled.

I could see from the expression on his face that he wasn't buying it, and I knew he knew crap when he saw it, or in this case, read it.

"Does it matter? I mean it'll sell regardless, won't it?" I asked.

"I thought it would be good. Not my cup of tea like you said, but decently written, you know? It's bloody rotten."

"Maybe it's a test. Maybe she knows it's crap and wants someone who'll be honest with her. I'm sure she's had everyone kissing up to her for a while now. Have you read her last book? Maybe that was crap too. Maybe she was a one hit wonder but no one cared."

"Maybe we're screwed," he sighed.

"Let me take it with me. I'll read it and see if I agree," I proposed.

"I'm only seventy pages in. I need to finish it."

"Run me a copy."

"That would be unethical. Here," he said handing it to me, "just read a few pages and tell me if I'm wrong."

I read the first ten pages and although I was somewhat distracted by the kids, there was very little doubt that it was awful.

CHAPTER 19

"What do you mean it's crap? What kind of crap?" Colleen asked, as we headed out to the highway in Dee Dee's extremely comfortable midnight blue Range Rover, with its tan leather upholstery.

"Just bad," I said.

"You have to be more specific. What's it about?"

"The first ten pages were nothing but one long description of a sleazy strip club with every lazy stereotype you can imagine."

"I've never been to a strip club, have you?" Colleen asked.

"I have, don't ask," Dee Dee laughed, adding, "they are pretty much a lazy stereotype."

"Ten pages worth?" I asked.

"Not the one I was in. I'd say three words could have summed it up. Dark, seedy and smelly."

"Smelly?" Colleen and I both questioned.

"It was really rank."

"Well there's a fourth word right there," Colleen observed.

"The point is, Gavin won't sell a piece of shit. He can't. It's just not in his nature," I said.

"Oh please, are you seriously telling me he's liked everything anyone he's ever represented, has written?"

"No, of course not, but he's been able to see that it was well done."

"Very little is truly well written," Colleen said, "and I'll even admit to questioning some of my own work when I say that. I mean, perfection is rarely achieved."

"I don't think he's expecting perfection, but the ability to keep your eyes open as you read would be nice."

"So he either has to give her notes, or keep his mouth shut and sell something he doesn't believe in," she reasoned.

I closed my eyes and sighed, because I knew he was incapable of keeping his mouth shut. One way or the other, he would end up telling her it was unacceptable dribble, and then she'd no doubt declare him a pompous ass void of good taste. The last thing he had told me on my way out the door was to clear my mind, get a decent night's sleep, and then write him a novel he could sell, because Sirri Bingington was not going to be the light at the end of the tunnel we had hoped she'd be.

The drive up to the lodge all but flew by, thanks in part to my falling asleep halfway up there. When I awoke a few hours later, I was cold and opened my eyes to see snow piled high on either side of the road.

"Did we know there was going to be snow?" I asked.

"Roman said there might be," Dee Dee informed me.

"I packed for sun," I said, to myself as much as anyone else.

The lodge was just off the main highway leading up to Yosemite, down a poorly paved road bordered by a high bank of freshly cleared snow. A large, A-framed log building with a picture window came into view. There was a hand carved wooden sign hanging above the arched doorway that read "The Riverrun Inn". It was rustic and yet managed to appear incredibly inviting. The lobby had highly polished wood floors that looked as though someone had simply split tree trunks, sanded them down a little to even them out, and then laid them side by side. They were unlike anything I had ever seen, but I loved them. The front desk was more of the same.

Colleen gave her name to the woman behind the counter, a woman who looked to be only a little older than Colleen herself, and she squealed with the delight of a school girl meeting her pop idol.

"The wedding, of course. You're Keith's girl!" she said, coming around to give Colleen a big hug. "I'm Nancy, Kim's sister in-law. Oh, Mike and Kim are so excited about this. They have told us to be sure you have whatever you want. Cal!" she yelled towards a back room.

A teenaged boy dressed in lose fitting jeans, an undershirt, and a corduroy jacket, came out looking disinterested at best. He was cute in a small town, unsophisticated way, and yet I suspected he could give a lot of attitude.

"This is my son, Cal, and he knows the grounds around here like the back of his hand. He'll show you to your rooms and when you're settled, he can show you around, although it's getting late," she acknowledged.

It was nearly six and Colleen said we would probably do most of our exploring in the morning if that was alright.

"Of course. You must be tired. Have you eaten? There are some fine restaurants around here," Nancy offered.

"We'll probably just order a pizza if that's okay," Colleen said.

"Yes, yes of course, there's a Pizza Hut not too far from here."

Cal took us to our rooms located on the second floor, and not only did every room have a beautiful four poster bed, but they each had adjoining balconies that looked out onto the rushing river. Surrounded by giant sequoias and massive rocks spotted with patches of snow, there were three deer grazing just across the water to complete the perfection of my view. Grabbing my phone, I snapped a picture and sent it to Gavin. Then I went down to Colleen's room and told her I might refuse to go home.

"I told you it was beautiful, and wait until you go to bed. There's a feather mattress on all of the beds. You'll think you've died and gone to Heaven."

"I can't wait!"

Unfortunately, I was uncomfortably engorged again, so while she ordered the pizzas, I went back to my room to try another hot shower. Sadly, the shower there was not great. The water pressure kept alternating between drizzly rain and pelting hail, and I couldn't get it warm enough either. I returned to Colleen's room to complain, and found her and Dee Dee lost in a sea of bridal magazines.

For the next couple of hours, we indulged in pizza and discussions of both the wedding and Colleen's bridal shower. She said she wanted to keep things simple, so it was agreed the shower would be held at Dee Dee and Roman's on a Saturday in April, yet to be determined. We also made a list of everything that was needed for the wedding, such as someone to perform the ceremony.

"You know who has volunteered," Colleen said rolling her eyes.

"Oh no," I laughed, knowing immediately that she was referring to our step-cousin, Jerry.

Aunt Beth, our mother's sister, had married a man nearly twice her age, and he'd had a son, Jerry, ten years older than Colleen. It was a well-known fact that Jerry had experimented with a lot of drugs, and during one particular acid trip, he claimed to have spoken with God, who had suggested he become a minister. He'd offered to preside over Gavin and my nuptials as well. I'd been able to turn him down by saying it was important to Gavin that we be married in the church.

"What are you going to do?" I asked.

"I told him that Keith's godfather is going to do it, but now we have to find him a godfather," she laughed, "and he hasn't even been baptized."

"Add that to your list," I told Dee Dee.

And she did.

We were all tired out from the night before, so we said goodnight around ten, and returned to our own rooms. I slipped into the big bed, melting into the comfort it provided, but then instantly missed Gavin and the kids. Reaching for my phone, I hit our number and waited for Gavin to pick up. I got Scott instead.

"How could you have not told me Corky is coming home?" he demanded, as I heard Gavin telling him to give him the phone.

"Since when do you care?" I asked.

"Since always! I told you that the other day."

"Exactly, stop telling me and tell Corky. Let me talk to Gavin."

He gave Gavin the phone, and he sounded exhausted as he asked why I hadn't called earlier to let him know we'd arrived safely.

"I sent you the picture."

"That could have been taken anywhere. In fact, it looks like a promotional shot."

"I know, that's how beautiful it is here, although I wasn't expecting snow."

"That's not going to be a problem, is it? You are still coming back tomorrow, right?"

"As far as I know. I miss you guys. How stupid is that?"

"Not stupid at all. I should hope you would."

"I know, but here I have this great opportunity to sleep, and I want you to be lying with me."

"I'll be there next time. Corky called, if you couldn't have guessed. You told her she could stay at our house?" he asked.

"Sure, you don't care, do you?"

"I wish you'd have discussed it with me first, Kelly. We aren't exactly at our best right now, are we? It's hardly the time to bring others in."

"Don't be silly, it's just Corky. She doesn't care if we aren't the perfect hosts."

"I care," he sighed.

"Gavin, she has no place else to go. She can't go back to that delusional friend of yours who seems to have forgotten everything he told her. He broke up with her, whether he remembers it that way or not. You know that."

"I thought I knew that, but I'm no longer so certain."

"It'll be nice to have her back. I've missed her."

"I know you have, I just hope it's not going to cause more chaos, and continue on indefinitely. At any rate, she's coming in tomorrow night."

"Yay!"

"Get some sleep. Have you written anything yet?" he asked.

"No, have you read anymore?"

"No, Scott's about to leave and then I'm going to attempt a few more chapters before I sleep."

Okay, I love you," I said.

"Love you, too."

CHAPTER 20

I was in the midst of an amazingly poetic description of Italy when the phone rang, and I realized I had been dreaming that I was writing, instead of actually doing it. Disappointed, I sighed and grabbed the receiver.

"Hello," I mumbled.

"Rise and shine," Colleen cheerfully chimed. "We need to find breakfast and take a hike."

"A hike? I thought we were just looking around."

"We are, get up," she insisted.

I wanted to write down the description that I'd been typing in my dream, but I could only remember that I had been typing it on what I now realized was an antique typewriter my father has, and proudly displays in his den. I could not come up with a single adjective to paint the picture I'd envisioned in my dream.

When I told Colleen about it at breakfast, she hugged me and told me it was a sign.

"A sign of what?" I asked.

"That you are really going to do this. I always have dreams before I start writing."

"I never have, at least I don't think so."

"And you've yet to write your novel," she pointed out. "I'm telling you, this is great. You are really going to do this."

I decided to go with the enthusiasm she was giving me, grateful that she had such confidence in my ability to write, even if I was less sure. Later, as Cal led us through the grounds surrounding the lodge, looking for the perfect setting in which Colleen and Keith should exchange their vows, I tried to work out the relationship of my main characters. My first obstacle was trying to decide if I wanted this to take place in the eighties, or if I should further distance the storyline from that of our parents by setting it in the present. I asked Colleen and she got annoyed.

"Are we doing this now? God, Kelly, one thing at a time. Could we focus on me for a minute? Do you mind?"

"Right, sorry," I said.

"How are we going to do this?" she sighed. "Maybe this is stupid."

"What? Why?"

"Have you seen where to set up chairs and a gazebo, or at least a trellis? And how are we going to get everything up here? I mean the flowers and the cake, and all the food. Where are we going to put anything?" she asked, clearly beginning to freak out.

"Just pick a spot and we'll make it work," Dee Dee assured her.

Colleen closed her eyes, pointed her finger and spun around a couple of times before opening her eyes.

"Great," she said, "we'll be married in the river. Good luck setting those chairs."

"Well," Dee Dee said, stopping to consider.

"No, just no," I laughed. "Come with me," I insisted, taking Colleen's hand. "For one thing you are too far from the hotel, and for another, everything is going to look different once the snow is gone."

"That's just it! This is impossible."

"No it's not. Look around you. It's gorgeous up here. Any spot we choose is going to be perfect. Just look for your two favorite trees and we'll set up a floral trellis between them."

She looked at me as if I were nuts, but I continued to drag her back towards the lodge, saying we wanted to be close enough to have access to the facilities, but far enough away that it wouldn't clutter the background of their wedding photos. After much debate we eventually settled on a spot near the river, with a beautiful backdrop of trees and boulders. Dee Dee promised her we would make it work, and took lots of pictures, both to show Keith, and so that we could later consult them when picking out flowers, and where to set the chairs, etc.

At the back of the lodge there was a good sized patio where they hosted summer bar-b-queues. We checked into using that for the reception, agreeing the patio was large enough to hold several tables, as well as a makeshift dance floor.

"You are going to have to keep the guest list down is all," Dee Dee warned.

"No problem," Colleen said unconvincingly, and I knew as she did, that we were in trouble.

My phone beeped and I looked to see who was texting me, finding the following message; "Inexplicable rubbish from beginning to end. Every letter written, a waste of time. Easily the worst collection of syllables I've ever read. It begs the question, why, why would anyone put this out?"

I cringed, and Colleen snapped her fingers under my nose to get my attention.

"Hello, could you put that away and help figure this out?" she grumbled.

"What are we figuring now?" I asked.

"How we're going to make this look pretty instead of dusty, and what do we do if it rains?"

"You move the party into the lobby," I mumbled, while I texted Gavin that I was so sorry, and then put my phone back into my pocket.

"It's not going to rain," Dee Dee told her.

"You don't know that."

"Nobody knows that, but you have to stop focusing on things that don't matter." I said.

"It's my wedding, Kelly!" she shrieked.

140

"Exactly. You are marrying the love of your life, right? So long as you are here, and Keith is here, that's what matters."

"Oh sure. I don't remember you saying such things when it was your wedding."

"Which is why I'm telling you now. Of course you want it to be beautiful and it will be, but the celebration is what matters, not how it looks. You can stress yourself out so bad that you miss the whole thing like I did, or you can trust Dee Dee and I to sweat the little stuff and concentrate on just appreciating that you have found somebody you want to spend the rest of your life with."

"What if I haven't?" she asked.

"What?" Dee Dee and I both chorused.

"Well, how do you know, I mean, really? I love him. I don't want him to leave, but will I still feel that way five years from now? What if things change? Look at you and Gavin. Are you living the life you thought you would be? No, you are not."

"It doesn't mean that I want to leave him."

"You aren't even having sex!"

"You aren't?" Dee Dee asked.

"Colleen!" I objected. "For your information we had sex the other night, and really, you have to announce it?"

"Was it good, or were you just doing it because I said you had to?

"God! Yes, it was sort of good," I said, rolling my eyes.

"Well, guess what, Keith and I have amazing sex every time, and I want it to stay that way."

"Well guess what, it won't. Not always, but sometimes it will be, and that's worth hanging around for, because believe it or not, sex isn't the only thing that goes into a marriage."

"Every time? Come on," Dee Dee laughed.

"Yes, every time," she insisted.

"What are we talking here?" Dee Dee asked, "multiple orgasms, he says he adores you, or what?"

"Both."

"Every time?"

"Yes."

"Yeah, that's just weird," she laughed.

"That's a load of crap," I couldn't resist saying.

"My point is this," Colleen sighed, "what if it changes and I'm unhappy? What if he strays, or I want to?"

"What if Martians land and force us all to dye our skin green? You are being ridiculous. You love him and he loves you, and unless you've seen something in him that the rest of us haven't, you are going to go through ups and downs just like everyone."

"I know, you're right. Maybe it's not perfect every time," she laughed.

"I'd have to seriously hate you if it were," Dee Dee said.

"So, it was good?" Colleen asked me.

"He gave new meaning to getting free milk from a cow, not to mention we were in the bathroom, so you know, you have so much to look forward to," I laughed.

CHAPTER 21

We left for home around noon, and pulled into my driveway just after six. Meg threw the front door open and fell against me, hugging me so tightly that you'd think I'd been gone for a month.

"I missed you so much!" she told me, as Jack ran over and pushed her. "Ow! Jackie!" she cried, as he did the same.

Hilary walked out from the family room, carrying a sleeping Nick, and said Gavin had just called to say he was meeting a client and would be late. Then she apologetically told me she had to be going, but would be back the next day.

On the drive home, I had been fantasizing about coming home and taking an hour to get down some ideas I'd had in regard to my book. It was with a surprising quickness that all hope flew right out the window.

I was starving, and asked Meg if they'd had dinner. She said they'd had some very stinky bad Mac n Cheese that didn't taste like mine at all, and that there wasn't even any hot dogs to go with it. Jack told me he wanted a cookie, and Meg reminded him that they'd eaten all of the cookies the day before. I went to the cupboards and they were practically bare again. I could have had soup or tomato paste. Instead I chose a piece of toast, although even that was an end piece.

Nick woke up and wanted to nurse, and I ached to be able to feed him, but told myself it would be stupid to do so. I tried giving him a bottle but as Meg told me repeatedly, he didn't want that.

"You try feeding him," I said in frustration.

He nearly rolled off her lap, and I had to grab him just before he hit the ground.

"Where is your father?" I groaned.

"He is out losing my college or something."

"What?"

"That's what he said when he left this morning." she shrugged.

Nick continued to wail, and I alternated between putting him down, to feeling guilty and picking him up again. I put Meg and Jack in the bath, and tried to distract Nick by dipping his feet, but that didn't work either.

Suddenly I heard Corky calling to me.

"Honey, I'm home!"

I grabbed Nick and ran out to the living room where she stood with Scott directly behind her, holding her bags. I wasn't expecting that, and from the look she gave me, neither was she.

"Hi, Honey," I smiled, as Nick continued to cry.

"Happy to see you, too, Nick," she laughed, hugging us both. "Where are my other babies?"

"Oh, in the bath," I said, running back to the bathroom.

Corky followed, and while Jack looked nervous, Meg all but leapt out of the tub and into Corky's arms, giving her a million kisses, and telling her she'd missed her.

"This is more like it," she beamed, squeezing Meg tightly, and asking Jack if he was going to say hi.

"It's Corky," I told him, and he just fussed for me to pick him up.

Scott came back and said he was going to leave, but touching Corky's elbow said, "I'm going to call you in a day or two."

She just looked at him and he walked away.

"What was that?" I asked.

"You tell me. I thought Gavin was picking me up, not him."

"Did he tell you that he didn't break up with you?"

"Yeah, who knew?" she laughed, shaking her head. Then she looked at Nick and asked, "What has got you so upset little man?"

"He wants to nurse but Mommy won't do that," Meg informed her.

"Boundary issues?" she joked.

"I've been told to stop."

"Yeah, I know. Dr. Denial was filling me in when he wasn't accusing me of having our break-up ass backwards."

"I can't wait to hear all about it," I told her, suggesting we get pajamas for the kids and throw them all in bed.

Not one of them thought that was a good idea.

Gavin arrived home as we were reading "The Cat In The Hat" and Corky was failing at attempting to get Nick to take a bottle. Once again, he looked exhausted. Still, seeing Corky, he smiled and told her welcome home, going over to hug her before coming over to me and saying the same.

"Where have you been?" I inquired.

"Hell," he mouthed out, leaning in to kiss my cheek.

"Can you get Nick to take the bottle, or should I give up and nurse him?" I asked.

"Sure," he said taking him, but he wouldn't settle for him either.

Corky and I put Meg and Jack to bed, and when we came back out Nick was still fussing, but Gavin was nodding off, and the bottle was slipping out of his hand.

"Gavin," I said, startling him awake.

"Right, sorry," he said, shaking himself awake and trying to force the bottle into Nick's mouth one last time.

"I take it you didn't get a lot of sleep last night?"

"Not a lot, no."

"What has happened to you people?" Corky teased. "I leave for a little while and you fall to pieces."

"Were you meeting with Sirri?" I asked.

Hearing my voice, Nick pushed the bottle away and began fussing again as Gavin groaned.

"Here," Gavin said pulling some money out of his pocket. "Go buy us a bottle of wine while I get him down and then I'll tell you all about it."

The minute Corky and I got into the car she beamed at me.

"God you are lucky!"

"What?"

"I want what you have so badly it hurts."

"I'm having a nervous breakdown you ass," I couldn't help laughing.

"I know, and I could do without that part, but shit, Gavin is right there with you."

"Yeah, that's not good."

"That's great!" she insisted. "You are so lucky, Kelly. He could have walked away but he's not, is he?"

I just looked at her and she continued.

"He not only loves you, but he has told me he'll do anything to help you because he can't stand to see you unhappy. Have you any idea how many guys would just ignore your unhappiness, or at the very least go find some little skank to take their minds off of it?"

"You haven't improved your opinion of men, have you?" I asked, backing out of the driveway.

"I just don't think you know how good you have it," she said, and I burst into tears because I so wanted to believe that she was right.

"What? Am I missing something?" she asked.

I shook my head, wiped my eyes, and told her I just did this sort of thing all of the time these days.

"You should work on that. Nick is beautiful, by the way."

"How can you tell?"

"I looked at him," she laughed. "Jesus, Kelly, you are taking things way too seriously. We have to loosen you up. We may need more than one bottle of wine."

CHAPTER 22

When we got back to the house it was so quiet that I was sure Gavin would be asleep, but he came wandering down the hallway, asking if we'd thought to buy any food while we were gone.

"Only cereal and milk because I need to do a real shopping tomorrow."

"Cereal and wine?" he frowned.

"It's a western delicacy," Corky assured him. "You place a bowl of dry cereal on the table and nibble it like a snack while drinking your wine. It's a big thing in all of the finest establishments."

"Is it now?"

"Oh, yes!"

Gavin smiled at me and I smiled back, grateful to have Corky in our lives again to lighten up all that had become way too serious.

While Gavin opened the wine and poured us each a glass, I filled her in on what had so far gone down between Gavin and Sirri Bingington. Then I asked Gavin if the book had at least made sense as he had read further.

"Sadly, no," he said.

"But it was her you were meeting with tonight, right?"

"It was."

"And how'd that go?"

"Not real well," he sighed, before taking a slow sip of wine.

"Take us through it from the beginning," Corky told him. "First off, where did you meet?"

He glanced over at me before mumbling that he'd met her at her house.

"Uh oh!" Corky laughed, "Were advances made?"

"Advances may have been made."

"What?" I shrieked.

"Don't wake the children. It's not as if I acknowledged them. I could be off my game here and imagining it all anyway. I'm really quite knackered."

"Start at the beginning," I told him.

Gavin sat across from Corky and I as we were curled up on the sofa. Taking another drink of wine, he sighed and said he'd asked to meet her in a more public location, but she'd guessed that he wished to discuss the book and she wanted privacy.

"I must say, at that point I was hopeful that this was another of her tests, and that what she had given me was a massive joke, although I couldn't make sense of its sheer volume," he told us. "She lives in the Bel Aire end of Beverly Glen Canyon, in a gated Mediterranean with manicured grounds. It's quite the show place, you'd abhor it," he smiled at me. "Pretentious as can be."

"Alone?" Corky asked.

"Alone," he confirmed.

"How old is she? She's older than us right?" she asked.

"She's forty."

"Does she look good? She's pretty, isn't she?"

"She's alright I suppose," he said

"Breathing and with ample bosoms then?" Corky laughed. "What was she wearing?"

"I don't know, some sort of billowy thing. I think it was a long dress of some sort."

"Meaning he couldn't see past the bosoms," she told me.

"Stop that. Do you want to hear what happened or not?" he asked.

"Sorry," she laughed. "I'm just teasing you, go on."

"Right, so she greeted me at the door and led me back to her study. She offered me a drink which I declined, and which she made anyway, telling me it was just in case. Then we sat on a sofa much like you are now, and her eyes sparked as she asked me to tell her what I'd thought of the book. She said she couldn't wait to hear! Well, I breathed a sigh of relief didn't I, because the smile on her face was so broad that it could only mean that she knew it was shit."

"Oh no," I moaned.

"Kelly, if you'd seen the smile you'd have thought the same," he insisted.

"Don't interrupt," Corky said hitting my leg. "Go on," she told Gavin.

"I told her I was going to be honest, and that I'd never read anything like it, which I suppose would have been fine if only I'd left it at that, but then I proceeded to let her know that I'd never been so bored in all my life."

I cringed as Corky laughed, and asked what she'd had to say about that. Gavin cringed too and went to refill his glass.

"It was bloody miserable from that point on," he sighed. "I said it was a joke, expecting her to say well of course it was, but instead she began weeping, and told me she'd spent months writing this, and nearly a year researching it beforehand. I couldn't stop myself from asking her, researching what, strip clubs? Male prostitution? And I told her I was only guessing that that was what the book was meant to be about, because it was so lost in descriptive details that a plot of any substance was impossible to unearth. I really thought even then she'd begin to laugh Kel, I promise you I did."

"Oh, God," I groaned, wanting to laugh, but it wasn't funny, at least to me, Corky though couldn't stop laughing.

"Then what happened?" she asked, eager to hear more.

"I apologized, and said I wished I could tell her it was fantastic, but it's not, and she told me to get out. I got up to leave and she followed me to the door, stopping me at the last moment to say that she couldn't believe I was being so hurtful. I apologized again and said I was disappointed too, at which point she fell against me sobbing wildly. It was terribly awkward."

"Terribly, terribly awkward," Corky giggled. "God love you Brits! Go on," she told him.

"I led her over to another couch in another room, desperately trying to come up with something positive to say, but I was coming up blank, when she told me that her previous agent hadn't thought it was crap. However a moment later, she admitted she'd severed all ties with him because he'd told her it wasn't commercial enough. And yes," he said to me, "I told her that is because it is crap."

"So that's that, then," I sighed.

"She's said she's going to take some time to reconsider, and that she has an idea for another novel, but she'll have to consider if she's up to showing me the outline or not. I've told her I'll understand if she wants to part ways."

"I'd think you'd be praying for it, if she's half as bad as you say," Corky said.

"She's a huge name in the industry, I need her," he sighed. "Scott said there had to be a catch that she was coming to an agency as small as mine. I should have known this was coming."

"Scott is a giant shit if he told you that!" Corky exclaimed, and I agreed.

"You're a great agent, Gavin, I know that, and the truth is, you didn't tell her anything that she didn't need to hear," I said.

"She was our ticket, I was so sure."

"I know," I swallowed.

"There will be others," Corky insisted.

Gavin said he was going to bed, and told us not to stay up all night, as was often our tradition. Corky and I finished our wine and I told her I wanted to hear what Scott had said on their drive from the airport.

"Apart from what the hell have you been telling people?" she laughed.

"Yes. I want all the details. Have you guys even spoken since you left?"

"Not unless you count the night I got drunk and wanted to hear his voice so bad that I prank called him with the old, is your dishwasher running, and told him he'd better catch it."

"Did he know it was you?"

She just looked at me and laughed.

"We were together for almost five years, of course he knew it was me."

"And you talked?"

"Oh God no. He said my name and I hung up and cried myself to sleep."

"When was this?"

"About two months ago, when I was agonizing over sleeping with that guy."

"What guy?"

"The guy, Mark. I know I told you. He was going to back the show, or maybe he even did for awhile, I'm not sure. He looked like James Franco in that movie where he cut his arm off."

"I remember you saying there was a guy hanging around who looked like James Franco, but you didn't tell me you slept with him."

"I didn't in the end. I couldn't. How stupid is that?"

"I guess we'll never know."

"He was a really good kisser," she smiled, "But it was just too soon."

"Which brings us back to Scott," I said, unable to hold back a yawn.

"You're tired and so am I. Lets save this discussion for tomorrow," she suggested.

"Really?"

"Yeah, so am I in with Nick?"

"Either that or out here, whichever you prefer."

"I'll take Nick's room with a real bed," she said, and gave me a hug. "I'm glad I'm here," she told me.

CHAPTER 23

Nick was awake at 3:30 am but distracted by Corky who informed him his roommate manners needed to be seriously adjusted. Feeling shy, he nestled into my shoulder and magically went back to sleep. I couldn't believe it, and told Corky she might have to live with us forever. When I climbed back into bed, Gavin turned and asked why Nick had stopped crying, scolding me for having nursed him before I could even deny that I had. When I told him the baby had just gone back to sleep, he was as shocked as I was.

The alarm went off the next morning and Gavin rolled towards me instead of away from me. Yawning, he asked if Corky and I had plans for the day.

"Not really."

"Hilary will be here, so in theory you could go out," he said, rubbing my thigh under the sheets.

I hadn't thought of that, but just knowing that it was a possibility allowed me to face the day with less dread than I had felt in months. Smiling, I was moved to kiss him, but due to stale wine and morning breath, we both frowned after the fact.

"Bad idea" I admitted.

"No, great idea," he smiled, "just lousy timing," he said as Meg and Jack both ran into our room.

"I'm hungry!" Jack announced.

"I can wake Corky?" Meg asked, as I heard Nick start to cry.

"She'll want to sleep," I said, getting up.

Sure enough I went down to get Nick and she covered her head with her pillow. I grabbed him as well as a diaper, and then shut the door behind us. Somehow through several morning scuffles and baby breakdowns, she managed to sleep until almost eleven. I was in awe. While she slept, I took Meg to school, caught up on laundry, made a detailed grocery list, took a shower, and scheduled Nick's six month check-up, while Hilary watched the boys for me.

Stumbling into the kitchen looking for coffee, Corky announced that my hotel had gotten much louder than in years past.

"I know, I've noticed."

Jack ran over to her and said hello, as she eyed him with suspicion.

"We're friends now?" she asked.

"Hi," he repeated.

"Is that all you've got?"

"Mine" he said grabbing his blankie from the kitchen chair she was about to sit on.

"I'll keep that in mind."

"Hi," he giggled again.

"Okay, back off now, Jack," I said, suggesting he go play with his blocks.

The phone rang and it was Colleen asking if Corky had arrived, and reminding me that we were to meet at Mark's Garden flower shop the next morning, to go over her bridal bouquet choices. I assured her I'd be there, and hung up, passing our conversation on to Corky.

"I read her books, did I tell you?" she asked.

"No, what did you think?"

"Well, first off, as you know, vampires are not my thing, but considering, I thought they were really good. Far more entertaining than I had hoped. What possessed her to write in that genre? That's so not her."

"I asked once, and she said it was just an experiment, but the more she got into it, the more she knew she might have something. She says what she is writing now is more mainstream, but she's getting shit for it. Her agent doesn't think it will be well received."

"Why isn't she with Gavin?"

"Because she doesn't believe in mixing in-laws and business, and I have to say, I'm okay with that."

"Yeah, that could get tricky, I guess," she agreed.

"Trust me, as you can bear witness to, Gavin is painfully honest and I doubt Colleen could handle that."

"But you can?"

"Absolutely. I have complete and total respect for his opinion. If he told me what I had written was awful, I'd trust that he knew what he was talking about."

"Sure, but it would hurt, wouldn't it?"

"Probably, but I don't want to put out crap, so you know," I shrugged.

She nodded her agreement as the phone rang again, this time being Gavin, who asked that I remember to take his shirts to the cleaners. I walked away to have a quick financial discussion, wanting to know how much I could spend in the grocery store, hoping to avoid another embarrassing incident. I didn't really care if Corky knew how much we were struggling, but I knew Gavin would be embarrassed by it. When I hung up, I went back and asked Corky if there was anything she wanted, or needed to do, and she considered before smiling a still sleepy smile.

"Let's see, get a job, get a home, get a life, but other than that, not really, how about you?"

"Domestic chores, grocery shopping, the cleaners, vacuuming," I frowned.

"I've heard you need to write. That demented guy that picked me up from the airport last night indicated it was a matter of life and death."

"It's a dream of mine, I cannot tell a lie. However, my children and husband expect to be fed on a daily basis."

"So we will multi-task!" she announced. "We shall shop for groceries and an opening line, or scene, or both if we are feeling particularly ambitious."

"God, I've missed you," I said, on the verge of becoming overcome with emotion.

As we ran errands that afternoon, Corky quizzed me on my characters, setting, and the all-important opening line. I was in the cleaners when I decided that my protagonist would be named Callie, and in the produce section of the grocery store when I declared her to be a frustrated interior designer without enough clients. On the way home Corky asked what Callie was doing as the book opened, and I instantly saw her stepping into a bath.

"Cool, see, you are on your way," she assured me.

We returned home to Nick's fussing and Jack's wanting to go outside. I took Nick from Hilary so that she could take Jack and Meg outside while we unloaded the groceries and figured out what to make for dinner. Settling on chicken fettuccini in butter and garlic, Corky said she would feed Nick while I took a little while to come up with my opening line.

"Just go lock yourself in your room and see what you come up with," she encouraged.

With everyone taken care of I had no excuse not to.

CHAPTER 24

"Following a twelve hour flight, a harrowing taxi ride to her hotel, and a confusing argument with the concierge regarding promised room service that apparently didn't exist, Callie filled the claw footed tub which was somewhat oddly stationed before a large picture window overlooking the Italian countryside. Throwing modesty aside, she undressed and slid under the warm water, allowing it to wash over her body as her tired tears washed over her cheeks."

It wasn't perfect, that was for sure, but it was the most I had written in a long, long time, and it set the scene I wanted. At least I finally had an image in my head. I wasn't sure about the word "stationed", but I didn't like placed or situated any better. I found my old thesaurus and came up with positioned, deciding that would be preferable. Then I realized the first line was too long, so I broke it into two. I ended the first line at tub, and then explained it's positioning in the next. I also decided that as tired as she was, she would set her modesty aside only so far. Lastly, I had her tears mirror the sliding instead of the washing over. As of when I went out to start dinner I had these three sentences:

> *"Following a twelve hour flight, a harrowing cab ride to her hotel, and a confusing argument with the concierge regarding promised room service that apparently no longer existed, Callie filled the claw footed tub. A tub that was somewhat oddly positioned before a large picture window, overlooking the Italian countryside. Throwing modesty aside, she quickly undressed and slid under the warm water, allowing it to wash over her body, as tired tears slid down her cheeks."*

Corky ran back to read it, and then all through dinner we debated whether or not tears could be tired. Gavin came home around eight and we asked his opinion, explaining that I had actually written three whole lines.

"Did you?" he smiled. "That's fantastic, and tired tears are involved, are they?"

"For the moment, anyway," I confirmed.

Meg, who had just been sent to bed, ran out to greet him, and he asked her if she'd read what I had written. Wrinkling her nose, she reminded him that she couldn't yet read.

"Right then, that tells me you must be young, and therefore should be tucked away for the night," he said, taking her hand and leading her back to her room amid weak protests.

Corky's phone buzzed and she showed me a text from Scott asking her to meet him for a drink.

"What's the story with him really? Has he been seeing anyone?" she asked.

"I have no idea. We haven't exactly been social of late. I don't think he was with anyone at Colleen's party."

"Who's that, Scott?" Gavin asked, returning to the family room where we were discussing the matter.

Corky nodded and he sat next to me, draping his arm around my neck in such a relaxed manner that it threw up in my face again just how long it had been since we had felt any kind of connection.

"He's very much in love with you, and has been for quite some time," Gavin announced.

"Gavin, regardless of what he is saying now, he is the one who wanted out of our relationship, not me," Corky stated.

"I only know what he has told me as recently as this weekend."

Shaking her head, she suggested we order up a movie.

"Can I see what you wrote first?" Gav asked me.

I got it for him and held my breath as he read it, relieved that he looked up at me after and smiled.

"That is a very respectable beginning, and yes, in this instance I believe her tears would in fact be tired."

"I told you," Corky said, turning on the TV and scrolling through the guide to find us a movie to watch.

When Scott texted for a second time, she turned her phone off, claiming not to be interested in anyone too lazy to make an actual call. Then, of course, the movie she chose to watch was The Notebook. Gavin couldn't help laughing, but decided to walk away as she and I have watched that movie many times before, and he is of the opinion that it is greatly overrated.

When it ended, Corky and I both sighed in unison.

"Do you want to talk about it?" I asked.

"What, how love shouldn't be so complicated?"

"Something like that," I said, unable to suppress a yawn.

"Kelly!" she laughingly objected.

"Sorry, I'm totally awake."

"You're a total liar, go to bed."

"No, really we can talk."

"We'll talk tomorrow," she insisted.

Unable to keep from yawning again, I apologized and said goodnight.

Gavin was not asleep, but instead on the phone with Scott, who among other things wanted to know why Corky was ignoring him when he was certain they had shared a moment as they'd first locked eyes at the airport. When Gavin passed this on to me, rolling his eyes as he did so, I couldn't help but laugh. I suggested he hang up, and promised that I would get to the bottom of it the next day.

Lying in the dark, Gavin told me he was proud of me for having made the leap into actually writing down my thoughts.

"What did you do today?" I asked.

"A lot of follow up calls and emails, a little marketing of both my writers and myself, the usual," he sighed, sounding less than enthused.

"You need to be attending conferences, don't you?" I asked.

He didn't answer because it was so obvious that it didn't require a reply. When he was with Trinity, he'd attended conferences all around the country, and even throughout Europe, actively looking for new writers. Clearly waiting for them to magically appear, regardless of his reputation, was not working. I wanted to tell him to go for it, but of course traveling is not cheap, and mixed with my issues, the timing was less than ideal. Instead I told him I loved him and went to sleep.

CHAPTER 25

Corky and I arrived at the Mark's Garden flower shop before either Colleen or Dee Dee, and looking around, discussed why my character had come to Italy only to be in that hotel room alone.

"I thought she was meeting her husband and checking up on him," Corky said.

"She thought so, too, but it turns out he's traveled to some small village to investigate a lead in his story."

"What is his story?"

"I think he's writing a piece on some politician with Mafia ties. It's probably not going to pan out. I think I'll pretend that not all politicians are crooks."

"So you are writing fantasy."

"A little bit," I agreed.

"So she's in the tub, what happens next?" she asked.

"She'll probably think about why she is there and possibly back to when she first fell for this guy, unless you think that's too rushed. Do you think I should leave that for later?"

"Build the suspense a little?" she considered.

"Maybe the suspense comes into play in not knowing why she is there and so miserable," I proposed. "Maybe you leave the reader thinking they had this great thing, and wanting to know what's happened. Maybe you don't find out until the very end."

"Maybe, although that might get irritating."

"If it does, I'll just have to restructure it," I said, checking the time on my phone and wondering where Colleen and Dee Dee were.

They came in a few minutes later, coffees in hand, and looked surprised to see us.

"You made it out of the house!" Colleen shrieked, running over to hug Corky and welcome her back home. "You look fantastic and rumor has it you got rave reviews!" she told her.

"Right up until they fired us all," she laughed.

"It's a terrible profession, acting. You should really give it up. Keith says he'd never go back. He's so much happier on the writing end of things."

"I didn't know he acted," Corky said.

"He did, before we met, but that's how he started out." she smiled, as one of the florists came over and asked if they were his ten thirty.

We were shown books of designs, all of which cost more than the down payment on our house, but Colleen didn't appear to be phased. Her only concern was what would look best out among the trees and boulders. The whole thing made me uncomfortable. The idea that you would spend money at all, to essentially put nature back into nature, seemed preposterous. Sensing my disapproval, Colleen sighed.

"What?" she demanded.

"Nothing."

"You think I'm being ridiculous?"

"No, it's your wedding and it should be whatever you want," I said, not wanting to spoil this for her.

"But?" she pressed.

"But nothing, honest. The wildflower package is lovely."

"Is it the money?"

"Colleen," Dee Dee intercepted, "she said it's nothing, let it go."

"You think it's immoral, right?"

"It's a wedding and they are expensive, I get that," I said.

"But?" she said again.

"But you are decorating the most beautiful setting in the world. For God sake , that's why you chose it, remember? And the idea that you have to make it more than it already is, is absurd. So there, I said it, okay?" I snapped, turning to leave.

"I knew you'd be jealous," she muttered.

"You guys," Dee Dee whined.

"And I knew you'd hope that's what it is, so that you don't have to look at how stupid you are being."

"Oh, I'm stupid? At least I'm not so stupid as to be having a nervous breakdown because times are tight," she snarled, as Dee Dee cringed, and Corky pushed me towards the door.

"*Let it go, Let it go,*" she sang, reciting that song from Frozen, a movie Meg had watched a thousand times or more.

I stomped out of the flower shop grumbling about what a predictable bitch Colleen was, only to have Dee Dee follow us to our car.

"She doesn't mean it, Kelly. She's just stressing today. We'll talk later, okay?"

"She does too mean it," I said, dissolving into tears.

"She and Keith had a big fight last night during which he accused her of being shallow. That's what this is about. Don't pay any attention to what she said. She loves you with all of her heart."

"Even though I'm having a breakdown?" I asked, rolling my eyes.

"She didn't mean it and she's going to regret saying that, truly."

"Whatever," I sniffled, getting into the car.

Corky said goodbye to Dee Dee, got into the car, and didn't say anything for about three minutes. Then she looked over at me.

"Who was that back there with Colleen?" she asked. "She physically reminds me of Dee Dee, and yet she practically appeared compassionate."

I was trying not to lose it. I couldn't shake the look of disdain Colleen had shot me when she'd said I was having a breakdown. I felt worthless and guilty. My hands began to shake as I admitted to myself that I was in fact incredibly jealous of Colleen. She got to do whatever she wanted, whenever she wanted. She had the successful writing career that had been all but promised to me, and now she was able to afford her dream wedding with a designer gown, million dollar flowers, and whatever else she wanted. For all intents and purposes, she was living the life I should be living. The life we had discussed living on countless nights growing up. She was my big sister and she didn't even like me.

Suddenly I couldn't catch my breath, and my eyes were so flooded with tears that I couldn't really see to drive. I quickly slammed on my breaks and three cars rammed into us, the airbags exploding towards us with the first impact. I think I screamed.

CHAPTER 26

There I was in the emergency room again, only this time instead of asking me if I was suicidal, they seemed to be trying to convince me that I was. Everything hurt, even though there didn't appear to be anything specific wrong with me. The pounding in my head I was told, was due to stress and a spike in my blood pressure. I was asked repeatedly why I had come to an abrupt stop in ongoing traffic, if I wasn't trying to injure myself. I told them I was attempting the exact opposite.

They refused to release me until my blood pressure was under control and I had calmed down, not that I was doing anything other than crying. I was given valium and a muscle relaxant, and warned that although they couldn't prove it enough to keep me there, I was a danger to myself, and quite possibly others. I asked to see Corky, who'd been the one to insist I get checked out. She hadn't liked the way I'd been breathing just before we'd crashed. I apologized profusely.

"Don't worry about it. I know it wasn't intentional, but from now on, I'll be the one doing the driving," she said.

"I could have gotten us killed, and that's what I was trying to avoid," I cried. "I don't know what I was thinking."

"It's fine, Kel."

"It's not fine at all. Gavin's going to kill me."

"Gavin is on his way down here to pick us up, and is just grateful that we weren't hurt."

"I keep screwing up."

"It's okay, you're tired, both mentally and physically, that's all. You are going to be fine, I promise. I'll take care of you."

"What if the kids had been in the car?" I gasped, horrified at the thought.

"They weren't, and they won't be until you are better. Stop stressing. We're lucky, okay? We get to walk out of here, and that makes this a good day."

"I love you," I cried.

"I love you, too," she said, as a nurse came in and handed me a prescription for more valium, along with a list of mental health facilities.

I was strongly urged to get help before any more accidents occurred. Something I was informed would be inevitable without the proper care. When I stood up to leave, I felt loopy, and suggested to Corky that she might want to share in my new found drugs. She said she'd be happy with a tall glass of wine.

"Like really tall. Like the kind of tall goblets they drank out of centuries ago. We're talking big," she joked.

Gavin arrived, rushed in and immediately hugged me protectively, while reaching out to also rub Corky's arm. Taking a deep breath he told us he was glad we were okay. It meant a lot to me that he was relieved for both of us. One of the best things about Gavin is his understanding of our friendship, and how important Corky is to me. I've always appreciated that he accepted her as the family that she is to me, from the very start, and likewise, I appreciate the way in which she has accepted him. There has rarely, if ever, been an issue of jealousy between them.

As per Corky's request, we stopped to pick up some wine on our way home, as well as filling my prescription. Gavin said he thought I should try taking the valium for a couple of days at the very least, to see if it wouldn't lesson my anxiety. Like Corky, he also forbid me to drive. Approaching the house, I saw Colleen's Porsche parked in the driveway and considered asking Gavin not to stop. Instead I cursed under my breath.

"Need to pop another pill now, do you?" Corky teased.

"Yes! I'm not ready to deal with her."

"Why ever not?" Gavin asked, oblivious to how the day had begun.

"They exchanged words at the florist," Corky informed him, as Meg threw open the front door and ran out to greet us, quickly followed by Jack and Colleen.

"What kind of words?" he inquired.

174

"Not nice words," I said, carefully getting out of the car, as Gavin cautioned Meg not to jump on me, and hurried over to put his arm around my waist, as if I needed help to walk.

Granted, the drive home had somehow managed to wipe me out, but I was hardly crippled, and perfectly capable of walking on my own. I wasn't even feeling light headed anymore. Still, there was something gallant about his efforts.

Hilary stood at the door, holding Nick, who reached for me as we drew closer. I took him from her, and Gavin asked if I wanted to go to bed. It was still only early afternoon.

"Yes," Corky said, before I could answer.

"It's two," I objected.

"And you need to rest," she insisted, taking Nick from me.

"I know, but..."

"The nurse has spoken, Kelly," Gavin announced, taking me back to our room.

"Kel," Colleen said, following us.

"Give us a few minutes, will you?" Gavin asked, cutting her off.

"I just want to apologize," she began, but again he interrupted.

"Give us a few," he repeated, closing our bedroom door behind us.

Once we were alone, he held me, and sighing, stroked my hair, mumbling that I'd scared him. Surprising myself yet again, I sobbed that I had scared myself too, and no doubt Corky as well.

"What happened, Luv? Why were you having a panic attack? That's what it was, right?"

"I guess," I nodded.

"What did Colleen say to upset you?"

"I don't want to talk about it."

"Right, but we must, mustn't we, because you can't keep holding things inside."

"I probably started it," I confessed.

"Be that as it may."

"She said I was jealous, and indicated that I was having a breakdown just because we don't have money."

"After she's been leading the charge that it's due to your needing to write? Well that's a right cheap shot. Says more about her than you, now doesn't it?"

"She's not entirely wrong. I am jealous of her success, and I hate myself for it."

"Whatever for? I'm jealous of her success as well, but I certainly don't hate myself for it. She's driving a Porsche, Kelly. She can buy pretty much whatever she wants now, can't she? Her career is going swimmingly. I'd be concerned if you weren't jealous. It's not like we want her to fail, or is it?" he asked.

"No, of course not, but I have you and the kids, and that should be enough."

"Rubbish! Absolutely not," he declared. "You really have gone round the bend, haven't you? These things that you have, as lovely as we are, they aren't what you thought you were getting, now are they?"

"So what?"

"So you aren't wrong to be jealous of someone who has seemingly achieved everything that you imagined you'd have by now."

"She's my sister. I should be happy for her."

"Given the chance, would you take it away from her?"

"Only for a minute after she made that crack about my breakdown."

"Exactly, so you've nothing to be upset about."

"Except for the fact that I can't even handle my life right now and she can."

"Not your life, she can't. And there's no telling how well she is handling her own, seeing as she's felt the need to kick you when you're down."

"Why are you being so nice to me, Gavin? I've smashed my car, and we aren't going to be able to get it fixed, let alone pay for the hike in insurance that we both know is coming. That accident was completely my fault."

"I know that, but as Corky pointed out to me when she called, we got very lucky today. We could have lost everything, and instead all we've lost is a portion of one car. Don't worry about it, it's not important."

I cried.

I cried out of relief and exhaustion. I cried out of love and guilt, and I cried because I wanted to believe that he would continue to feel so lucky, but was pretty sure that he wouldn't. I was pretty sure it would pass.

He told me to get some sleep, tucking me into bed and going out to inform Colleen that I was too spent to handle anymore drama. I heard her start to object, but he obviously moved her away from the hallway as they continued to talk. I couldn't hear anything else he said to her. Instead I closed my eyes and did my best to shut out the world. Sleep didn't come instantly but it did come, and I didn't wake up until a few hours later when all hell broke out.

CHAPTER 27

I'm not sure what woke me first, Nick's shrill screams, Jack's crying, or Gavin's yelling "Bloody Fuck!" As I sat up, Meg ran into our room, and looking panicked, told me Corky was burning us up, our whole house!

I jumped out of bed, but was nearly stopped cold by how stiff and sore my back and neck felt. As if sensing that, Meg grabbed my hand and dragged me out to the kitchen, just as the smoke alarm in the hallway began screeching. We'd disconnected the one in the kitchen because it had a tendency to go off every time you turned on the stove.

Jack rounded the corner, throwing himself at me while hysterically crying, and frantically attempted to scale my legs. He was terrified of the high pitched siren the alarm sounded. I achingly pulled him up into my arms, and looking out to the kitchen, saw Gavin tossing my best frying pan into the sink. Corky looked on as she held Nick in her arms, who upon noticing me, also began to fuss.

I told Meg to grab a dish towel, and then I took it and waved it in front of the alarm, trying to bat away the smoke. Again, doing so was incredibly painful. Gavin came up behind me, took the towel out of my hand, and draped it over the alarm, instantly shutting it off. Jack, however, continued to wail, all the while trying to crawl back into the womb, he was so freaked out. Gavin attempted to take him from me but he was not having it, so we both did our best to calm him. I moved into the living room, sat on the couch, and held him tight, promising him it was okay. Gavin collapsed down onto the couch next to us, looking exhausted, and we listened to Meg telling Corky that she should just leave the cooking up to me.

Corky joined us a minute later, having fixed Nick a bottle, and smiling, said, "I'm Baaaack!"

This was not the first time she had nearly burned down our house. Meg was right. Cooking was not her strong suit.

"Pizza then?" Gavin proposed.

"With chicken!" Meg suggested.

"You'll want yours plain, right?" Corky asked me.

I attempted to nod but couldn't really move my neck. Seeing me grimace, Gavin asked if I was okay.

"Not even close," I said, looking at Corky. "Aren't you sore?"

"I've doubled up on Advil and wine, so it's not too bad."

"I'll get you the same," Gavin offered, jumping up.

"You can't mix the valium with alcohol," Corky warned.

"Can she have the Advil?" he inquired.

180

"Sure, probably the wine too, but they say not to mix the two."

"So the Advil, can she have it?" he asked, suddenly sounding impatient.

"Yes," she told him.

"Daddy's grumpy," Meg sulked.

"He has good reason," Corky told her, mouthing out to me that we'd talk later.

I didn't know if that meant even more had gone on, or if she was just not wanting to rehash things in front of the kids. Jack finally sat up, wiped his nose on his sleeve, and tearfully told us he was hungry. He wanted to know if dinner was ready, and got mad at us when we laughed at him.

Gavin returned a few minutes later on the phone, and while handing me some Advil, informed us that Scott was going to pick up the pizzas for us. Corky rolled her eyes, and went to get me some water. Gavin hung up and quietly informed me that Scott was worried about Corky. She returned before I could inquire as to why that was.

As soon as Scott arrived, Corky made a point of avoiding him by micromanaging the kids and me. If I hadn't felt so miserable, it would have been comical. I could tell it was amusing Gavin, while annoying the hell out of Scott. I crawled back to bed as soon as we were done eating, and listened to Corky play the role of super nanny, while telling Scott to help or get out of the way. Gavin came back to check on me and I told him I wanted the wine to go with my Advil because on it's own, it wasn't doing any good at all.

"They think you are suicidal, you know," he told me.

"That was made clear, yes."

"But you aren't now, are you?"

"Of course not."

"Good, then stay out of the wine. I'll get you a valium," he offered.

I tried to shrug but it literally brought tears to my eyes. I didn't understand how Corky could be functioning as well as she was. She brought Jack and Meg in to say goodnight a little while later, telling me she'd be back once she had them tucked in. I told her to hurry. When she returned, she brought with her a glass of wine that Gavin had told her not to share with me. She closed the door and climbed into bed with me, confessing that she did in fact feel as though she'd been run over by a Mack truck. Not only that, but she told me she'd been warned that we'd both feel even worse the next day. I didn't want to hear it even though I'd suspected that would be the case.

"What's up with you and Scott?" I asked.

I don't know, I might hate him," she said, and I couldn't help but bite my tongue to keep from laughing. "Okay, so I probably love him more, but that's stupid, Kel, because he's an idiot."

"Well, sure, but he's been that for a while," I teased.

"I know. I called him this afternoon after I called Gavin," she confessed, "because suddenly my whole life was passing before my eyes. I guess it was a delayed reaction, but then the crash was so sudden and unexpected that I didn't have time for it when it first happened."

"So from the hospital?"

"Yes. I was thinking I was just going to tell him that he had to figure out where they'd towed your car, and that he should deal with the practical stuff that I imagine people deal with after a crash, while I made sure you were okay. It didn't come out exactly as I'd planned," she smiled, taking a gulp of her wine.

"How did it come out?"

"It was something more like, Oh my God, what the hell is wrong with you? What is going on? I almost died! Kelly almost died! We could be dead! We were hit by three separate cars! We're at the hospital and I can't even call you, because you aren't in my life, and that's because you removed yourself. You are such a spoiled little baby commit-a-phobe that you are letting life pass you by. Well screw you Scott! And by this time I was crying of course," she added, "Just screw you. I don't want a loser who runs when things get intense. I'm intense. Life is intense. Deal with it."

"He didn't ask if you were hurt, or why you were at the hospital?" I inquired."

"Yeah, sure he did. He asked repeatedly, but I told him he wouldn't care, and to just forget about it. I hung up and he called right back, so I went cold on him, and said we were both fine, and that he might want to call Gavin, unless he felt Gavin was getting all intense too, in which case maybe he should run away like he always does."

"Well, that seems fair," I laughed. "Not that I'd really blame him if he did run away by now, because this is not fun."

"You'd tell me if you were suicidal, right?" she asked, in all seriousness.

"Of course I would. I'm losing my mind, but I don't want to die. I just don't understand why this is happening. This isn't me, is it? I'm not this much of a drama queen, am I?"

"I always thought you were the steady one in your family," she assured me.

"Me, too."

"I have to be honest about it," she told me, "I can't really wrap my head around it. I mean, Gavin told me you were in a really fragile state, but I didn't know what he meant, and I was just jealous that you had someone concerned enough about you to care. I mean, I love you, and I'm glad you do, but I was sure he was exaggerating."

"I remember overhearing my mom talking to one of her friends when I was around ten," I said, "and they were discussing the wife of someone that my Dad had worked with, who she said had had a nervous breakdown. I always wondered what that meant. I imagined someone sitting in an insane asylum with a blank expression on their face. I didn't think that you would just get upset all of the time and have melt downs. I feel as if I have the coping mechanism of a two year old. Jack and I are now equals, only I fear he's about to surpass me. And it's not just emotional either. I feel myself physically coming unglued.

Every day I tell myself I can do this, and then I step out onto the high wire and I start to panic. I physically couldn't breathe this morning."

"I know. That's what freaked me out. Just before you stopped the car, like a split second before, I realized you were having a full on panic attack, but after we crashed I started wondering if it was something else, because that's so not you. That's why I insisted you let them take you to the hospital, because I was suddenly thinking, what if it's a brain tumor or something."

"It's so weird," I told her. "I mean everything hurts, of course, but I feel like if I just get some sleep, I could get up in the morning and be normal, but then that's what I thought this morning."

"And from what one of those doctors was saying, that's the problem. He said you can't just pretend nothing is going on. He said you are like a house that's been knocked off its foundation and that now you are unstable and unsafe."

"God! He called me a house? I really have to get my body back."

"I think you have to find a shrink."

"We tried that. He told me I'm bipolar! I'm so not bipolar!"

"Of course not, but just because he was the wrong doctor, you don't quit."

"And we pay for it how Corky? Our insurance is crap."

"So you ask for help. Let's just find someone decent, and if you like them, then we'll figure out how to pay them. That really can't be your focus. Your focus has to be surpassing Meg in the coping arena. We both need to raise the bar to at least a five year old status. I'll send you to the shrink and learn how to deal vicariously," she concluded.

CHAPTER 28

The following day I was no longer the only one in pain. Corky and I were both completely miserable, and spent most of the day doing nothing but moaning, and occasionally watching an episode or two of *Friends*. I was incredibly grateful for Hilary, even if Jack was not. He wanted me to do everything from feeding him, to changing his diaper, but I just couldn't. I was so stiff and achy that I felt ready to break in two. I popped Valium, and Corky continued to pop Advil and wine. Gavin was gone for most of the day, but when he came home and Hilary left, he was all but swallowed up by his children. He came to bed at nine, exhausted and frustrated that I hadn't done anything all day.

"I can't do this for you Kelly," he told me.

"What are you talking about?" I groaned.

"You have to want to get well. Do you want to get well?"

"Of course I do, have you discovered a magical cure that you have neglected to mention?"

"A doctor, Kelly. I can't choose for you. You need to get on this, don't you, so that we can concentrate on other things."

"Oh, I'm sorry, Gavin, my breakdown is boring you? I'll get up first thing and take care of it," I sarcastically told him.

"It's been a long day," he sighed.

"Every day is a long day," I mumbled, feeling defeated.

"So you'll take care of this tomorrow. No more lying around." he announced.

"And we'll pay for it how?"

"However we have to. I'll rob a bloody bank if I must."

"That would be something, wouldn't it?" I said, and he looked over at me and actually smiled.

"Well yes Sweetheart, it would."

He leaned in and kissed me the gentlest kiss, but when he reached for me I recoiled. He sighed and turned his back to me, pulling the sheet around himself. I promised him that I did want to get well, and said I'd figure out how to get help the next day, but he was done talking, and I was all but left alone.

I laid awake for hours thinking about what the most practical approach back to health would be. I still couldn't believe this was real, and that I couldn't turn it around on my own. I didn't want to obsess about money, and yet it was almost impossible not to. As small as our house was for the five of us, it was in a nice, safe suburb of Los Angeles, and with that came a large mortgage. We had three kids to provide for, and now a nanny to pay as well. I concluded that I needed to write and generate some income while doing so.

Having been published in the past, I considered writing articles for a parenting magazine, or embellishing my breakdown for the entertainment of others. I concluded the latter would be easier if I really were bipolar, as that quack had said. After all, it was the soup d'jour of diseases, at least for the moment. I knew I didn't want to do either of those things though. I wanted to write my novel.

I thought about Devon telling me to talk to that Estelle woman too, and wondered if it wouldn't be more cost effective to go lock myself in a hotel room, and just write the damned novel I'd been wanting to write for so long. I imagined how wonderfully peaceful it would be to have a fully stocked mini bar, a big bed all to myself, and the time to actually think. It sounded like heaven.

 I finally drifted off to sleep, but instead of dreaming of hotels and peacefulness, I dreamt of being in that tunnel in Paris with Princess Diana, and I knew it was not going to end well. I startled awake just as we crashed, and she slumped over onto my lap.

Terrified and breathing hard, I couldn't catch my breath again, and the fact that Gavin either refused to, or just didn't notice, left me feeling crushed and alone. I got out of bed and shuffled out to the living room to cry, and once I was all cried out, I sat staring out the window in a tired numbness. It seemed abundantly clear that no matter who was around, or how much they did or didn't love me, I was on my own. Somehow, I had wound up going round the bend, as Gavin would say, and somehow I was going to have to be the one to find my way back. I just didn't have a clue how I was going to do that.

Morning arrived as it always does, and I moved through it in a daze. I fed Nick a bottle, put in a load of laundry, and got Meg and Jack cereal for breakfast. I couldn't bring myself to play with them, but I set Meg and Jack up in front of Sesame St., and took Nick back to ask Gavin if he shouldn't be getting up. He was already in the shower, so I put Nick on the floor, much to his dismay, and made our bed. As I did so the phone rang, and seeing that it was Colleen, I debated not answering, but at the last second, grabbed it and said hello.

"Kelly, are you just going to refuse to speak to me?"

"I answered," I defended.

"Did Gavin tell you how sorry I am?" she asked.

"No, about what?"

"He didn't tell you?" she shrieked, so loudly that I actually had to hold the phone away from my ear.

"Nope," I sighed, as he walked out asking what I was doing to Nick to cause him to fuss.

"Why have you put him on the floor?" he criticized. "It's no doubt filthy. I can't imagine that you've mopped in weeks, if not months," he said, picking him up and plopping him in my lap before returning to the bathroom to shave.

"Christ, he sounds charming," Colleen muttered in my ear, as Nick twisted and cried, but then settled to chew on my arm.

"It's morning," I defended.

"Are you feeling any better?" she asked.

"Sure, why not?" I said thinking again that no one had a clue.

"You weren't hurt, right?"

"We could have been killed," I quietly said, more to myself than her.

"Thank God you weren't."

"Yeah, do you need something?" I asked.

"My sister would be nice. I didn't mean anything I said that day Kelly, you know that. You didn't either, right?"

"I love you Colleen, I've got to go," I said, hearing Meg and Jack calling me.

"Mommy the TV isn't working" I heard Meg yell as I hung up.

I knew without looking that the cable had been cut, and wondered what would be next.

CHAPTER 29

Gavin's need to provide for us once again goes back to the way he was raised. Although his father is an acclaimed playwright, and has had some financial success, he has also been careless with his money. More often than not, he has neglected the practical things, such as bills and mortgages, in exchange for extravagant gifts and alcohol.

When Gavin and I married, one of the things he prided himself on was the fact that he had a good job, a savings account, and a retirement plan. He knew (or at least assumed) that he would be able to provide for us, always. My parents, who were both well provided for throughout their childhoods, and who have always been able to provide for us as well, have no concept of what it is like to go without. They have offered to pay for things in the past, and although admirable, they find Gavin's refusal to accept help during tough times to be silly. To be honest, I alternate back and forth myself. Regardless, I knew better than to mention the fact that the cable bill hadn't been paid. Meg did not. I had told her the TV must have broken, but she had to know why, and as soon as Gavin walked out, demanded to know if he could fix it.

"What do you mean, it's broken?" he asked.

"It just says words and a phone number," she told him.

"Oh," he said, with a heavy sigh.

He looked at me, clearly expecting disappointment, and I wanted to cry, I felt so bad for him. I rubbed his back and apologized, feeling it was more my fault than his, but that only annoyed him further.

"Whatever are you apologizing for? You really must stop that," he snarled, before addressing Meg. "It's an oversight on my part, Meg, I'm terribly sorry. I'll have it fixed later today."

"Fix it now," she whined.

"I can't. I'm going to have to go into the bank I'm afraid. It'll be back on this evening."

"Daddy, fix it!" Jack pleaded.

"I have to be going. You'll address what we discussed last night, won't you?" he said to me.

I wanted to scream, "How?" but instead I followed him outside, and asked him to talk to me. He didn't have the time to do so, or so he told me, as he all but ran to his car. I knew I should have asked him weeks ago how bad our finances really were, but it was such a sensitive subject that I never had. Just as with my sanity, every day I hoped for the best, praying that things would turn around. Unfortunately, things were obviously only getting worse.

The kids of course, didn't care about jobs or minds lost. They wanted what they wanted, and now that it wasn't available, the TV was the only thing they wanted. Meg kept turning it on again and again to see if it was fixed, and Jack had one meltdown after another. Nick fed off of both of them, and Hilary looked almost as overwhelmed as I felt. Unable to stand it any longer, I told Hilary to take Meg to school this second!

Realizing how harshly I had said it, I was mortified.

"I'm so sorry," I apologized. "I shouldn't take this out on you. I'm so sorry," I repeated, as she continued to stare at me with an expression of shock.

Corky, having heard me snap at her from the other room, suddenly appeared, telling Hilary that she had this, and with that, she threw her arm around me, and pulled me back into the hallway. Jack ran after us, throwing himself at me and wailing. Corky ignored him, and looking me in the eye, asked, "What are you doing?" I sat down, pulled Jack into my lap and cried.

"Shit," Corky cursed. "Kel, get up."

"Mommy," Meg began crying. "What's wrong with Mommy?" she asked Corky, having now followed us as well.

"She bumped her elbow," Corky lied. "Really hard, but she's fine. You are fine, right Kel?" she encouraged.

I nodded, but pulled Meg into my lap as well, and we all just cried for a minute, until Jack lifted his head, gave me a kiss, and wiping my tears, told me "All better."

It was so sweet that I kissed him and Meg both, and forced myself to get up.

"I love you," I told them. "I have to go get help. I'll get better, I promise."

"You'll get all better, your elbow?" Meg asked, looking confused.

"Sure. I have to call Uncle Dev to ask for the doctor's number," I said, going back to my room.

I laid down on my bed and wanted nothing more than to pull the blankets over my head and disappear. I remembered that Devon had given me Estelle's number, but I had no idea what I had done with it. Just as I reached for the phone, I remembered that I'd put it into my cell phone. It was sitting right there on the nightstand, and although I picked it up and found the number, I didn't know what to say.

Corky came back with Nick a few minutes later and told me Hilary was taking Meg to school and Jack to the park.

"I don't know what to say," I told her.

"About?"

"To Estelle."

"Oh," she said, clearly relieved that I was planning on calling her. "Easy, just say you got the number from your brother, and that you are going through a very rough time, but he was sure she could help you."

"Okay," I agreed, assuming I'd just get a machine anyway.

When she picked up, it threw me, and I stumbled over my words so much that Corky took the phone and told her it was a bit of an emergency. She arranged for me to see her that very afternoon, even though I kept telling her I had no car, and no way of getting there. Hanging up with Estelle, Corky took a deep breath and informed me she was going to call Scott and make him take me.

"Gavin says Scott's worried about you. Did I tell you that?" I asked.

"He should be," she mumbled, but then she laughed, and told me she'd had a sex dream about him the night before. "We're all crazy," she announced.

CHAPTER 30

Estelle's office is above the garage of her house in Encino, which was less than ten miles away from our house. A moderate sized Cape Cod house with a well manicured front lawn, it screams comfort. There is nothing pretentious about it, and likewise, her office is the same.

I had been told to approach the office by the stairs to the right of the garage, and as I knocked on the door, I was doing my best to calm my breathing and to keep from shaking. Estelle opened the door and reached for my hand, both greeting me and pulling me in. She was in her early fifties, tall, curvaceous, and had a pleasantly casual air about her. Dressed in a long skirt, paired with a light, loose fitting sweater, her long dark hair was swept to one side.

"You must be Kelly, I can see the resemblance to Dev. How is he doing?" she asked.

"Good, I guess," I said, taking in her office.

There was no desk, or anything formal. Just two couches and an overstuffed chair. One wall had a long, tall book case with a hundred books or more. In another corner there was a tall wooden file cabinet, and the back wall included a big window that overlooked part of the backyard. A yard bordered by large, full trees.

"Have a seat," she encouraged. "Anywhere is fine," she smiled.

I chose one of the couches, and she told me to feel free to put my feet up and get comfortable, as she herself curled into the opposite corner of the same couch. I tucked my feet under me and instantly felt just that much more at ease.

"I have to confess, I've been racking my brain, trying to remember what Dev ever told me about you. I know you all write, but you are the one who is married, right?"

"Yes," I nodded.

"To an English guy, right?"

"Right."

"Any kids?"

"Three."

"Oh," she said, surprised. "Goodness, it hasn't been that long since Dev and I talked. You've been busy. How old are they?"

"Almost six months, two, and four. Two boys and a girl."

"Planned?" she inquired.

"No," I said, as my lip began quivering.

"That upsets you?"

"I don't know," I said as the tears flowed.

"I'm not here to judge you, Honey. Anything you say, short of posing a serious threat to yourself or someone else, is strictly between us, and I can promise you, after doing this for thirty years, I've heard it all. Why does that upset you?"

"It's not how it was supposed to be," I cried, quickly adding, "I love my kids, I really do."

"Of course you do."

"They are perfect, and Gavin, my husband, he's a really good guy."

"Sure."

"I'm just so unhappy and I can't get a handle on this, and I feel so guilty."

"On what, exactly, or do you know?"

"I don't know anything," I sobbed.

She got up, grabbed a box of Kleenex off the top of the file cabinet, and placed it between us. I blew my nose and struggled to turn off the waterworks.

"Back up and tell me how it was supposed to be," she suggested.

"Gavin was going to be the top literary agent in the world, and I was going to be a successful novelist, and later on, like a few years from now, we were going to have two kids. Preferably two of the same gender so that they could be close throughout their lives."

"You and Dev aren't close?" she asked.

"Sure we are, but growing up, I had more in common with Colleen, and I'm sure he'd have rather played firemen than Barbies."

"Right, right, of course. I do recall his telling me there were times when a brother would have been nice," she laughed. "You strike me as an intelligent person, and please don't take this the wrong way, because my third child was a surprise as well, but if you didn't want kids until later, how did you end up with three so quickly?"

"Meg was an accident, and then Gavin fell in love. He couldn't wait to have another, and things were going really well for him at the agency, so he convinced me that we should have our second, and then once Jack was weaned, we'd get a nanny and I'd have time to write. He said we were just reversing the order of things. I was in love too, so I willingly went along with it, but Jack was colicky, and Meg was two, and we never had time to discuss a nanny, let alone get one. The one night we got some time to ourselves, Nick was conceived, and like Meg, that was while using protection! Then the agency fired Gavin when he made the mistake of criticizing them. Now we are drowning in every way imaginable."

"Do you think you suffered from postpartum depression after either of the first two pregnancies?" she asked.

"I don't think that's what this is. It goes deeper than that."

"Postpartum depression can be extremely deep, not that I am saying this is that, but certainly it is something to consider. What do you think is causing it? And by it, what, if you can put it into words, is "it"? " she asked.

"An inability to handle my life. Colleen, my sister, says it's just not being able to write, but I fear it's that with a lot of disappointment in myself because I'm not who I want to be in any arena. I'm not the wife I want to be, I'm not the mother I want to be, and I'm not the writer I want to be. And I can no longer cope with even the simplest of things. I nearly got my friend and I killed the other day because I was having a panic attack and slammed on the brakes, and I don't have panic attacks."

"Ever?"

"Never before."

"Do you have any clue what caused it?"

"I might have been upset that Colleen, who is in the midst of planning her wedding, accused me of having a nervous breakdown just because we don't have money, but she and I have always fought. I don't let her get to me, not usually."

"But I take it money is a big stress right now? Is your husband working?"

"He's gone out on his own, but most of his previous clients stayed with the big agency, so our income has been drastically reduced."

"So she hit too close to home."

"I guess, maybe," I considered.

"Just for a moment, lets go through symptoms. Are you able to sleep?"

"Not for the past four years."

"Has it been worse lately?"

"Sure."

"Eating? How is your appetite?"

"I don't know, I guess it varies between overeating and not eating at all."

"Do you feel panicky about the kids? Worry excessively?"

"Jack has croup every few months and I might have felt, no, I definitely felt less able to cope with it this last time. I worried that it was somehow my fault."

"Have you thought about harming any of the kids, even in just a fantasy kind of way?"

"No, of course not. I would never."

"Of course not, but you know, someone might fantasize about putting them to sleep for a few years, or things like that."

"No."

"Have you had any blood work done since the last little guy was born?"

"No, " I said, explaining about the quack who had suggested it, but whom we'd decided was nuts.

"You should go to your doctor and let him or her know what is going on, just to rule out anything physical, and then we can talk about treatment options. I'm not a big fan of medications if they can be avoided, but sometimes they can give you a much needed temporary boost to get you moving, and therefore able to work on what is really going on. Do you have insurance?" she asked.

"Some," I said.

"So take care of that first and then come back and we can work out a payment plan that won't add to your stress. Consider today on the house," she offered.

I of course, cried.

CHAPTER 31

"All sorted out now?" Scott asked, as we headed home.

"Sure," I mumbled.

"So what's the deal, Corky wants to get married, or what?"

I just looked at him and rolled my eyes. He didn't say another word. He didn't bother coming in, either. He just dropped me off and beat it out of there. Corky met me in the kitchen with a glass of wine in one hand, and Nick in the other. Hilary was in the backyard with Meg and Jack.

"This looks worse than it is," she said, referring to the wine, "but my back was bothering me again, and this guy cries an awful lot."

"Okay," I said, taking Nick as he hollered and leaned towards me.

"So?" she asked.

"Scott wants to know if you want to get married or not," I answered.

"Seriously?"

"What's the deal, he asked."

"What did you tell him?"

"What should I have told him?"

"To grow up."

"I rolled my eyes."

"Close enough. So what did Estelle say? Do you like her?"

"She was great. Very nurturing, and she says we can work out a payment plan."

"That's great."

"I hope so," I said.

It seemed almost too good. The truth was that I had felt an instant connection to Estelle, and her saying she would work with us, without my even having to bring it up, felt like such a blessing, that I was sure the other shoe was about to drop. I dreaded going to the doctor because with the way things had been going, I was sure I'd be told there was something wrong with me. It would no doubt be expensive and incurable too.

Making good on his word, the TV was working by four, so when Gavin came home at six, Meg declared him the best daddy ever! Like Corky before him, he looked at me and said, "So?" I told him the same things I had told her, and he appeared to be greatly relieved. Again like Corky, I was still in pain. Every bone in my body continued to ache, but I couldn't help wondering if the valium wasn't just adding to my feeling so lethargic and numb. As soon as the kids were in bed, instead of trying to confront Gavin on our finances as I suspected I should, I went straight to bed.

As suggested, I made an appointment with my OBGYN the very next day, although they couldn't squeeze me in until the following week. Once Nick was down for his morning nap, Corky suggested I take a nice, relaxing bath and figure out what was going to happen next in my novel, while she took a walk to sort out her life. She said we'd meet back when she returned, have lunch out in the backyard, and share what we had each worked out.

The bath took a few minutes to relax into because Jack had overheard us talking, and decided he wanted to take a bath with me. When I told him I needed to think, he told me I did not. Corky insisted I just go, but then about the time Jack began to settle, she left for her walk, and I could hear that he'd decided he wanted to do that, too. Eventually things quieted down and I was able to close my eyes, drifting off to thoughts of Callie in the claw footed tub in Italy.

I knew her tears centered around her husband, and decided his name was Ben. As I'd discussed with Corky, I was sure he was a journalist and off researching a potentially dangerous assignment. I could only imagine that she would worry about him, that is if she knew what he was investigating. After a while, I concluded she probably did, and by the time my water was getting cold, I had the beginnings of my next section.

Missing Ben as she did, Callie questioned how she had come to be in this picture perfect village, minus the one person she had come to see. Such was the nature of Ben's job as a journalist. Dependability, she was finding, came in short supply. His was a job she found exciting, but at times frightening.

Climbing out of the tub, she wrapped herself in the plush white towel that had been neatly folded and left on the bed. Jumping under the duvet, she said a prayer that Ben would be safe and fell fast asleep.

It wasn't Shakespeare, but at least it moved the scene forward. I was pretty sure Ben was going to return drunk as a skunk, and he was no doubt going to startle the hell out of her when he did. I would have attempted to write more, but I could hear that Nick was up and Corky was returning. I got dressed, and feeling better than I had in days, went out to see what Corky had figured out.

"Everything and nothing at all," she said when I asked. "How about you?"

"Callie is married to Ben and his job intrigues her, but scares her at the same time. Now that I think of it, he drinks too much."

"Did you write or just think?"

"I wrote a few rough lines," I said, as Meg arrived home from school.

"OOH, go get them!" Corky squealed.

"Let's feed the kids and put them down for naps first, and then we can go outside and really talk," I suggested.

"Mama, I'm too big for a nap," Meg pouted.

"God Kel," Corky observed, "you look a thousand times better. Maybe Colleen is right. Maybe you really do just need to write."

"Writing is so much better than reality right now," I sighed, immediately feeling guilty for having said it aloud.

"What?" Corky asked.

"That's a horrible thing to say," I said, hugging Nick who did a nose dive for my breasts, deciding he wanted to nurse.

"Why, because it's true? It doesn't mean you don't love your kids," she said, hugging me.

"I'm so lucky, though."

"And it's good you know that, but it doesn't magically make everything alright. You're not a bad person just because you are struggling right now. You're going to get through this, I promise."

"Okay, I'm just going to nurse him, this is stupid," I announced. "I haven't had that much Valium, have I?"

"Google it first," she suggested, as Hilary hesitantly told me Gavin had asked her to be sure I didn't slip back to nursing Nick.

"I can give him a bottle," she offered.

"So can I," I said resentfully.

"Don't shoot the messenger, Kel," Corky advised.

"I'll feed him a bottle," Meg volunteered. "Mommy let me do it. I'm a good helper. Let me."

"And after you'll take a rest, right?" Corky encouraged.

"But I'm big," she whined.

"Which is why you just need a rest and not a nap, but everybody needs a rest sometimes."

"And after I can have a treat?" she bargained.

"I saw a new bakery on my walk," Corky told her. "If it's okay with your mommy, maybe we can go there after everyone's nap."

"Okay, that's a plan. That's a great plan, right, Mommy?" Meg checked.

"Sure," I agreed.

"Good, then it's all settled," Corky said, slapping a high five with both Meg and Jack.

Of course, Jack just looked confused.

CHAPTER 32

Lunch consisted of saltine crackers with peanut butter and a glass of wine, set among the overgrown grass and scattered weeds of the backyard.

"Do you own a lawn mower?" Corky laughed. "It's a wonder you haven't lost Jack out here."

"It is almost as tall as him, I know. Meg claims to like it."

"Oh, well then, by all means allow the ruin to continue."

"It really is awful," I frowned.

"How can you expect to get your life in order if you can't get the house in order? This is your home, and it should be beautiful. It used to be beautiful."

"I know," I sighed. "So what did you discover on your walk?"

"That your house is a disaster in the midst of a really nice neighborhood, but let me read what you wrote first," she said, putting her hand out for the laptop I had brought out with us.

She read and considered.

"It's not great, I know..." I started.

"No, It's fine," she said as I grabbed it back and reread it.

"I think I should fix this last line to read, *Exhausted from her flight and the events of the past few days, she hurried under the duvet, said a prayer that Ben would be safe, and fell fast asleep.*"

"Ooh, better, what has happened in the past few days?"

"I'm not sure yet, but Ben is going to come in and startle her before we find out, so you'll have to wait and see."

"This is good, Kelly. We just have to find a way to keep you going. You need more than an hour's time."

"That's just it. It takes a while to be able to clear my mind enough to concentrate, and as soon as I hear the baby or Jack starting to fuss, I'm thrust right back to reality and the spell is broken."

"So maybe you need to be one of those coffee shop writers. There's a Coffee Bean two blocks away," she pointed out.

"Maybe. I guess I could drop Meg at school, go there for a few hours and get home before she's dropped off," I thought aloud.

"Exactly! You have to make the time, and with Hilary here, there is no reason not to."

"We trust her, right?" I checked.

"Hilary? Sure we do. She seems very nice."

"Okay, so now that we have solved all of my problems, how are you? Did your walk help you to figure things out?"

"I may need a full series of walks," she sighed. "I'm not really an actor, am I?"

"You didn't start out that way, but I don't know, you get parts," I offered.

"Not big parts, and I don't love it, do I? It doesn't feed me like writing does you. I need to find my passion, and in the meantime I need to call my commercial agent and tell her to get me a role like Mr. Clean. You know, a part I can play over and over and make a living off of."

"Mr. Clean is an animation!" I laughed.

"Fine, then that insurance lady, Flo. I'll be the next Flo, or the dish soap lady, whatever."

"That's still acting, though."

"I know, but it would take very little of my time so I could explore what my real passion is."

"And Scott? Does he factor into this at all?"

She stuffed a cracker in her mouth, buried her head in her knees, and groaned, before looking back up at me and smiling even though her eyes were filling with tears. I hugged her and told her she could do worse, which made us both laugh.

"I don't want to love him," she cried.

"Why not, because he hurt you?"

"Uh, yeah."

"If he couldn't hurt you, he wouldn't be worth loving," I told her.

"What kind of twisted logic is that?"

"It's not twisted at all. Let's face it, Scott is intelligent, funny, both intentional and not," I teased, "well built, good looking, and apparently worthy of sex dreams, so come on," I said, as she smiled, clearly remembering her dream.

"But he's also immature, arrogant and awkward. He hasn't a clue as to how to express true emotion."

"So in other words he's a guy."

"Exactly! I find that really confusing and difficult to deal with. Gavin's not that way."

"Of course he is. Gavin has a whole slew of issues that I have no idea how to handle."

"Like what?"

"Like his hang ups on money. I have no clue how much trouble we are in right now, and I know if I confront him he'll not only get angry, but he'll be hurt."

"Yeah, he is touchy about that," she conceded. "What else?"

"He shuts down and shuts me out. I don't know what he's thinking half the time," I said, suddenly on the verge of tears myself. "I love him so much, but sometimes I wonder why."

"He's really scared Kelly, and he feels like a failure. He feels as though he's pushed you into this breakdown by running over your needs to get what he wanted."

"He's told you that?"

"He asked me last night if you are going to be okay, and then it all came out. He loves you so much. He's a really good guy. I'm kind of in love with him myself, but then I've told you that before."

"He told you he thinks it's his fault?"

"Yep. He says he pushed you, and then he blew it by losing his job. I asked him how he's doing client wise, and he says there is promise, but everyone is between projects right now so it's a matter of being patient. The book signing he had to go to the other night went well, he said."

"I hate that he feels guilty, and I hate that I don't know that he shouldn't. I know everybody makes mistakes, but if he'd just kept his mouth shut," I groaned.

"This was going to happen regardless. You put your dreams aside and it's reached up and bit you in the ass. It's hard, but blame is only going to make it harder. You have to forgive him, and yourself, and move forward."

"I know, you're right. Maybe you need to do the same with Scott."

"Mr. "What's the deal?" she laughed. "God! He's such a jerk!"

CHAPTER 33

The following day was a Saturday, and thinking about what Corky had said about the house, I asked Gavin if we couldn't work on the yard. He looked less than enthused and pointed out that Corky was still sleeping. He said it would be rude to turn on the lawnmower and disturb her.

"She's the one who has told me our house looks like shit," I told him.

"Please don't curse in front of the children," he sighed, as Jack drove his toy car across the floor, repeating "shit" over and over.

"Stop it, Jack," I sulked.

Gavin glanced up from his phone and told Jack the same as Meg asked if it was a bad word.

"Of course it's a bad word," I snarled. "You know darned well it is."

"No need to take it out on her," Gavin objected.

215

"Fine, I'll just do the yard myself and you can deal with the kids, since you are such a perfect parent!" I announced, dropping Nick in his lap and marching out to the backyard.

Taking a shaky breath, I looked around trying to remember what the yard had looked like before it had been taken over by weeds. There had been a time when I'd had the beginnings of a vegetable garden, but now it was all but buried. I went to the garage to look for some gloves, clippers, and the lawnmower, and Gavin met me in there, carrying Nick and being followed by Jack.

"What are you doing?" Gavin asked.

"I'm going to take back my house in the hope that I can then take back my life."

"More sage advice from Corky?" he questioned.

"Yes."

"I'll mow the lawn later," he promised, trying to hand me Nick.

"Well I'm going to rip out weeds now,"

"Kelly, please, it's been a very difficult week, hasn't it? Can't we just work our way into this a little slower? I've barely had a chance to wake up, and some breakfast would be lovely."

"You want me to make you breakfast?"

"More than you know. Seriously, I will mow the lawn today. I promise."

"Front and back?"

"Yes, yes, whatever."

"It has to get done today."

"I know."

"Even if a client calls you in crisis. We have to come first today."

"What is that supposed to mean? I haven't put you first this week? I'm doing everything in my power to put you first. What more do you want of me?"

"I want you to help me get this house back to what it was."

"And I've said I will."

"Good!" I glared, taking Nick and muttering to him as we walked inside that I'd just get back in the kitchen where I belonged.

Once again, in retrospect, I can see that it was over the top to resent the man for wanting to be allowed to wake up and eat before jumping right in to yard work, something he'd never enjoyed. At the time, however, I was miserable and questioning why I had married a man who was clearly stuck in the 1950s. I bit my lip to keep from crying as I balanced Nick on my hip and cracked eggs with one hand like a short order cook.

The smell of toast and eggs woke Corky, and Gavin managed to charmingly, yet sarcastically, thank her for setting me on a warpath of yard work.

"If we all do it, it'll be fun," she assured him, asking Meg if she was going to help.

"Help what?"

"Make the backyard nice again."

"And the front," I insisted.

"How?" Meg asked.

"By getting rid of all of the weeds and overgrown grass," Corky told her.

"Okay," she shrugged.

Once breakfast was cleaned up, I put Nick down for his morning nap, took the baby monitor outside, and all but Jack began pulling weeds. Jack kicked a ball, more often than not at one of us, trying to get us to play with him. Gavin kept stopping to do so, in between answering his cell phone as well as the house phone, both of which kept ringing. When his mother called, he went back inside completely. In just over an hour, we were hot and sweaty, and I could hear Nick fussing and Gavin ignoring him.

"This is hopeless," I grumbled, going in to get him up from his nap.

By the time I had changed the baby, filled a pitcher with some ice water, and returned to the backyard, Scott had appeared, and was showing Meg the proper way to pull a weed out by the root. Corky was ignoring him, busily stuffing the weeds we had already pulled into a big garbage bag. Noticing me, he stood up, took the pitcher and put it down on the old wooden picnic table that we were slowly unearthing, saying he'd go get some cups. As soon as he walked away, I looked at Corky who shrugged and continued stuffing weeds.

It was hard to accomplish anything with Nick and Jack, so I took them back inside just in time to hear Gavin telling his mom that he'd keep her posted. Hanging up, he looked at me and said she really wanted to come over and help.

"I think it upsets her that we've hired Hilary," he said. "I suspect she's jealous."

Why that made me cry, I have no idea, other than it struck me as sad that my parents were close enough to be involved with their grandchildren but chose not to be, and his mom wanted to be, but couldn't. Gavin looked lost, and didn't have a clue as to why I was upset this time.

"I put her off," he said defensively. "It's not like I told her to hop on a plane."

I cried harder, and sobbingly tried to make him understand, but after a minute he just hugged me and suggested I take some valium. I wanted to scream.

CHAPTER 34

We made a fair amount of progress on the yard that day, and Corky insisted on buying us some flowers as a way of saying thank you for allowing her to stay with us. Scott volunteered to go with her to lift the potting soil, since he assumed her back was still sore from the accident. She told him to suit himself, but insisted on taking Meg with them so that she could help choose the flowers.

We were all exhausted, but Gavin said if I'd let him take a quick shower, then I could take a relaxing bath while he watched Jack and Nick. He even suggested I light some candles and put on some music to shut out the world. I took him up on it, but instead of being able to think about writing or simply relaxing, I couldn't stop thinking about Corky and Scott. I was dying to be a fly on the wall. I knew Meg was still too young to be a good spy.

Gavin came in about a half hour into my bath and said Scott was on the phone wanting to know if they should pick up some Chinese food for dinner.

"The kids will eat chow mien, won't they?" he asked.

"Sure, so long as they get some plain. Tell them to say they want only the noodles. You have to be really specific," I warned.

He nodded and walked out, but Jack ran in and began stripping off his clothes, wanting to join me, and just like that, my alone time was over. Gavin apologized, but I thanked him for having allowed me to have as much time as I'd had. Jack and I snuggled and played for a few minutes and then got out and put on our pajamas early. For some reason he found that really funny.

Gavin found it odd, saying we'd be having dinner with Corky and Scott. I maintained that neither one of them would care, and that in fact, given the choice, they would also eat in their pajamas. He said he felt it was rude, but before we could debate it any further, they returned with a full pallet of flowers and of course the Chinese food.

"You don't care that I have my pajamas on, do you?" I asked Scott.

"Why would I?" he asked, although he sounded cranky.

"Gavin thought you might, that's all." I shrugged, turning to Corky and mouthing out "is he mad?"

She made cuckoo signs behind his back and I dragged her off to our room.

"Kelly, what are you doing?" Gavin objected. "Let's eat."

"I'm just getting Corky some pajamas" I laughed, closing the door behind us. "What happened?"

"Nothing. He's just annoyed that I'm ignoring him. He feels I can't do it forever and didn't appreciate it when I asked him what's the deal? Of course, he under estimates me."

"Because this is your plan, to just ignore him? What happened to forgiveness?"

"I discovered I'm not there yet," she said, getting undressed as I gave her a pair of my favorite pajamas to put on. "Why are we wearing pajamas?" she inquired.

"Because I don't feel like having to get undressed again later and Gavin's making a big deal about it."

We went out to the kitchen and Meg announced that she wanted pajamas, too. Gavin told her absolutely not, insisting she still needed a bath, and that he wished to eat dinner, not hold a pajama party. Corky and I both found that amusing even though he did not.

After dinner, Gavin and Scott went outside to have a beer while I gave Meg a bath and Nick a bottle. Corky read to Jack, and once Nick and Meg were also in pajamas, we went outside to debate where we would plant the flowers the next day. I wanted them in one corner all bunched together in a burst of color, while Gavin felt they should go out front where the kids wouldn't be kicking balls through them. Scott felt a patio was needed and that the flowers should be in big planters on the patio.

"There is no patio," Gavin said, stating the obvious.

"But we could add one. How hard could it be?" Scott asked, pulling out his phone.

"Who are you calling?" I asked.

"I'm Goggling it," he said, which reminded me, that was what he and Corky had in common, their love of Google.

"Right, this is hardly the time for such projects," Gavin said. "We are putting the yard back together, not further damaging it."

"Oh calm down, I'll do all the work," Scott growled.

"You're right about that," Gavin muttered, as I told the kids to say goodnight.

They complained, but I put them down anyway and asked Corky if she wanted to watch a movie with me. We chose another of our favorites, *America's Sweetheart* with Julia Roberts, Billy Crystal, and John Cusack, among several other favorite actors of ours. Gavin and Scott came in halfway through, saw what we were watching, and asked how many times we'd seen it now. We shushed them and they both sat down and watched with us. When it ended, Corky said perhaps her passion lied in screenwriting. Scott laughed and she stared at him blankly.

"Oh, you are serious," he said, trying to wipe the smile off his face.

"Why are you still here?" she asked,

"Blow me," he muttered.

"Alright now, there's no reason she can't give it a shot," Gavin said.

"Writing or blowing him?" I laughed.

Corky hit me, while Gavin smiled.

"I can write, you know," Corky insisted.

"Of course I know!" Scott exclaimed. "I'm the one who has told you, you are more suited to writing than acting, remember? I'm just not sure screenwriting is it for you."

"Because you know me so well."

"I fear I do."

"I'm sure you could write a screenplay," I told her.

"A monkey could write a screenplay," Scott said, "it's the quality of what you would write that is in question."

"Why do you think she couldn't?" Gavin inquired.

"Because there are rules to screenplays, and she is incapable of doing what is expected."

"I'll bet you're expecting this," she said getting up, flipping him off and walking out to the living room.

"You really don't know her," I told him, getting up to follow her.

CHAPTER 35

"I could write the play version of that movie," Corky told me. "Not that I would write a play, but you know what I mean. I could write about all of the drama that goes on when you are a part of a touring group, working out the kinks in a play."

"I'm sure you could," I agreed, "although could you do so without alienating people?"

"Well clearly names would be changed and characters embellished, or in some cases pulled back, because even though things happened, some of it was unbelievably over the top."

"So do it. Don't let Scott, or anyone else stop you. You and I both know you can write."

"I can."

"So on Monday, we'll drop Meg at school, and then we'll both go to the Coffee Bean and write."

"Damn straight we will! This calls for wine. Have you been drugging it up today," she teased, "or can you join me?"

"I can definitely join you," I said.

When Scott left about a half hour later, he said he'd be back the next day to put in our patio. I looked at Gavin who raised his hands and said he was having nothing to do with it. The two of them said their goodbyes and closing the door, Gavin looked at us and shook his head.

"He insists he can do it in one day, and that we should think of it as his gift to us for having to put up with Corky," he laughed.

"Why are you friends with him?" Corky demanded, adding," certainly you could find better."

"He's a fantastic friend and you know it," he scolded. "I'm going to answer a few emails and go to bed. Will you be joining me?" he asked me.

"After I finish my wine."

"You haven't had any valium?" he checked.

"None. I think it depresses me."

"Then throw it out. I'm tossing it right now," he said, marching off.

"Go right ahead," I told him.

Sure enough, Scott showed up the next day with bags of sand, and stacks of bricks. He had a plan that included leveling a section of the yard, pouring sand, laying bricks on top of it, and then pouring more sand to somehow secure the bricks further. I was pretty sure that was going to make for a very wobbly patio, but I admired his initiative and determination. While he worked on the patio, I talked Gavin into sanding down the picnic table. Then while the kids were napping, I painted it a beautiful blue green, making it look fresh and new. Corky went out apartment hunting.

She returned a couple of hours later saying she had put in an application at a new building only three blocks away. While I loved the idea of her being within walking distance, Scott shook his head in disapproval. We ignored him and went inside to fix dinner.

In the end the patio looked nicer than any of us had expected, especially with the newly painted table set upon it. When Hilary arrived the next morning, she was shocked by the transformation the back yard had undergone. She said it was like day and night. I was frustrated that we had yet to do anything with the front yard, but both Gavin and Corky insisted we would get to it the following weekend.

I explained to Hilary my plan to drop Meg and to go write, even though Corky was now refusing to get up and join me. Used to being able to sleep late, she insisted she'd meet me at the Coffee Bean after another hour's sleep. I wasn't really surprised that she would renege, so I gathered Meg and left. Unfortunately, at her school I was approached by the director, who reminded me we were behind in payment.

227

"I meant to talk to Gavin about that this weekend," I said, embarrassed and trying to come up with a lie that could buy us more time. "I was in an accident last week and I haven't been as present as I should be."

"Be that as it may, and of course I'm happy that you weren't seriously injured, but we need payment this week or we are going to be forced to give Meg's spot to someone on our wait list."

"Of course. I'll see to it that you get a payment by Friday at the latest."

"I'd appreciate that because unfortunately, she won't be allowed back on Monday if we don't."

"No problem," I said, kissing Meg goodbye and hurrying out of there

I was completely humiliated, and couldn't leave fast enough. Sitting in the car, I tearfully texted Gavin that Meg was going to be kicked out of school if we didn't pay them immediately. He texted back that he'd be going to rob that bank now.

Taking several deep breaths, I drove to the Coffee Bean, pulled out my laptop, and walked inside. There wasn't a table to be had. Annoyed, I pulled out my last five dollars and ordered a tall latte that I was forced to take to a table outside.

The noise was ridiculous, as this particular Coffee Bean was on a very busy corner of Ventura Blvd, but I tried to convince myself I could ignore it. I told myself to think of it as white noise, and opened my laptop. I turned it on and my phone rang. It was Gavin asking what we owed the school and what they would settle for. As I told him, I was pretty sure what the director had been saying was that they wouldn't settle for anything less than the seven hundred dollars we owed them.

"Bloody hell," he moaned.

"Maybe we only need Hilary for mornings," I proposed.

"No. I'll find it. I don't know how just yet, but I'll find it. I'm sorry, Kelly" he sighed, then asking, "Where are you?"

"Outside at the coffee place."

"On that busy corner? Go inside."

"All of the inside tables are taken."

"Right, okay, well I have to go," he said, sounding as stressed as I felt.

"Okay, love you," I said.

I put down my phone and pulled up what little I had written, only to have three fire engines come screeching down the street. Their sirens were deafening. Once they passed I reread what I had written and tried to come up with a description of Ben. I couldn't picture him. Was he tall, short, blonde or brunette? My phone rang again and this time it was Devon, just checking in. I told him I'd call him back when I got home because it was all but impossible to hear him. Like Gavin, he told me to go inside.

Next Corky showed up, and once again we had to discuss what a crappy table I'd gotten. She said she'd go in and stake out a better one. Five minutes later she got one and frantically waved to get my attention. Laughing at her animation, I went inside, had a sip of my rapidly cooling five dollar latte, and in walked Colleen and Dee Dee.

"There you are!" Colleen exclaimed. "We've got to talk."

CHAPTER 36

"Change of plans," Colleen had announced, and two days later as I nervously sat in the doctor's office having blood drawn, I couldn't stop thinking about her news.

Keith, she had explained, had been talking to a friend who'd decided to move to Montana, and he'd offered to sell them his three acre property, with the most amazing five bedroom, six bath house, she had ever seen. Now the wedding was going to be held there, at their new 2.75 million dollar estate. She had assured me it was a bargain.

I wanted to be happy for her, and yet it had literally turned my stomach. Still, I'd said all of the right things, or at least I hoped I had. I'd said it was amazing, and that I was so happy for her, and she, too, had said the right things. She'd excitedly told me how much the kids would love it, and said we could come over any time we wanted to use the pool, or to just hang out. She said we'd have weekend bar-b-ques, and sleepovers, and maybe they'd even get some horses.

As the nurse poked me and drew my blood, I couldn't help but wonder why I was sitting there, and Colleen was living my life. When my doctor came in and heard how things had been spiraling out of control, he was sympathetic but had no easy solutions. He told me physically speaking I was worn out, but he had no quick and easy solutions. He offered me an antidepressant, but I didn't want drugs, I wanted the life I had been promised. For the past two days I had been choking every time I thought about telling Gavin what Colleen and Keith had done now.

Corky was as speechless as I was. She'd tried to give me a pep talk that day, after Colleen and Dee Dee had left to go meet Keith at the realtor's office, but then she'd admitted she had nothing. We'd both been walking around in a daze ever since and Gavin was so stressed out about how he was going to pay Meg's school that he hadn't noticed.

I thanked the doctor for his concern and offer of help, but said I'd try talking to Estelle before turning to medication. Then I sat in the car, finally calling Devon back, and begging him to tell me that Estelle really would be able to help me.

"I figured that's why you hadn't called back. As soon as Dad told me they'd bought that place I feared that would be the nail in the coffin, so to speak," he confessed.

"I don't want to be this green eyed monster of jealousy, but she's killing me," I cried.

"I know, Kel, but you can have everything she has, and you will, it just hasn't happened yet, that's all."

"I was trying to believe that, but then she gets this and all we get are overdue bills."

"It's going to turn around, I promise. Talk to Estelle because she's really good at putting things into perspective."

"Okay."

"Seriously," he stressed.

"I will. Are you okay? How's New York?"

"Eh, it's okay. I'm getting a little tired of the hustle/bustle atmosphere. It was fun for a while, but now it feels monotonous."

"So come home. Why can't you write from here?"

"I told myself I'd give it a year, but maybe, we'll see."

"Your piece on the Mayor was really funny," I offered.

"You read it?"

"I did," I told him, "and it made me cry I was so proud of you, but then crying has become kind of my thing, so you know, don't be too flattered."

"But you thought it was good?"

"Sure, didn't you?"

"I always amuse myself," he laughed, "but I worry sometimes that it doesn't translate."

"You are brilliant!" I assured him.

"As are you, Kelly. Your turn is coming, just wait. You'll be more famous than any of us."

"Ahh but for what?"

"Whatever you set your mind to."

"So long as it isn't an episode of *Snapped,* " I said.

"Right, try to avoid that," he advised.

"I'll do my best," I promised.

I went home and was surprised to find Gavin there so early in the day. I naturally worried that something was wrong, but he showed me a thick manuscript, and said Sirri had sent it to him. He explained that it wasn't hers, but was from a friend of hers who was looking for representation, and knowing that he'd be stuck reading it all night, he'd decided to come home early to see if I needed a break. To say I was shocked would be an understatement.

CHAPTER 37

While Gavin helped watch the kids that afternoon, I made an appointment with Estelle for the following day, as well as did the shopping, and picked up the dry cleaning. I did not, however, find any time to write.

Corky took a meeting with her agents, both theatrical and commercial, but came home discouraged. She said they'd told her she could possibly play a mom role in a few things, but for the most part, she was a little too pretty for average, while not being pretty enough for glamorous. She was advised to either lose fifteen pounds and dye her hair blonde, or to gain fifteen pounds, but right now neither of them had anything for her. They thought writing was a great idea though, telling her she was really funny and that they would go see her movie.

Over dinner Gavin told us both that we needed to focus and rededicate ourselves to our writing, informing us that Scott was on his way to Paris to research an art heist he'd be writing about for a major publication.

"Paris? He gets to go to Paris!" Corky shrieked. "He hates the French."

"Scott does?" Meg asked, reminding us, "It's not nice to hate people."

"Corky is mistaken," Gavin said. "She meant French bread. He hates French bread."

"Nice save," I mumbled.

"He has no business getting to visit French bread," Corky grumbled.

"You really must stop all of this nonsense," Gavin told her. "He'd have probably taken you with him, had you been nice to him."

"Sure he would."

"Colleen and Keith have bought a three million dollar house," I suddenly blurted out.

"Bloody fuck!" Gavin exclaimed, before quickly putting his hand over Jack's mouth and telling him not to repeat that.

Of course as soon as he removed his hand, he did.

"I'll put you to bed right now," Gavin warned.

"Buddy fuck!" Jack beamed again, as Corky and I both struggled not to laugh.

"Stop it Jackie, Daddy shouldn't have said that," I told him.

"Even if it was the correct response," Corky defended.

"Buddy fuck, no, no," Jack said, as Gavin reached over and pulled him out of his high chair.

"Gav, he'll stop," I said, as Jack screamed, but he insisted on putting him in his crib. "He's to have a time out at the very least," he stated.

"That's really not fair," I called after him.

"Nothing is right now," Corky said. "I can't believe that idiot is in Paris. How many times have we said we were going to go to Paris?"

"Somewhere in the range of a hundred and fifty," I replied.

"I have a book with Eloise in Paris," Meg commented, as Gavin returned.

"I'll let him out in a minute," he told me, looking sulky while stuffing a spoonful of mashed potatoes in his mouth.

We all ate in silence for a minute, although in truth it was anything but silent because Jack was going nuts in the other room. Sighing, Gavin got up to go deal with him. I told Corky that I should have kept my mouth shut, but as she pointed out, he was going to find out one way or another.

We didn't discuss it any further. Jack tearfully came back to the table, choosing to sit on my lap rather than returning to his high chair, and once he was done eating, Gavin went back to our room to read.

Corky received a call from the owner of the apartment building she'd put an application in on, telling her it was hers if she still wanted it. She was no longer sure she could afford it, and asked if she could see it again the next day. It was agreed that we would both go look at it in the morning and decide if it was worth all the money they were asking for each month.

Later, when I went to bed, Gavin was nearly done with the manuscript . I crawled under the covers and he closed it.

"Is it any good?" I asked.

"It is. It's quite good assuming she doesn't do anything hideous in the last twenty pages."

"Is it marketable?"

"Very."

"That's good."

"How long have you known about the house?" he asked, adding, "I assume from the way you spit it out that it's been festering for a while."

"Since Monday."

"Three million? Do you suppose it's nice or dreadfully gaudy?"

"Oh, I suspect it's very nice. The house itself is up on a ridge in a gated community above Hidden Hills and she says the pool has a slide built into the rocks. They have three acres and she says they might get horses."

He kissed my shoulder before asking if I thought they had a guest house bigger than our house, and if so, did I think we could move in.

"You'd tell me if we were going to lose the house, right?" I asked, hoping he wouldn't get mad.

"I wouldn't do that to you, Kelly. How can you think that?" he asked, although much to my relief it wasn't said defensively.

"I know you are doing everything you can, I'm just scared," I confessed.

"I'm trying to refinance and that will free up some cash to hopefully tide us over. It should go through no problem, but with the way things have been going, I must admit it's leaving me quite unsettled."

"Are we going to be able to pay school? Was I wrong to call Estelle today? I should have waited," I sighed.

"I'll make it work somehow. Who knows," he said returning his attention to the manuscript, "perhaps this will be the book that turns things around. Although, I'd rather it were yours."

CHAPTER 38

The title of the manuscript he read that night was *Looking Out For Me,* by Maria Risner, and he arranged to meet with her later in the week. He told me again the next morning that it was well written, and suggested I skim it at the very least, because he felt it might inspire me to get serious about my own book.

"I am serious about my own book!" I objected.

"Are you? Because I've yet to see any pages."

"You think it's so easy."

"I think I came home yesterday and you chose to run errands. And although I appreciate the clean shirts, truly, and the dinner we had, I think were you seriously intending to do this, you'd have gone to write."

"Because you don't understand what is involved."

"Are you going to write today?" he demanded.

"I'm going to try, but I have to take Meg to school, and check out Corky's apartment, and see Estelle and I don't know!" I said, quickly becoming overwhelmed and frustrated.

Gavin walked over and hugged me as I started blubbering, while telling him I wanted to write, but life was getting in the way.

"I'm not purposely trying to upset you. I'm telling you that I believe you are more talented than any writer I have ever represented, and quite frankly, Luv, I need your book. I know life is giving you fits right now, and that it is difficult to put this first when we are all pulling at you. I know I'm just as guilty as the rest, but put yourself first, Sweetheart. I'll kick and scream just as the children will," he admitted, rubbing my back, "but you mustn't pay any mind. Do what you need to do."

"I'll try."

"No, do it," he insisted, adding, "I'll bring you a check for Meg's school tonight."

"Thank you."

"Let's do our best to have a good day, shall we?" he said.

Or asked, as I wasn't sure if he was seriously suggesting we both make the effort, or if he was just speaking British. Either way, he went to work, and I was left with three children and a sink full of breakfast dishes. Granted, Hilary arrived a few minutes later, but I didn't notice the dishes washing themselves.

I quickly did them, and then telling Meg to get dressed, rushed
back to our bedroom to look at the manuscript. Unlike Gavin, I
am not a fast reader. I pay attention to every word and piece of
punctuation, and can read no other way. I decided I would just
read random paragraphs to get a sense of her style. Before I
knew it, Meg was standing in the doorway, asking why I
wasn't dressed, because Hilary had told her she was going to be
late for school if we didn't leave immediately. Gavin was right,
I thought to myself, this was definitely well written.

"Is Corky up?" I asked.

"I don't think so."

"Go wake her and remind her we have to go look at what might
be her new apartment," I told her, promising that I would get
dressed while she did.

In the end I had to agree to drop Meg first, and then swing
back to pick up Corky who was less than awake and ready to
go. The apartment was nice, but not spectacular. The
advertised wood floors were laminate, which is a pet peeve of
mine, but Corky said she could live with them. I said I could
live with her living with them, too, I just couldn't do it myself.
She called me a floor snob.

There was a nice fake fireplace, but in L.A. that's really all you
need, and the bedroom had a reasonable sized closet. There
was a guest bathroom as well as the master bath, but the
kitchen was so tiny, the two of us barely fit. Still, the
appliances were new and the reality was, Corky wasn't much of
a cook. As she joked, the less to burn down the better. I loved
the location, so I told her that for selfish reasons I would

encourage her to take it, and only wished I could say I'd spot her when she came up short on rent.

"I have a few months worth put away," she reasoned, "and who knows, if I'm lucky I'll land a bland mom role, or have to stop eating all together, thereby becoming glamorous by default. Either way it's a win/win."

"Cool, so take it."

"I think I will," she decided.

She signed the papers and was told she could move in the week after next, or that weekend if she wanted to prorate the rent. She chose to wait, because she wanted time to go through the storage unit where she had thrown all of her stuff when she'd given up her last apartment.

On the way home I told her about the Maria Risner manuscript, what little I had read. I explained that it appeared to be about this girl going off to college, trying to cope with being on her own for the first time, while running into strange people and trying to figure out where she fit in.

I'd intended to read some more when we got home, but as soon as we walked in the door, Jack attached himself to me, all but begging for some attention. Gavin's words came back to me, but I knew I didn't have time to write, because I'd have to go see Estelle in a while. So instead, Jack and I swung on the swings, gave Nick a ride in the wagon, and then made grilled cheese sandwiches for lunch.

Corky suggested I could go see Estelle, and then go to Coffee Bean to write before coming home. As she pointed out, she would be there when Hilary left, even if Gavin wasn't yet home. I could think of a million excuses for why it wouldn't work. One of them was the fact that I literally did not have a dime to my name. I had all but emptied our joint account at the grocery store again, and I was out of cash. I was going to have to postdate a check to Estelle as it was and I felt terrible about it, but vowed to bring it up in therapy. Therapy that I was suddenly dreading.

CHAPTER 39

I called Devon again on my way out the door, this time to ask him how therapy works and why he had talked me into this.

"You've already met her," he pointed out, saying, "therapy is easy. She'll ask questions if you don't have anything specific to discuss, or don't know how to start it."

"The whole thing is only upping my anxiety," I complained.

"Don't be a baby," he teased.

"Thanks, that's helpful."

"I love you, Kel, just relax. It'll be nice, you'll see."

"Okay," I agreed, but by the time I got to Estelle's I was just shy of a panic attack.

Devon was right about her, though, because not only did she sense my uneasiness, she addressed it immediately. She told me to have a seat, offered me a bottle of water, and then sitting next to me, suggested we start by taking a couple of deep breaths. With that out of the way, she smiled and reminded me that she wasn't there to judge me, and asked what was stressing me out so much that I was nearly hyperventilating.

"This, therapy, money, my life, just for starters," I said.

"Okay, so let's put money out of the way as far as this is concerned. I'm going to tell you upfront that if you are struggling financially you probably can't afford my rates," she stated unapologetically. "When you get back on your feet and can afford to pay, you will. For now, I have other patients who pay me very well, and as wonderful as that is, I don't do this strictly for the money. I want to help you. It's what I do, and what I am good at, and what makes me feel good about myself, so please, seriously, do not let money ever stop you from coming here, or getting the help you need."

"That's so generous. I don't know how to thank you."

"You don't have to. So what else is stressing you out?"

"I'm so stunned by what you just said, I don't even know," I mumbled, trying to figure out if she could possibly be that nice or if I was somehow misunderstanding what she had just said.

"You mentioned money, therapy and your life. Which should we address first, therapy or your life?" she asked. "I'd vote for life, but it's your choice."

"My life should be pretty perfect. I'm sure most people would think it is."

"From the outside looking in?" she asked.

"Yes."

"But what do you see?"

"God, I don't even know," I admitted, trying to think. "Okay," I sighed after a moment, "here is an argument I have had with my husband numerous times, and he brought it up again this morning."

For the next hour we discussed both motivation and passive/aggressive behavior, as well as ways to find the time I needed to put myself first, and what that even means. I was able to open up to her with remarkable ease, and by the time I left her office I felt that with any luck at all, I might one day find my balance, and get back to being me.

Still too embarrassed to go write at Coffee Bean when I couldn't even afford a cup of coffee, I drove up into the hills, parked my beat up, damaged car, and set my laptop on the seat next to me. Then I tried to come up with how Ben would enter the story. I concluded I needed to describe the stillness of the room, so that when he burst in, it would be just as jarring to the reader as the characters themselves. After a lot of over thinking, I forced myself to start typing.

> *Callie slept deeply, the room bathed in the thick darkness of its predawn hour. Encased in the warmth of silence, the sharp crack of a door slammed against the wall, and shook her awake, causing her to scream as she bolted upright, gathering the blankets tightly around her body. In that first rush of confusion, she wasn't sure if this was an earthquake or intruders, but she was consumed by fear.*
>
> *Ben lurched forward, and as they each took in what was actually happening, their reactions could not have been*

more opposite. "Baby!" Ben beamed, his heart racing, delighted to see her as he stumbled drunkenly across the room. "What is wrong with you?" Callie shrieked, her own heart beating against her chest so fiercely that it hurt. As she struggled to catch her breath, Ben fell against the bed reeking of stale whiskey.

As always it wasn't quite as smooth as I wanted it to be, but I reasoned with myself that it got the point across. These people were a mess. I finished out their encounter before my stomach began growling at me because I was hungry. I wanted to write more, if for no other reason than to prove to Gavin that I could, but I also knew that in order for it to be any good, I would have to be able to concentrate. My stomach told me in no uncertain terms that I would not be able to, so I conceded to defeat and headed home.

I walked through the front door and Corky held out her phone to show me a text from Scott. There was a picture of a Paris jewelry store with the question, "Should I go in?"

"Who is he?" she cried.

CHAPTER 40

"Tell him to go in and buy big!" I laughed.

"I swear I'm tempted to marry him just to teach him a lesson," Corky said. "I'll be all like, oh Baby, yes, yes, yes! I can't wait! I'm calling my mom right now!"

"Let's call Gavin and ask him what he'd do if you did," I laughed, pulling out my phone as Meg ran in from the backyard to greet me.

"You wrote, didn't you?" Corky observed.

"A little bit, and Estelle was amazing," I said, hitting Gavin's number.

"Who are you calling? Come swing with me," Meg whined, pulling on me.

"Hang on, I have to ask your daddy something," I explained, as he answered, clearly braced, and asked what was wrong.

"Nothing, in fact I have good news for a change, but first things first, have you talked to Scott today?"

"No why?"

"He's sent Corky a picture of a jewelry store and asked if he should go in."

"Alright," he laughed.

"How should she proceed? She's tempted to tell him she's calling her mother right now to pick a date."

"Sarcastically speaking I presume" he checked.

"Yes, I am fairly certain that she is being facetious."

"It would serve him right if she did, now wouldn't it? They really shouldn't play with one another's feelings."

"Thank you, so that said, what do you think he'd do, if she did?"

" What is he saying?" Corky demanded.

"I trust he would know that she wasn't serious," he said, as I waved both Corky and Meg off.

"Because he's not?" I asked.

"Oh on some level he may be, but I hardly think he's ready to put a ring on it, as they say. I suspect he is just testing the water. Not to mention pushing buttons."

"And his reasons for doing so would be what?"

"That he's bothered by her, I would imagine. He thought he understood where he stood with her and then she turned his world upside down."

"His world or his ego?"

"Yes well, I'll not be getting into that," he declared, adding, "You sound like yourself, Kelly. Are you having a good day?"

A lump immediately rose up in my throat, and tears burst forth as much out of relief, as anything else. For a moment I couldn't speak, and I walked away to tell him in private what Estelle had said about paying for therapy, and how grateful I was. He too was grateful, agreeing it was wonderful news in light of our current situation, but he also admitted that he wasn't entirely comfortable with it. I just reminded him that like she had said, when we could pay, we would.

He advised me to tell Corky she shouldn't engage in a battle of words and emotions, especially when communicating through trans-Atlantic texts. I asked how his day was going and he rattled off a list of issues with one of his more difficult authors, but said he was hopeful he'd be home by six thirty at the latest.

Although Corky confessed that she agreed with Gavin's advice not to engage, she said she couldn't help but be a little disappointed. This sparked a "what if" conversation where we amused ourselves with several versions of how she could respond, and what each response would leave Scott thinking.

Hilary left while I was making dinner and Corky was reading what I had written. It didn't take long to become overwhelmed again as Nick fussed in his bouncer, Jack complained that he was hungry, Meg whined that Winnie Winters (I kid you not, that is the child's actual name) had not been a good sharer at school that day, and the boiling water on the stove splashed up to burn me as I poured the pasta into it for our spaghetti dinner. Hearing me curse, Corky came out to help. Of course she said if I were a supportive friend I'd burn more than myself. When I looked at her like she was crazy, she said, "You know, because I nearly burned down your entire kitchen." I ran my arm under cold water, but it didn't do a lot of good.

"I'll distract you," Corky offered, telling Jack and Meg to settle down while pulling a very grateful Nick out of his bouncer. "We need to discuss your mommy's book. Are you aware of the fact that your mother is writing a book?"

"Mommy!" Jack half cried, half groaned.

"Jack, have some Cheerios while dinner is cooking," I said going to the pantry.

"Sagetti!," he cried.

"It has to cook," I told him.

"What kind of book?" Meg inquired. "One for me?"

"No, for grownups," Corky told her.

"Mommy!" she complained, "that's boring."

"No it's not," Corky defended. "Geez Meg, Ben has a drinking problem we have to figure out. Why is Ben such a mess?" she asked me.

"I'm not sure. I think he's immature and a little self indulgent, plus I think he likes the image of the hard drinking, hard hitting journalist. I'm sure he has father issues."

"What does his dad do?"

"He's a politician of course," I said, as it suddenly came to me that his father was probably somehow involved in what he was investigating. "The question is this, is he trying to bring his father down, or is he the one guy he always thought was beyond reproach, and therefore he's devastated to learn that he has something to do with this?"

"I don't know, either way could be interesting. Does Callie know his father?" she asked.

"Sure, they are married, so she must know him some."

"Interesting," she nodded.

"No, you should have a dragon in it," Meg told me. "That is what makes books interesting, and a little girl who is it's friend."

"Plot twist!" Corky laughed, as the house phone rang.

It was Colleen, who excitedly told me she had the keys to their new house and that I had to come check it out the next day.

"Already?"

"Sure, we're all friends so we don't need to stand on protocol."

"I guess."

"I'll pick you up at ten. Tell Corky she should come, too!"

CHAPTER 41

The house had massive potential, but was a little dated, and were it mine, I thought, I'd want to renovate. I could tell as we went through it that Colleen was bothered by something and I couldn't help but wonder if it was the way Dee Dee was running the tour. She acted as though it was her house, discussing what furniture would go where, and what paint colors would go on the walls. I reasoned that she was an interior decorator by trade, so it was only natural that she would offer advice, but this was stated as if she was the only one who would have any say.

As she and Corky headed out to the pool area ahead of us, I pulled Colleen back and asked if everything was okay.

"Of course it is," she said, somewhat defensively, and not at all convincingly.

"Okay, well I'm just checking."

"It just looks different than I remembered, she sighed. "I mean it's so big, and the hill is so hilly. How are Meg and Jack going to play around here without rolling down to the next zip code? What if this is a horrible mistake?" she asked.

"It's not really kid friendly, is it?" I observed.

"Even the slide into the pool looks like a death trap now. I wanted this to be for all of us. I imagined it as a place where we could all relax, and that's not going to happen with the kids falling over mountainsides, and being eaten by rodents. I'll bet there are all kinds of rodents out here. Oh crap, do you think there are snakes?"

"God, I hope not, but yeah, there could be," I frowned.

"Shit!"

"So you'll get a good exterminator."

"Then Nick will put a chemical laced plant in his mouth, not to mention I don't think exterminators can do anything about snakes."

"Is it bats that get rid of snakes?" I questioned, trying to remember.

"I don't want bats!"

"No, I wouldn't think you would," I laughed.

"It's not funny," she cried.

"I know, all three of my kids are in peril," I teased.

"You seem better," she said.

"Hopefully things are turning around. I don't know, we'll see. This will be okay," I said rubbing her arm.

"Keith will kill me if I say I don't want to move, and we've signed all the papers anyway. Do you think we could get out of it?"

"Maybe, but maybe not. I can't remember if there's a grace period. Maybe there is, but then you said this was a friend's, right? That could be awkward."

"Keith would kill me," she repeated.

"How is Keith?" I asked, suddenly remembering Dee Dee having told me something about a fight that day at the florist.

"He's stressed. Warners has backed out on his film. Well, postponed it, and he's not happy because he was counting on it shooting this summer. I don't know what difference it makes though, because he'll still have his other film in production. I mean, I think this simplifies things, but apparently I don't understand the film world," she said, rolling her eyes.

Suddenly she was on the verge of tears.

"I had this image of walking down that staircase in my wedding gown and it was going to be regal, but now that I'm seeing it again, this place looks like something out of an eighties soap opera!" she wept. "I'll look like a character out of that show Dallas. All we are missing is the fountain out front where our mom and Keith's mom can get into a big fight and push each other into it."

"I could totally see that happening," I admitted, as Dee Dee and Corky came back to see why we hadn't followed them.

"What's wrong?" Dee Dee asked.

"Everything!" Colleen wailed.

We all did our best to console her, but she was beside herself. By the time we left, she was declaring the house to be the tackiest place in the world. Not only that, but she was also threatening to embrace this whole eighties themed wedding, by insisting we all get big perms and wear Madonna style clothing.

When she dropped us at home, I gave her a hug, and suggested perhaps she too, should be talking to Estelle. She said she was going to runaway to New York instead, lock herself in a room at Trump Towers, and write in between walks through Central Park. I was dying to scream, "Take me with you!" but I managed to resist. Corky looked at me as they drove away.

"That went well," she commented.

"Do you think she and Keith are okay?" I worried.

"Do you suppose anyone is okay?" she threw back at me.

It was a question I would throw at Gavin later that same night. We were lying in bed, getting ready to sleep, but I couldn't stop thinking about both Keith and Colleen, and the characters in my book. Then I thought about Corky and Scott, and both my parents as well as Gavin's, and I just had to ask if he thought any relationship was truly solid.

"I would like to think ours is," he said.

"As would I, of course, but it all seems so dismal at times."

"Us?" he questioned.

"No, relationships in general. I mean who do we know that is happy?"

"Your parents seem perfectly happy to me."

"Now, but they weren't always."

"I think it is possible to be happy with one's spouse and not happy all at once. I mean certainly we can be annoyed with one another, or even hurt by something, and still be committed to the relationship. Still know that there are far more good days than bad. It's rather like life itself, isn't it? Not every day is roses, and all that."

"I think that might be what my book is about. I think Callie is going to find out that's how real relationships work. I just hope Keith and Colleen are okay."

"Best they find out now," he reasoned.

"I suppose."

"You mustn't take on the world's problems."

"She's not the world, she's my sister."

"And she's quite capable of working this out for herself, as is Corky. You need only worry about yourself and your book. I expect ten pages tomorrow," he announced.

"There's a challenge I won't meet."

"Dreadful thing to say. You'd best go back to Estelle immediately," he teased.

"I'll definitely do my best to write, but ten pages is asking a lot. Of course if I were in a room in Trump Towers..."

"Dream on, Luv," he said.

CHAPTER 42

Nick was up half the night fussing and teething. Even after I gave him some Tylenol he took a while to settle, and due to the fact that Corky was attempting to sleep in his room, I wound up bringing him back to bed with Gavin and me. Unfortunately, snuggled in against me, Nick decided he wanted to nurse, and so we had to debate that again. Gavin was adamant that I not give into him, reasoning that it would equate a giant leap backward and we were moving forward. In the end, he got up and walked Nick to sleep, putting him back into his crib once he was out. Of course Nick was awake and fussing again by five, and by seven I was exhausted, as was he himself.

When Hilary arrived, Gavin said he could take Meg to school for me, and suggested I go back to bed for an hour or two before attempting to write. I gratefully took him up on his offer, but Nick refused to go down for Hilary, and after a while I had to get up to be sure he was okay.

We took his temperature to see if this wasn't more than teething, but that didn't seem to be the issue, and Corky who had been disturbed, teased that he was just being a mama's boy. He eventually fell asleep, so having him settled, Corky and I went to the Coffee Bean to write. I told Hilary to call if she needed reinforcements.

At the Bean, by the time Corky had bought us both coffee, and we'd secured a table and pulled out our laptops, it was after eleven. I knew Meg would be home in just over an hour, and I was having trouble letting the morning go, worrying that Nick was going to wake up miserable again, but Corky immediately began typing furiously. That, too, proved distracting. When my phone rang, and I didn't recognize the number, I answered to hear Keith at the other end.

"Kelly, what the hell happened at the house yesterday?" he asked.

"I'm not sure," I hesitated, unclear on how Colleen would want me to answer.

"Colleen has just flown off to New York."

"She said she was going to," I admitted.

"Why?

"I think she's just freaking out."

"Meet me for lunch, can you?" he asked.

"I'm not sure, Nick is having a rough day."

"Don't you have both Corky and the nanny there? Please?"

"When?"

"Like an hour from now? I'll meet you down the street at Art's so that you can go right back home," he said, referring to the deli that was only a few blocks from our house.

"Okay, assuming Nick isn't going nuts, I'll see you there."

"Great, thanks."

I told Corky I was going to go check on Nick, meet Keith, and that then I'd try writing that afternoon, assuming I had any brain function left. She wished me luck and continued typing as if she were possessed.

At home, Hilary was surprised to see me so soon, while Nick was contentedly lying on the floor next to her and Jack, as they worked on a wooden puzzle.

"See?" Jack beamed, "I do it," he said pointing to the puzzle.

"You are getting big," I told him.

"I getting big," he nodded in agreement, before telling Hilary, "Do more!"

Nick rolled onto his stomach and hollered for me to pay attention to him, so I grabbed him, gave him some kisses, and took him to sort laundry before I needed to leave again. I promised Hilary I wouldn't be gone for long and then, because it was a nice day, I chose to walk down to the restaurant.

Keith is ridiculously good looking. His chiseled cheekbones and strong jaw line, accompanied by the contrast of his almond colored eyes and honey blonde hair is almost too much. He dresses really well too, and naturally draws a lot of attention from women. I was not the least bit surprised to find one of the waitresses flirting with him when I walked up to his table. He stood and kissed my cheek, waiting for me to sit before he sat back down. We ordered cokes and then discussed how good all of the food at this particular deli was. Once we'd ordered our food, he told me I looked better than the last time he'd seen me.

"Knock wood," I told him, and smiling, he knocked on his forehead.

"So your sister," he said, "what happened?"

"What did she say happened?" I asked.

"She just announced she was going to New York to write because this is all too much, but when I asked what "this" was, she said everything. When I asked that she elaborate, she just assured me it's a girl thing and that I wouldn't understand."

"And you've come to me instead of Dee Dee?"

"I tried her but she told me to give her some space and not to be so damned suffocating. I'm not suffocating, am I?" he questioned.

He looked so confused by the prospect that it reminded me of how much I liked him, even if I didn't know him as well as I'd hoped I would by now.

"I don't know, are you?"

"I don't think so, and if I am, that's the first I've heard of it. Dee Dee seemed almost angry," he reported.

"I don't know what that would be about. Can I just say before we go back to Colleen though, how much I appreciate your taking my kids overnight the way you did."

"Oh please, they are great. I just felt bad that we didn't take Nick too, so that you could really sleep. I can't wait to have kids," he told me.

"Where is Colleen on that?"

"Not as ready as me, but she'll come around, don't you think? She certainly adores your kids."

"I know, but now that I think about it, I've never heard when, or even if, she wants kids. How weird is that? We must have discussed it sometime."

"She'd like to wait a couple of years, and I'd like to meet in the middle. We'll work it out," he said, confidently.

"So she didn't say anything to you about the house?" I inquired.

"No, I asked if something had happened and she said, what do you think? but then refused to say anything else. She couldn't get away fast enough. I didn't get home until nine and she said she had to go catch the red eye to New York."

"I'm not sure how to proceed here," I frowned, "because she'll kill me if I betray a confidence, and yet you deserve an explanation."

"Spill it, sister," he joked, but then more seriously said, "I love her, Kelly, and I just want her to be happy."

"So if that's true, I hope you both don't hate me for saying this, but she showed us around the house yesterday and realized it wasn't what she thought it was. In fact, it reminded her of the kind of houses they had in Dallas. The show, not the city," I specified, "and then she began freaking out that Meg and Jack would fall off the mountainside and be eaten by rodents."

"She saw rodents?"

"No, but you have to admit with all of that land, there are bound to be some."

"Did you like the house?" he asked.

"Yes and no. I mean, there is a lot about it that is beautiful, but I had to agree with her that it's a little dated and not kid friendly at all."

"The pool has a slide," he offered.

"I think she is probably just having pre-wedding jitters. I doubt it has anything to do with you, but more with the realization that she is making huge decisions that will affect the rest of her life, and it's overwhelming. Plus I probably haven't made any of it look so great lately."

"She really hates the house?"

"Maybe, but you didn't hear that from me."

"Do you think she could learn to love it? I just sank a whole lot of money into that thing."

"I know. I'd give her a day to calm down and then ask again why she needed to get out, without bringing me or this conversation into it," I added.

"We could make it kid friendly, don't you think?"

"To some extent, sure."

"I paid cash for that and the owners used it to do the same for their ranch in Montana. I can't ask for it back."

"And she probably knows that, which is why she feels she can't tell you, but again, you didn't hear it from me."

"Hates it?" he asked, incredulously, adding, "she was all excited about getting married there and walking down those stairs in her gown. She said I'd cry when she made her grand entrance."

"Oh you'll cry alright, because by the time we left she said it would be an eighties wedding to rival Madonna and Sean Penn's, and she was threatening to make us all get curly perms"

He buried his face in his hands and shook his head, asking what he was going to do. I felt bad for him, but at the same time happy for Colleen that she was going to marry a good guy. I told him to hold off on doing anything until I talked to her. I promised him I'd call her later in the day just to check in and to gauge her mood, and then I'd let him know if it was safe to broach the subject.

Our lunch arrived, and we ate while trying to figure out why Dee Dee had been so hostile towards him. As I told him, I could see where Dee Dee had mellowed, and yet it only seemed natural that she would at times revert back to her old, irritating ways. He agreed and thanked me for giving him a clue as to what was going on. It was a nice lunch but then I walked back home, only to be bombarded by Meg, who had more tales about the dreadful Winnie Winters. Apparently, she was turning out to be quite the adversary.

CHAPTER 43

I called Colleen but got her voicemail, so I told her Keith was concerned, and to call me back. Writing did not appear to be in the cards that day, as Nick got fussy again, and Meg was being rather cranky herself. I dreaded Gavin's coming home and being disappointed in me, and resented the fact that I knew he would be. It didn't help that Corky had outlined her entire script, and written up the first five scenes. Not only that, but it was good.

I told her I hated her, and she told me it had simply flowed out of her more effortlessly than anything she had ever written before.

"You know what they always say, write what you know," she grinned, "and this is still fresh enough in my mind that I know it backwards and forwards."

"Crap, if I go by that I'll have to write about dirty diapers."

"I'll bet you could," she said.

"I'll bet you could," I childishly mimicked, as I threw a dish towel at her.

Nothing if not predictable, Gavin gave me a look of expectation as soon as he came in. I just groaned. Corky cheerfully told him to leave me alone, and then suggested he read what she had written.

"Nothing?" he asked, and I walked away. "Kelly," he sighed.

"You shouldn't pressure her so. She's trying," I heard Corky tell him.

I went back to our room, closed the door and tried Colleen again who picked up this time.

"Why didn't you call me back?" I whined.

"I was writing."

"Seriously?"

"No, not really. I was with Dev. We went to this bar and studied people, making up stories about them. It was fun."

"Nice for you," I sighed, before thinking to stop myself from saying it out loud.

"What's wrong? You aren't depressed again already, are you?" she asked.

"I failed at writing today, and Corky wrote an entire outline for a script that is going to be really good," I whined. "And now I'm a disappointment to Gavin and she gets to be the clever one, and it's like our childhood all over again. Oh crap! Do you think I've married our father?"

"God no," she laughed. "What makes you think Gavin is judging you? And just by the way, that was my childhood you just described. You were the one who could do no wrong and Dev was his boy, so you know..."

"Yeah, I know," I agreed, because the truth was, my father had always praised everything I had ever done. "I could see it in Gavin's face, that's how," I informed her.

"Well, if he's disappointed, it's only because he believes in your writing. I should have brought you with me," she speculated, as I thought she sure should have.

"Why would you just run out on Keith without any explanation?" I demanded.

"He called you?"

"We had lunch."

"Really?" she said, adding, "that's interesting."

"It was kind of. I like him."

"Well, that's good, because he's family, or close enough, anyway. He likes you and Gavin too."

"So do you still hate the house?"

"Yes! And Dee Dee says I can't tell him."

"Why not?"

"Because I said I wanted it. And okay, so I know I did, but I just remembered it so differently. It looked homier and more intimate with furniture and everything, and of course Dee Dee says it will again when we get our stuff in there, but it's old and isolated. We'll be all alone up there on the hill like a couple of old hermits. You aren't going to come out there. You said yourself the kids will be in danger, and now Dee Dee has announced that she and Roman want to have a baby and have started fertility treatments, because if it were going to happen naturally, it would have by now, and of course she just has to tell me that I should do the same, because thirty-seven is old, and I haven't had any scares, so I probably can't get pregnant on my own either, and I'm not even ready for kids!"

"I know, Keith told me you want to wait a couple of years."

"What the hell, Kelly? When did I get old?"

"You aren't that old. Lots of women older than you have babies."

"I'm old! I looked it up and everything says I'm old to ancient."

"So worst case scenario, you'll adopt."

"Dee Dee says they don't like old either."

"Well, Dee Dee isn't in charge of everything and doesn't get a say in your procreation."

"Do you not know Dee Dee? Of course she does. At least in my life."

"So what? Here's what I saw today. Keith is a good guy who loves you, and I may have told him you hate the house, and he didn't even scream. He says he can't get his money back, but he didn't scream."

"He was okay with it?" she asked.

"Okay might be a little strong," I laughed, "but he certainly didn't accuse you of forcing him to buy it, or say you were an idiot, or anything like that."

"What did he say?"

"He asked if I thought you guys could fix it."

"Really, he wasn't mad?"

"He didn't seem to be."

"Do you think we can fix it?" she asked.

"Shit, you have the number one book series in the country, you can do anything you set your mind to."

"So can you. I truly believe that," she told me. "Our parents might have a few flaws, but I was thinking about this as I was laughing with Devon, they have raised three great kids, and let's be honest," she laughed, "I'll bet no one saw that coming."

I could only agree. I laid back on our bed and we reminisced about various times our parents had sat us in cafes, bought us milkshakes, and then left us there to go to a restaurant two streets over for a relaxing dinner. At the time it hadn't been a big deal, but now as a parent, I couldn't imagine ever doing the same with my kids.

Gavin came in towards the end of our conversation, and sitting next to me, waited for us to finish up. When we did, he asked if everything was alright.

"Sure," I shrugged.

"Have you a plan for dinner?"

"Cereal?" I proposed.

"You're angry with me," he smiled.

"No I'm not. I'm frustrated, that's all."

"I don't mean to pressure you. I know the kids and your family have to come first sometimes."

"I'm discouraged, but I'm going to try again tomorrow."

"And that's it, isn't it? You just have to keep trying."

"Did you read Corky's stuff? It's good isn't it?" I asked.

"It is, very, but then she's able to leave all of this behind, isn't she?"

"That she is."

"You'll get there," he promised.

CHAPTER 44

Over the next three days Corky finished her entire script, while I wrote about three words. Gavin signed Maria Risner and began submitting her novel, *Looking Out For Me* to publishers. He also booked an appearance as a speaker at a writing conference, filling in for one of his former colleagues at Trinity, who had been scheduled to speak, but had a family emergency. He was away all day Saturday, but came home energized and excited by how well it had gone. Vowing to get more speaking engagements in the future, he took the cash they'd paid him and threw it on our bed. Grinning, he asked me if I wanted some.

"How much is that?"

"$2500. This," he said, separating the 2000 from the 500, "has to go on bills, but we can either split the 500, or put it towards the front yard."

"Let's do this," I suggested. "Three hundred goes to the yard, and we each get a hundred for ourselves."

"I like the way you think," he said.

On Sunday, Scott returned. Corky had gone out to write, Jack was down for a nap, and Meg was giving Nick a ride in the wagon. Gavin and I were debating whether or not our front lawn could be saved with massive amounts of water, or if it had to be replaced completely, when Scott drove up in his old 4-runner. After saying hello, Gavin asked his opinion on the grass, and he considered, before saying water was worth a shot. I trimmed some bushes while the two of them sat on the front porch watching the kids, listening for Jack, and discussing eccentric billionaires who steal art. Corky returned, declaring her script complete. Scott scoffed at the idea.

"What?" she demanded.

"Is it formatted? Is it the proper length?"

"No Scott, of course not. I've written it as a 375 page limerick, what do you think?" she asked, rolling her eyes as she pushed by him to go inside.

"It's actually quite good," Gavin told him, as Scott laughed at her.

"Doesn't really surprise me," he admitted.

"So why are you giving her a hard time?" I demanded.

"I enjoy it?" he suggested.

"Whatever, it's your loss."

"I know it is," he mumbled.

"You could try winning her back with kindness," Gavin told him, adding, "just a suggestion."

"I somehow doubt that would work," he said, getting up and following her inside.

"What's he going to do?" I asked Gavin.

"I haven't a clue."

I sat next to him on the steps and confessed that I was tired of gardening now. Nick had long since fallen asleep in the wagon and Meg was quietly drawing in the dirt with a stick. Gavin leaned in to kiss me and we began making out for a minute, reminding me that we hadn't been able to relax and enjoy each other like that in ages.

Suddenly, both Scott and Corky burst out of the house.

"Jack is waking up," Corky announced, as they rushed over to Scott's car, got in and drove away.

"Look out!" I laughed.

"What was that?" Gavin asked.

"Sex, remember that?"

"Rather fondly," he smiled, as I went in to get Jack.

Scott dropped Corky off later that night, not bothering to come in. She immediately walked to the kitchen, asking if we had any wine.

"I do believe you've drunk it all," Gavin called out to her. "Do you need me to go get you more?"

"Yes please," she said.

"I'll be back," he promised, and off he went.

Once he was gone, Corky walked into the den where I'd been watching TV, sat next to me, and rested her head on my shoulder.

"Are you alright?" I asked, turning the TV off.

"I wish," she sighed.

"Did you talk, or just have sex all afternoon?"

"And evening," she smiled, sitting up.

"And it was enjoyable?"

"I wouldn't have continued if it weren't."

"Good, so?"

"So he asked what I want and I don't know, do I?"

"What does he want?"

"He says he wants me, but when I asked what that means, he got all uptight and said that was a stupid question."

"To which you replied?"

"Screw you?" she laughed.

"And did you?" I laughed back.

"No, I told him to bring me back here."

"Do you still love him?"

"I don't know," she groaned, and I just looked at her because I was pretty sure she did. "Ok, so yes, but seriously, Kel, as the song goes, what's love got to do with it?"

"It's the foundation. It just means that should you decide you want to move forward with him, you have something to build on."

"Yeah, I guess that makes sense," she agreed.

"Were words of love exchanged?" I inquired.

"Oh hell no," she laughed.

"You should tell the people you love that you love them, "I told her.

"Always?"

"Yep, I think so."

"Can it come in a text?" she laughed, pulling out her phone.

"Oddly enough, I think it can," I said.

CHAPTER 45

Estelle gave me an assignment the following day, telling me to go do something, anything for myself. I said writing was for myself, but she said she didn't believe that it was. At least not right now. She said it sounded to her as though I was writing to compete with Corky, Colleen, Devon and every other writer I knew, not to mention to please Gavin.

"I'm not saying it can't be enjoyable under ideal circumstances, but it sounds to me as though you need to cushion yourself from all of that pressure. Go to a movie, lay out at the beach and read a trashy magazine for pleasure, get a manicure, whatever you want, but pay attention to you. Give yourself permission to be completely selfish for at least a couple of hours," she encouraged. "And whatever you do, don't feel guilty about it."

I promised I would give it a try. Then I went home and Corky told me Colleen was back and wanted to meet at the bridal shop the next day. I wasn't about to return to the scene of the crime, so to speak.

"I was carted off in an ambulance the last time I was there. I'm not going back," I told Colleen when she called again.

"You have to. We have to pick dresses. You and Dee Dee have to agree on something and Meg needs a dress too," she insisted.

"Meg does not need a designer dress, and you can send me pictures of dresses, but I'm not going back there."

"You have to be fitted. Come on, this is Hollywood. They probably won't even remember you."

"It's not going to happen."

"It's my wedding, Kelly. You have to."

"I love you and will go with whatever you choose, but I can't go back there. I won't," I told her.

Round and round we went, but I remained firm. We hung up and an hour later my mother called to complain that I had upset Colleen. She said it wouldn't kill me to be more understanding. I told her my head was exploding and that I had to go. Gavin massaged my shoulders and Corky poured me a glass of wine, while they both told me to let it go. When the phone rang again, I announced that I wasn't home, but it was for Gavin. Sirri Bingington was calling.

They talked for twenty minutes and when they hung up, Gavin said she had decided to send him the outline for another novel she was beginning, because she appreciated that he had taken Maria on as a client.

When we went to bed that night we were both exhausted, but Gavin insisted things were turning around. He said Estelle was absolutely right that I should do something nice for myself. He said I'd earned it. So, as I fell asleep, I decided I would go get my hair cut, and maybe even get a manicure as well. I wanted to feel good about myself again.

Things were getting so much better that Nick actually slept through the night and when he began to fuss at 6:45 the next morning, I practically felt refreshed. I got him up and changed him, fixed him a bottle, and took him back to our bed where Jack had already moved into my place. I pushed him over and told Gavin of my plans.

"We'll have to have sex if you do all that," he teased.

"Too soon," I shuddered. "I like sleeping through the night."

"It is rather nice, isn't it?" he agreed.

Meg came in and complained that we were snuggling without her, but Gavin pulled her up to join us, telling her we were doing no such thing. Looking over at me as Jack crawled around in our blankets, Nick contentedly drank his bottle, and Meg sang us a new song she'd learned at school, Gavin smiled.

"This is everything to me," he said.

At that precise moment I had to agree that it was pretty perfect, but within a minute or two Jack was trying to push Nick out of my lap, and Meg was complaining that we weren't paying attention to her songs. It fell apart quickly.

Gavin got up to shower, and I took the kids out to get breakfast. Once they were semi-settled, I began flipping through a few magazines looking for a good haircut. I was leaning towards a slightly layered, shoulder length cut, when

Jack, who I had allowed to sit at the table like a big boy, fell off his chair and bit his tongue.

Between the screaming and the blood, you'd think it was much more serious than it was. Fortunately, he recovered quickly. Gavin went off to work, and as soon as Hilary arrived, I went to take a shower, minus any guilt.

CHAPTER 46

My hair cut made me feel ten times lighter, even though it wasn't a dramatic change. It just felt fresh, and by the time I had treated myself to a manicure as well, I felt like a new person. I literally bounced into the house, calling for Corky to show off how great I looked.

"In here," she yelled, with what I couldn't help but sense was an amused tone.

I walked into the family room to discover her sitting with my mom, who held a glass of wine in one hand, and Meg's naked baby doll in the other hand. She looked tired and confused, as Meg excitedly told me her grandma was here.

"We are going to buy me a beautiful dress," she beamed.

"I can't thank you enough for pulling me into this," my mother sarcastically told me, as Corky motioned for me to turn around so that she could see the back of my hair.

"I like it. It looks really good," she told me.

"Yes, yes, you look beautiful as always," my mom said, finishing off her wine, and standing. "Let go get this over with."

"Get what over with?" I asked.

"We have to go get Meg's dress, and you have to try on a couple of things. I've promised Colleen I'll hand deliver you."

"Why and to where?"

"Because apparently I'm her mother, and this is what mothers do when their daughters get married. I was all over your wedding, or so she has informed me. Let's just finish up."

"Where?" I repeated.

"The dress shop, Kelly, so have a glass of wine if you need liquid courage, but get over yourself. No one cares if you were having a bad day the last time you were there," she said, rolling her eyes.

"I care and I told her I wasn't going back there."

"So I have heard ad nauseam," she said, looking at Corky.

"I've tried explaining," Corky said.

"Mom," I whined, "I was carted away!"

"You had an incident. Big deal. Just let it go. That was then and this is now. I still have a long drive ahead of me and I'd like to get home before *The Price is Right,* so let's go."

"An incident? Is that what we are calling this?"

"Save the drama, Honey. The point is that you are doing better. If you don't make a big deal of it, no one else will."

"Should I just leave the boys alone? Because Hilary has to leave in a half hour, and if you think I'm doing this without Corky, you are out of your mind."

"So ask her to stay," my mother hissed at me.

I walked out to the backyard where Hilary was watching Jack run around, and shaking my head and laughing, asked if she'd had the pleasure of meeting my mom.

"Yes," she smiled.

"She is insisting that I ask you to stay late tonight. Please say that you can't."

"I really can't," she told me.

"Thank you," I said returning with the news, as my mother showed me a text from Colleen all in capitals, saying, WHERE ARE YOU? "Tell her to come to me." I said sitting on the couch and pulling Nick into my lap.

I kissed him and discussed which nail salon I had gone to with Corky, as my mother texted back and sighed a lot. Meg told me she wanted to do her nails, too, and for the wedding, she thought maybe Colleen should do face paint of a lion on her cheek. Corky and I were amused even if my mother was not. Colleen texted back to bring the kids.

"Oh sure, maybe Jack could run out in the parking lot again," I said.

"You take a stroller and tell him to sit still," my mother said.

"You don't know Jack, do you?"

"I'll hold onto Jack," Corky offered, telling me to give up, because in the grand scheme of things, this wasn't worth the argument.

I conceded against my better judgment, and off we went to the dress shop. Meg was excited, but both Jack and Nick were hungry and cranky. I fed Nick a bottle in his car seat on the way there, but Jack said he wanted noodles. Corky tried promising him she'd buy him some if he was good, but at barely two years old, and in a dress shop, that was asking a lot.

When we arrived, Colleen thanked me profusely, whispering in my ear that she'd explain later, not that I knew what she was referring to at the time. Dee Dee came out in this fuchsia dress and asked what I thought. I told her I thought the color was too much. She looked annoyed and went back to the dressing room while Colleen told me she had narrowed her bridal gown choices to two, and was going to model both to see what I thought.

"Look around," she said, adding that she would be right back.

"Don't you dare like the ruffle dress she's chosen," my mom said, as Corky walked away laughing. "You'll be laughing for a whole other reason when you see it," my mother told her.

Dee Dee returned first, this time in a long, sleeveless lavender gown, with a scooped neckline and a purple sash at the waist. I liked it. It was understated, yet pretty, while being the kind of dress that wouldn't override the bride. I said she looked great and that I'd gladly try on the same.

Colleen came out in a dress that was strapless and fitted to the waist, but then had layers of ruffles cascading into a full skirt, that although a little fluffy, certainly weren't anything to laugh at. She looked beautiful, and despite the daggers I felt aimed at my back from my mother, I told her so.

Meg and Jack began chasing each other, and I told them to settle down. Meg said this was boring and she wanted a dress. My mother took her over to a rack of dresses for Jr. Bridesmaids, and I went to try on the lavender dress. It bunched a little across my chest but I was assured it could be fixed, and overall I liked the way it looked. I waited to show Colleen who came out and was stunning in her next dress.

Again strapless, this one had hand painted rose petals across the bust, as well as in the back and towards the bottom of the full, princess style skirt. It was breathtaking, and as I told her, perfect for the castle like stairs in her new house.

" That's the one. You are gorgeous! " I said.

"It is, right?" she smiled, admiring herself in the mirror.

"I want mine just like that!" Meg announced.

The eager salesclerk immediately pulled out a similar, mini hand painted dress, that cost twelve hundred dollars.

"Oh no!" I said.

"We'll take it," my mother shocked us all by saying.

"Mom! She's four. She's going to spill punch on it. Are you mad?"

"It's Colleen's day. If you want it, I'll get it. Consider it my show of support," she told Colleen.

"Get it, get it!" Meg squealed.

"Sweety, you haven't even tried it on," Colleen said, and Meg immediately began tossing off clothes.

"It's immoral," I said.

"Maybe it'll be scratchy and she won't like it," Colleen suggested hopefully.

Thankfully it was much too big, and I told the salesclerk not to dare say they could fix it. Colleen promised Meg we'd find her a beautiful dress somewhere else, and although disappointed, she agreed.

My mother couldn't leave fast enough and Dee Dee wasn't far behind her. Colleen and I changed out of our dresses and agreed that this was a huge hurdle to have out of the way. Then we all went out for noodles.

CHAPTER 47

Dee Dee called the following day to say we had to arrange Colleen's bridal shower, and asked what I thought our theme should be. I suggested it be friendship and that we leave it at that because this wasn't the movie *Bridesmaids,* and we weren't preadolescent teens. Corky felt that was harsh, and admittedly, I was met with silence on the other end of the phone. After a few seconds, Dee Dee informed me that we were having this shower in less than ten days.

"You are going to have to help out a little, Kelly, because I am working, you know? I have a lot of clients, plus Keith and Colleen's house. I'm very busy."

"I am trying to work myself," I said, annoyed by her self-important attitude, "but if you tell me what you need, I'll do my best."

"I'll send over a list," she said.

We hung up, and I laughed with Corky about how Dee Dee was reverting back to her old ways. We both agreed the new and improved Dee Dee had been too good to be true.

Meg was cranky again that day, and I couldn't drop her at school fast enough. Once I had, I met Corky at Coffee Bean, where she was going to Google how to format her script, while I worked on my book. We had no more than sat down when Hilary called to inform me Meg's school had called to say she'd thrown up. I had to go get her, and from there we spiraled into disaster, once again.

The stomach flu hit our house like a tornado, spinning through a deck of cards. Gavin came home later that same day feeling ill, and by midnight he was throwing up as well. Nick was the next to fall, followed by Corky, and then me. Jack was the only one not affected, but all that meant was that he was running around wreaking havoc, while the rest of us were fighting over toilet bowls. All told, we were laid out for a week.

Dee Dee took it personally, of course, while Colleen said she wished she could help out with Jack, but she couldn't afford to get sick. Scott brought us juice and groceries once or twice, but just when we began recovering, Hilary was struck down.

Four days before Colleen's bridal shower, I was expected to organize the food, flowers and place settings, while Dee Dee handled the beverages, entertainment and invitations. Needless to say, writing took a backseat to the preparations, even though my mind constantly wandered to thoughts of Callie and Ben, interrupting whatever I was supposed to be concentrating on.

Corky helped out as best she could, but she was attempting to settle into her new apartment, not to mention being in heat, and confused by her feelings for Scott, while at the same time trying to avoid him. He had almost single handedly moved everything out of storage and into her new place for her. Then he'd been offended by what he perceived as her lack of gratitude. She insisted it was no such thing. She was just exhausted by a week of the flu and being stressed out about how few auditions she'd had since returning to LA.

The night before the shower itself, she called me in tears because she'd tried asking Scott something about her script and he'd supposedly gone off on her.

"What do you mean he went off on you?" I asked.

"He told me one minute I'm a writer, and the next I need an audition, and then I'm off to something else, and what? What am I off to?" she cried.

"I have no idea," I admitted.

"He's just mean. All I wanted to know is if I finally had the formatting right, and he says how would he know, after he's been acting like the format expert all of this time."

"I'm sorry," I said, looking at Gavin who was reading another manuscript. "Scott's upset Corky," I informed him.

"She's upset him as well," he said, not bothering to look up. "He'd like her to make up her mind."

"Did you hear that?" I asked Corky, passing on what he had said.

"About what?" she demanded.

"About what, she'd like to know," I told him.

"Where their relationship is going and when it might arrive, as it were," he sighed.

"You mean what she asked him six months ago?"

"Precisely."

I passed that onto her, and she said it was typical that now he would want this. I could only agree, but said the fact remained that he did.

"What if I just want sex?" she asked.

"He would love you forever and ever," I couldn't help but laugh.

"Maybe I want a respite. Maybe we just have a strictly sexual relationship until, say July, and then we reassess."

"You could try it."

"I think we need a grace period, and at the same time the physical attraction is crowding things, so we'll just give it the attention it's demanding and then regroup in July."

"Sounds like a plan," I said.

Of course when I hung up, Gavin wanted to know what the plan was. As soon as I told him, he lunged at me and said he wanted the same.

CHAPTER 48

The bridal shower went off without a hitch, at least on the surface. The truth is I was ready to kill Dee Dee, who would ask me to do things and then re-do everything herself. The one thing Colleen had specifically requested was that we include Meg in everything. As her flower girl, Colleen wanted her to feel special, and saw to it that she did. Meg was excited to wear her new party dress, and to be allowed to go to a grown up party. She sat next to Colleen, beaming up at her as Colleen proudly showed her off to all of her friends, and told them what a great kid Meg was. I loved seeing how happy she was. Right up until the moment Dee Dee pulled me aside and suggested I send Meg into the kitchen with her housekeeper, because the entertainment was about to get x-rated.

"Oh, you did not hire a stripper," I said.

"Two," she grinned, signaling for her housekeeper.

"You knew Meg would be here!" I objected.

"And you knew there would be entertainment. Who did you think I was going to hire, Polly Pockets? Carmen will watch her."

"Unbelievable," I said, taking Meg's hand and telling her we had to go outside for awhile.

"Why?" she whined, as Colleen asked where we were going.

I just shook my head and passing by Corky, asked that she come find us when the show was over. Then I fielded questions from a four year old as to why we had to leave the party. When I said they were doing grown up things inside, she wanted to know what kind. When she heard hoots and hollers, she really wanted to know. I was so annoyed.

Colleen came out and apologized afterwards, claiming that Dee Dee's infertility drugs were the cause of her irrational mood swings and irritability.

"She just wasn't thinking," she defended.

"I'm not saying a word," I said, trying my best not to spoil the day for her.

"And I really appreciate that. The stupid thing is, she has gone out of her way to come up with solutions to make our house more kid friendly, and she thought it was great that I wanted to include Meg today. She just had a brain freeze. Don't hate her."

"It's your day. Let us eat cake," I suggested, trying to distract Meg, who was now asking Colleen what they had been doing inside without her.

"You want to get this?" Colleen laughed.

"Already tried, but seriously, how do you explain this?"

"Do you want to cut the cake?" she asked Meg, and that finally served to distract her, at least for awhile.

Later, after the party was over and we were cleaning up, Dee Dee also apologized, although it came with the disclaimer that she didn't know what the big deal was. I just shook my head and said I was letting it go. On the way home, Corky insisted that I'd been lucky to miss it, saying it had been over the top and kind of gross.

When later that night Gavin informed me he already had a first offer on Maria Risner's book, I found it depressing instead of exciting, as he did.

"That's great," I sighed, unintentionally.

"What do you mean? It is great," he insisted.

"Which is what I just said."

"Not as though you meant it."

"I'm sorry. It's been a long day, that's all," I told him.

He looked at me, now sighing himself, and I of course burst into tears because I could all but hear him screaming, "Just write!"

"It's not that simple!" I cried, returning my attention to the dishes I'd been washing.

"It is if you decide to make it your priority," he insisted.

"Really?" I challenged, whirling around to face him.

He was already walking away, and now furious, I decided to do the same. I marched past him, went back to our room, grabbed my purse and my laptop and then walked out to my car. I was pulling out of the driveway when he stepped outside, calling me back.

I ignored him and went to the Bean, where after ordering the largest coffee they had , I set up at a table, and began writing profiles of each of my main characters. I developed all kinds of background information about their families, schooling and previous relationships. Although I knew it might never make it into the book, the information gave me insight as to who these people were, and why they might do the things they would eventually do.

Scott and Corky came in, arm in arm, two hours later.

"Gavin says you've made your point, and that you should go home," Corky informed me.

"That's nice, but I'm not finished."

"Clearly, but you can't really stay here until you finish."

"No, but I can until the words stop coming. Go away," I told them.

"He doesn't like the idea of you being out so late. Just go home and work there," Scott insisted.

"Go away," I repeated.

They bought coffee and then returned, saying I should go write at Corky's because they were going to Scott's. As they pointed out, I could have the place to myself. I was instantly intrigued.

"That could work," I agreed.

"Sure it could, let's go," Scott said, pulling out his phone and calling Gavin to let him know of the compromise we'd come up with.

He was less than pleased. Apparently the kids were having a difficult night.

CHAPTER 49

Writing at Corky's was a brilliant idea. It was quiet and comfortable. I was able to put on some music, curl up on her couch, and concentrate on nothing other than how my story should proceed. Once I had reread my profiles, I went back to that Italian hotel room where Ben and Callie had stalled out weeks ago.

Ben attempted to explain where he had been and what he had been doing, while at the same time trying to seduce Callie, who wasn't in the mood. Eventually he passed out and she vowed to address his drinking the next day. As in life, that didn't go so well. Ben was hung-over, Callie was jetlagged, and Gavin began calling and texting me every five minutes, telling me to come home. At one in the morning I took pity on him and packed up.

I found Jack sleeping in our bed, while Gavin was in the nursery putting Nick down. He met me in the hallway and muttered that he hoped I had at least been productive.

"I was. I think I made some significant progress," I assured him.

We went to bed, where looking at Jack, I was told not to ask, and advised to just go to sleep.

The next morning, although Gavin was definitely dragging, I felt reenergized. Jack was delighted to wake up in our bed and to see that I had returned.

"You back! Mommy back!" he told Gavin.

"Yes, fantastic," he grumbled.

"I don't think you mean that," I laughed, kissing his cheek and asking what he wanted for breakfast.

"Bangers and mash."

"I don't think we have any sausage."

"Of course not, because you won't buy them," he said full of irritation. "You never make what I ask for, so why bother offering?"

"What did you do last night to put your father in such a lousy mood this morning, Jackie?" I asked.

"I looked for you, and you all gone," he said sadly.

"But I came back," I reminded him.

"Mommy back!" he exclaimed again, cheerfully.

"Yes, well, I was here all along, now wasn't I, Jack?" Gavin sighed, getting out of bed.

"Do you want me to run to the store? Do you have time? I'll go get you the makings for Bangers and Mash," I offered.

"Too little, too late."

"We could have them for dinner," I suggested.

"Perhaps," he said.

Nick began calling, so Jack and I went in to say good morning, only to be repelled by the odor wafting out of the nursery. When even a two year old is stopped in his tracks, you know you have a serious problem.

"Is it?" Jack asked, wrinkling his nose.

"Oh my God," I choked, plugging my nose. "Go ask Daddy to start the bath."

"Okay," he said, running in the opposite direction.

It was a rough way to start the day, but once Nick was cleaned up, he as well as Meg, who had been disturbed by my groaning and complaining, were in good moods. She entertained him while I poured cereal and made Gavin some eggs. Having had a shower, he was also in a better mood and asked if I'd be writing again that day.

"Absolutely. I figure Corky will still be sleeping at Scott's. I should have all morning to myself. Her apartment is ideal."

"So the book will be complete by tonight?" he teased.

"Oh, definitely. Bound and printed."

"You have a title then?" he inquired.

"Are those important?"

"Rather."

"I may need an extra day in that case."

"Alright, but don't fuss about."

"Of course not."

"What are you talking about?" Meg asked.

"Nonsense and such, don't worry about it," Gavin told her.

"It's not important?" she asked.

"On the contrary, it's really quite important."

"Perhaps that will be the title of my book," I mused, "On the Contrary."

Gavin considered, and nodding, said he liked it.

CHAPTER 50

After dropping Meg at school, I swung by Coffee Bean on the theory that coffee had been a part of what had made writing pleasurable the night before. I wanted to relax and fall right back into creating, so I bought a large latte, and then continued on to Corky's. I unlocked the door, balancing my coffee, my purse and my laptop, and burst in on what clearly was meant to be a private moment. Corky and Scott were on the very couch that I had been so comfortable on the night before, and not only were they were deeply entwined, but clothes were coming off.

"Oh crap," I said, trying to quickly pull my key out of the lock so that I could retreat.

"Oh God," Corky groaned, attempting to push Scott away.

"I'm sorry. I'm leaving," I told her.

"No wait, it's fine," she said, disentangling as Scott asked what she was doing. "Stop!" she ordered, although I wasn't sure which of us she was talking to.

"I thought you'd still be gone," I explained.

"Oh shit," Scott said, finally catching on and sort of rearranging himself, as he added, "Morning, Kelly."

"Scott," I said, trying not to laugh as I stared at my feet.

"You should go," Corky informed him.

"No, what?" he asked.

"We're done here," she laughed.

"We can't move to the other room?"

"Definitely not."

"But..."

"Gone, over, not coming back. Go home," she told him.

He took a deep breath, but then he kissed her and said he'd call her later, before playfully pushing me on his way out. Once he was gone, we both burst out laughing. Then Corky announced she was going to bed.

"Wait up, are you saying you didn't sleep at his place?"

"Hardly."

"So what did you do all night?"

"What do you think we did?"

"All night?" I asked, disbelievingly. "You guys had sex all night, came back here, and were going to have it again?"

"Oh yeah, he's a machine," she laughed.

"All night?"

"We took breaks, but sort of, yes."

"That sounds seriously redundant," I couldn't help laughing.

"We are seriously redundant, haven't you noticed?"

"So no talking, just sex?"

"Some talking, but nothing serious. We're just having fun for awhile."

"Okay," I shrugged.

"Sit down and write."

"There?" I frowned.

"Oh please, grow up, you interrupted. Nothing tawdry has happened there, yet anyway. I'm going to bed."

"Can I listen to music?" I asked.

"Sure, turn it up," she smiled.

So I set myself up much as I had the night before, and waited for inspiration to strike. It did not come instantly, and I thought about calling Gavin to ask if I was crazy, or if having sex all night didn't just sound tiring. Then I worried that I was getting old and that he might be tempted to stray if I made such a call.

I quickly dismissed that idea as insulting to his integrity, and told myself to get back to Callie and Ben. It took a few more minutes, but then Ben woke up in a bad mood, and Callie told him she hadn't flown half way across the world to have him be hung over. This sparked a fight in which she brought up several past grievances, and Ben walked out, only to return twenty minutes later with flowers and apologies. I learned that day that Ben and Callie thrived on a fiery drama that they interpreted as passion.

I wrote until noon, at which point I decided to go to the store to buy the sausage that Gavin was so fond of, planning on making him his bangers and mash. I also decided I would seduce him that night, because I'd concluded it had been far too long since I had been the one to initiate sex. Of course things didn't go as smoothly as I'd hoped.

Nick's stomach was still off, so while I was making dinner, he had another messy diaper. Gavin changed him, but it was amongst a lot of complaining, and eventually insistence that I help. After dinner, Gavin had to attend another in-store appearance with one of his writers and while waiting for him to return, I got sleepy. I dozed off, jerking awake every couple of minutes to see if he was home. By the time he arrived, I was seriously over it. I told him to imagine that he had come home two hours earlier, and that we'd had a real good time.

CHAPTER 51

The weekend came and went, and I never once managed to write. On Saturday I had to take Meg to a birthday party, and on Sunday Gavin decided we should take the kids to the zoo. He said he'd been reading Jack *Five Little Monkeys* while Meg and I were at the party, and Jack had insisted that the alligators in the story weren't real. He wanted to show him that they really did exist, plus he was sure he'd love getting to see the monkeys.

It was a hot day, and by the time we got home, the kids were tired and Gavin and I were exhausted. Meg and Jack had run us all over that zoo, while Nick had bounced between Gavin and I, refusing to sit in his stroller for reasons unknown. Every time we attempted to force the issue, he cried so much that we felt the eyes of every other parent in the zoo, looking at us as though we were somehow abusing him.

On Monday, I was determined to get in some writing before my appointment with Estelle. I arranged to go over to Corky's, because she finally had an audition. As was so often the case, the audition was all the way down in Santa Monica, so I knew I'd have a fairly decent chunk of time. In the morning I dropped Meg at school, bought my coffee, and let myself into Corky's. I double checked that I was alone, and then sat down to write. Fifteen minutes in, I got stuck.

I was trying to define what exactly Ben was investigating. I contemplated it's having to do with sports, and more specifically, soccer. I decided Italian politicians were willing to throw games in America, in order to build up the sport, or something to that effect anyway. I knew I needed to have more detail in order to make it believable, and spent a long time trying to Google corruption between the U.S. and Italy. It wasn't until Corky came back that it hit me, I should have just called Scott. Research like this was right up his alley.

"Is he working on anything right now?" I asked Corky, knowing he had already turned in his article on the Parisian art heist.

"No, and he's bored, so the only possible danger is that he'll get way too detail oriented and drive you crazy," she warned.

"I'll give him a deadline so that he doesn't have enough time to get carried away."

I called him up, told him what I needed, and he said he'd be right over. While waiting for him to show up, Corky entertained me with tales from the land of the bland mom. She said she had been horrified to find herself in a room full of boring looking women, all trying out for the role of a mousey mom. She said we had to give her a serious makeover, because she could never go there again. Although I thought she looked fine, I agreed to meet her at our favorite beauty supply store later that afternoon, following my appointment with Estelle.

Once Scott arrived, I read him what vague descriptions I had of Ben's investigation, and he agreed that more details were needed, but complimented me on the concept. He felt sports was a good way to go, and said he would figure out and research a few good scandals for me. I thanked him, and when Corky was out of the room, suggested he find a way to make her feel attractive. He said he would, but then as I was leaving, I heard him teasing her about being bland. I wanted to run back and clobber him, but I was late, and just brought him up in therapy instead.

Estelle was of the opinion that Scott was either being controlling in his teasing of Corky, or more likely, just being a guy.

"Don't get me wrong, guys are great," she laughed, "but they aren't wired the way we are. When they tease, I think they genuinely are only trying to kid around. They can't imagine worrying about such things, and even if they did, they'd appreciate their friends making light of it in order to show them how silly they were being in the first place. We of course take it all way too seriously. Never having met your friend, I can't say for certain, but I'm willing to bet she's not bland at all."

She was right, of course. Corky has the best peaches and cream complexion in the world, and her eyes are warm and friendly. She has a great body, too, not to mention a casual sense of style that I try to emulate, but don't think I pull off as well as she does. Corky looks better in a simple t-shirt and a pair of jeans than anyone has a right to. She is also instantly likable. She gets along with everyone. She doesn't always love everyone, but she can deal with them far better than I can.

As always, I felt much better by the time I left Estelle's, and I passed on to Corky what she had said about Scott's teasing.

"He's such an ass," Corky said, rolling her eyes, "but I think Estelle is right, he doesn't get it."

We went to the counter of our favorite brand of makeup, and Corky told the makeup artist/sales clerk that she wanted to look sultry, and as far away from bland as possible. The girl told her that would be easy, and proceeded to cover her face with what could only be described as comically dramatic eye liner, shadow, and a deep, red lipstick, that quite frankly had us laughing. As over the top as it was, though, I could see where if she dialed it way back, it would actually be quite flattering. I asked for some makeup remover wipes and toned it down for her to show her how stunning she really was. We chose a subtler lipstick, grumbled about the cost, and then Corky made her purchases.

Gavin called just as we were leaving, and told me he'd asked Hilary to stay late so that we could go to dinner with Scott and Corky. I asked Corky if she knew of this plan and she said no, but then Gavin said that was only because he and Scott had just come up with it.

"Go home, put on something pretty and meet us at that new place down the street," he told me.

"What new place?"

"Angelo's Steak house."

"Gav, that's expensive," I said.

"Kel, let me worry about that," he replied.

"Babe,"

"I have it handled. Meet us there by 6:30 pm" he instructed.

CHAPTER 52

I wasn't sure what Gavin was up to but as Corky and I discussed, a steak sounded real good, and an evening out would be great. I dropped Corky at her apartment, agreeing she'd get dressed, walk over to our house, and then we'd walk down to the restaurant together.

As soon as I got home, I was swallowed up by the kids. Nick wanted me to hold him and Jack had to show me how he had mastered climbing onto the swing outside all by himself. Meg had more stories to tell about school, and in particular about her teacher who had told her she was going to have a baby at Christmas time.

I gave them exactly ten minutes and then handed Nick back to Hilary, telling Jack and Meg I had to get ready to go. Meg followed me to our room, saying she would choose what I should wear. I was agreeable as far as the green dress she choose, but I told her I could not pair it with red high heels. She felt strongly that it would look festive.

"It's spring, almost summer, not Christmas. I'd look like an ornament," I laughed.

"But I love those fancy shoes," she whined, adding, "and Daddy loves them, too."

"Well I'm sticking to these sandals," I said pulling out some dressy, gold shoes with a slight heel.

"Oh, Mommy, those are hideous awful!" she exclaimed.

"Thanks for the vote of confidence, but I'm wearing them anyway."

"No, don't! They are ugly."

"Meg, that's not nice, and they are not."

She actually began to cry, and silly or not, I began second guessing myself. I finally told her we'd let Corky decide, and I went into my bathroom to apply a little makeup. She didn't approve of that, either. There were more tears about how I was pretty with just my plain old face. When Corky arrived, Meg ran out to quickly try and convince her that I was making myself ugly. Corky came back to my room with Meg in her arms, looked me up and down, and declared me beautiful. Meg buried her head and wept. I checked her forehead for a fever, but she was cool as could be, so I declared her to be tired, gave her a kiss goodbye, and suggested she get over it or go to bed.

Corky put her down as her weeping turned to angry wails, and the two of us beat it out of the house. We were running late, so we rushed as we walked, discussing the fact that we knew we'd still probably arrive before either Gavin or Scott. The restaurant itself was doing very well, and there were at least a dozen people mingling outside, waiting for tables. I gave our name to the maitre d and was pleasantly surprised when we were shown to a table at which both Scott and Gavin were already seated.

Gavin stood up, kissed my cheek and told me they'd ordered us some wine. Picking up his menu, he told me everything sounded delicious, and asked if I was going to have a steak.

"What is going on?" I smiled.

"What makes you think something is going on?" he smiled back.

"We haven't been able to go out in ages."

"We haven't had a nanny."

I looked at Scott who was also smiling.

"What?" I demanded.

"You both look lovely this evening," he laughed. "Not bland at all."

"You are pathetic and were the subject of my therapy session," I informed him, before turning back to Gavin. "What?" I whined.

"I've finally had a truly successful day is all, and it's been a long time coming, so I thought it would be nice to celebrate."

"How successful?" I grinned.

"I think you'll be rather pleased," he said leaning in to kiss me again.

It had been a long time since I'd seen him this happy, so I knew he'd acquired one of his writers a nice publishing contract. The question was, how nice?

"Go on, who's deal have you set?" I asked.

"Deals," he beamed, "in the plural."

"Really? Oh, I am definitely having steak," I said, wanting to scream with excitement. "Details! Give me the details."

"First there is Graham Wickham, whose contract I've renewed for another three books, with an advance of $75,000 for each book. And then there is Maria Risner, who is to receive a $30,000 advance on her novel, with which I am very pleased."

"As you should be. That's incredible! You are good," I said proudly.

"He's not done," Scott smiled.

"There's more?"

"There is," Gavin said, looking smug. "I was talking to Dean at Kensington with whom I've set the Wickham deal, and your name came up. He would like to offer you a contract as well. He thinks your book sounds very intriguing."

"I haven't written my book, Gavin," I said, feeling a slight panic rising up in my throat.

"I know. Might be just the push you need, don't you think? We have a meeting tomorrow to go over things."

"Things?"

"Yes, details, number of books, money, deadlines, those sorts of things."

"Certainly he isn't going to hand me a contract without reading anything."

"Your reputation precedes you, not to mention the reputations of both Colleen and your Dad. Devon's making quite the name for himself too, you know. This could, and should be huge!" he said, squeezing my knee as our wine arrived.

"How huge?" I choked.

"Deliciously huge," he smiled, raising his glass.

CHAPTER 53

The sun seductively caressed my back as I sat on the sofa staring out at the sea. I was in Italy doing research for my book, and Gavin was in an adjoining room on the phone with a fellow agent. I heard a scuffle outside our door just before it burst open with what appeared to be the entire Italian police force falling over one another, all trying to serve me a warrant for my arrest. I attempted to call to Gavin as they handcuffed me, but no sound came out and they dragged me away.

Gavin shook me awake, saying I was having a bad dream. Then he kissed my shoulder, patted my behind, and told me to go back to sleep. My heart was beating out of my chest as I lay there trying not to panic, but knowing I was losing the battle. Earlier, when we'd gone to bed and Gavin had wanted to victoriously make love to me, I had alternated from being lost in the moment, to simply being lost and overwhelmed. He was selling a book that I had barely begun to write!

Sitting up, I took a deep breath and told myself now was the time to act. The house was quiet, I couldn't sleep, and I had a book that needed to be completed. I climbed out of bed, grabbed my laptop, and reviewed a conversation I'd had with Scott over dinner in regard to Italian law. I quietly headed out to the kitchen and set my computer on the small table. I put on some coffee, grabbed a hostess crumb cake, and sat down to create. Although I was fine-tuning the scandal, I also began developing a new character.

Anna, I decided would be the name of the girl helping Ben to connect to all of the people he was investigating. She was of course Italian, voluptuous, and of much concern to Callie. Ben regarded her as just one of the guys, but Callie was threatened and in constant competition for Ben's attention. It built conflict, and yet I wanted to balance Callie's insecurities with her determination not to lose Ben. I didn't want her to come off as clingy and irrational. By the same token, I didn't want Anna to appear conniving or even after Ben in anyway. She was merely a free spirit, caught up in an adventure.

Before I knew it, I had been writing for close to three hours and Nick was beginning to fuss and stir as the sun was starting to flood the kitchen with light and warmth. Even at the crack of dawn, I could tell it was going to be a triple digit day. I quickly backed up what I had written, and then went to say good morning to Nick.

Gavin looked smug as hell when he got up and I told him of all I had accomplished. So much so that I began to wonder if there was really going to be an offer from Dean, or if he had just said that to motivate me. When I questioned him, he laughed.

"Of course there's a deal, although admittedly, if I'd known it would work this well I might have made it up."

"What happens if I get stuck though?" I fretted.

"I don't know, we'll figure it out. What were you dreaming about last night?"

"I was being arrested, but you were too busy setting deals and trying to outdo some agent to even notice."

He just nodded as if that made perfect sense.

"You don't find it surprising or even a little alarming that I would be arrested and you would be too busy to notice?" I asked.

"What was your crime?" he casually inquired.

"I have no idea."

"Perhaps it was I who called the police," he laughed.

"What for?"

"Assault most likely," he teased.

"I should assault you, you uncaring jerk," I laughed, playfully strangling him and forgetting for a moment that we were always surrounded by little children.

"What are you talking about?" Meg inquired. "You are kidding or fighting for real?"

"We are kidding," I assured her, as Gavin asked her if she knew what assault meant.

"I think it's bad behavior."

"Indeed it is," Gavin said, kissing the top of her head. "See to it that you are never a part of that sort of thing," he instructed her.

316

"Okay," she beamed.

We had a nice morning, but by the time I'd dropped Meg at school, I was ready for a nap. I presumed Corky would still be sleeping, so instead of getting coffee and going to write, I quietly let myself into her apartment, curled up on her couch and fell fast asleep.

I awoke to Corky and Scott arguing in her kitchen. Clearly he had spent the night and they had yet to notice me on the couch. Not only that, but Gavin and I appeared to be the subject of their disagreement.

"All I'm saying is that he might want to take a step back and look at how overwhelmed she's been before thrusting her out into the world," Corky said.

"Because you underestimate her. She can do this and she needs to do this," Scott insisted.

"Of course she can do this. I'm not disputing that, but she's had a nervous breakdown you ass, and you don't just magically get over that."

"How the hell would you know? Are you an expert in the field?" he demanded.

"In the field of Kelly, yes! Yes I am!'

"Oh so you know better than her husband?"

"Of course I do."

"Because all guys are stupid?"

"I didn't say that."

"No but you sure as hell indicate it on a daily basis."

"I do not! Jesus, get your period and relax."

"You did not just say that," he exclaimed.

"Yeah I did," she laughed.

"Fuck you."

"I wish you would," she said, followed by a muffled giggle.

"Cut! Time out," I said sitting up, and causing Corky to yelp.

At least, I hoped it was me causing it.

CHAPTER 54

I was nervous as hell to meet with Dean, even though as it turned out, we were only meeting through Skype. I hadn't been able to put a face to the name, although Gavin insisted I'd been introduced to him on at least two occasions. As soon as he popped up on Gavin's computer screen however, I remembered him instantly. A man in his early sixties, he had bushy grey hair, a round face and a booming voice that rang out with a cockney accent to rival that of the actor, Michael Caine.

Dean was a merciless flirt, and immediately told me how beautiful I looked and what a lucky man Gavin was to have me as his wife. From there, he told me how fortunate it was that Gavin had gotten in touch with him because he'd been wondering if I had been continuing to write. He told me, as I remembered his having said in the past, how much he'd enjoyed my collection of short stories, and said naturally with all of Colleen's success, he'd been waiting to see what I would do next.

"Mostly I've been having children," I laughed, "but lately writing has become not just a desire, but a much needed escape."

"Fantastic news for your fans," he announced, as if I actually had fans.

The reality was that my "collection" as he called it, although critically acclaimed, had done only moderately well when it had come out over five years ago. It had long since been buried by the millions of books that had come out since then.

"I can't wait to read this new novel," he continued. "Gavin says it's a romantic, political thriller. Just the sort of story that will appeal to men and women both. A bloody great concept, I must say," he enthused.

"Okay," I said through a forced smile, while looking to Gavin and wondering what he was getting me into.

"It is," Gavin confirmed. "It's wonderful."

"I'd expect nothing less. I'm looking forward to reading it myself," Dean said, adding, "I'll let you go Luv, give my best to your Dad. Gavin and I will work out all the contract specifics. No need to make you listen to us go back and forth," he chortled.

"It's been a pleasure as always," I told him.

"Go write," he smiled.

"I will."

"Call me back in a few minutes," he told Gavin.

"Will do," he said, signing off, and then turning to me with a big smile, he asked, "any specifics you'd like to demand?"

"Such as?"

"A research trip to Italy with your husband," he suggested.

"Where you call the police on me? No, thank you," I laughed.

"Realistically, when do you think you'll have the first draft complete?" he inquired.

"I have no idea. I mean Colleen is getting married in just under three weeks!"

"Right, so that can only be helpful to have that out of the way, don't you think?"

"Sure, but I don't know. I can't totally take over Corky's, and our house only works in the middle of the night."

"I've got it," he grinned. "I'll tell him you need a bungalow at the Chateau Marmont for the month of June."

"Fan-bloody-tastic!" I laughed. "I'm sure that would be no problem."

"You don't know if you don't ask," he laughed.

"Fine, I'd like it stalked with cupcakes from Hanson's Cakes as well, and so long as we are asking, I'll need a personal trainer too, not to mention a nurse to shake me out of my diabetic coma, and let's see, what else?"

"Alright, don't get carried away. I'll come down and give you a workout," he teased, "and you shan't be needing a nurse because I'll be eating at least half of those cupcakes for you."

"Taking your 15% as it were.?"

"We're married. I'm taking 50%," he smiled. "Now go home, kiss our babies, and make me dinner. I plan to be home with your deal in just a couple of hours."

"Yes sir!" I saluted.

He kissed me and I sighed, thinking about how nice it would be to be able to make demands.

"Stop by Hanson's on your way home," I told him.

"Will do," he promised.

For the rest of the day I was filled with a nervous energy, wondering what kind of a contract Dean was going to offer, truly not having read one word of what I was writing. It seemed ridiculous to expect much of a deal, and yet I couldn't stop fantasizing about how amazing it would be to have all of our financial worries lifted. At least for a while.

I began replaying our conversation with Dean over and over in my head, trying to gauge what, if anything, had been said between the lines. I worried about Gavin's having sold it as a political thriller, and told myself I might have to do even more research. Still, if I had the time to really think, I reasoned that I could certainly build suspense, and after all, that's what thrillers were based on, right?

Meg and I decided to make lasagna for dinner, as that was a dish she loved to help me with, and by adding just a little spinach, it was a way to get her and Jack, not to mention Gavin and myself, to have a vegetable. We prepared it, threw it in the oven and then went out to play in the backyard. Gavin snuck up on me, grabbing my hips as I was pushing Jack on the swing. I startled, and turned to see him smiling.

"You are going to be very pleased with me," he promised.

CHAPTER 55

I was sitting at the kitchen table the next morning, holding my head and sipping coffee, when the phone rang. Looking at the caller ID, I saw that it was Colleen.

"Yes?" I asked, unable to wipe the triumphant smile off my face, even as hung-over as I was.

"You little bitch! Is it true? It's true, right?"

"Whatever could you be referring to?"

"A quarter million for one book? When you haven't even been published in five years?"

"Oh I'm getting more than that," I laughed.

"Seriously?"

"Gavin has talked them into a cottage at the Chateau Marmont for the entire month of June, as well as a few other perks."

"Like what?" she demanded.

"Like a babysitting clause that says they will pay up to $2500 in overtime, should I need to write after hours on nights when Gavin can't be home."

"No way!"

"Way!" I told her. "And to be fair, you are partly responsible for it, so thanks."

"Oh my God! That is genius. I didn't know you could ask for things like that."

"I don't know that most people can, but Gav is not most people."

"Oh brother," she laughed. "He rocked your world last night, didn't he?"

"Well, yes and no," I couldn't help but chuckle. "He's promised better when we sober up and have a cottage at the Chateau Marmont all to ourselves."

The truth was that we had celebrated with multiple toasts once the kids had been safely tucked away in bed. We were both giddy with excitement and relief. When I'd eventually called Corky to share the good news, she and Scott had come over to celebrate with us, bringing two bottles of Champagne, one for each of us. We'd all taken turns gulping out of the bottles while slapping high fives. We'd joked about throwing money in the air and making it rain, but between the four of us we'd only had five bills, totaling all of thirty one dollars. When the champagne was gone, we'd moved on to a bottle of wine, all the while making plans to go to Italy together, possibly in the near future. Gavin also made promises to get Corky a good deal for her script, so that in the future she'd have more than a dollar in her pocket. By the time she and Scott left and we'd finally made it to bed, we were both too drunk to do anything other than pass out, but just before we did, promises were made.

In the morning, although we both had the equivalent of a bale of filthy, dry cotton in our mouths, and pounding jackhammers in our heads, we'd rolled toward one another and smiled, bad breath be damned. There, several hours later, we were still giddy. We both knew for the first time in what felt like an eternity, that we were going to be okay. We weren't going to lose our house. We weren't going to lose our health insurance or have to pull Meg out of school. We weren't going to have our credit cards refused or our electricity shut off. All of the things that had been weighing so heavily on our minds had magically disappeared, literally overnight.

Colleen congratulated me, but also reminded me that we had a million things to take care of before she could be married. She insisted she would need my complete attention over the next couple of weeks and made me promise I would put the book on the backburner. I said I would, even though I had no intention of not writing. Buried under my joy and relief was a panic attack just waiting to surface. I promised to meet her at her favorite hair salon the next morning to go over hairstyles for the wedding.

As soon as we hung up. I forced myself into the shower. Then I took Meg to school, bought my coffee, and went over to Corky's. I found her sitting on her couch, nursing a cup of coffee of her own, but her eyes were red from crying.

"What's wrong?" I asked, rushing over to comfort her.

"Scott doesn't want to have fun anymore," she wept.

"What do you mean?"

"He loves me!" she wailed, as if that were suddenly a bad thing.

"Well Corky, he's told you that before so why are you so upset?"

"He doesn't want to have fun!" she repeated.

"What does that mean?"

"That he sees me as a bland mom. He wants to marry me and have kids, and be everything that he thinks you and Gavin are, but I know," she sobbed. "I know all that you have been through, and I'm not you. I'm selfish. I can't do that. I love your kids and Gavin, too, but I'd end up killing someone. That only works for you and it didn't even, did it?"

"So he asked you to marry him?"

"We had a huge fight. I think he hates me, and my new neighbor threatened to call the police. Everything is awful!"

"Call the police? What? Oh come on, it's not that bad really," I insisted.

She wept uncontrollably, and not only did I see my writing time wither and die, I also realized that as much fun as we'd all had the night before, clearly we had drunk way too much.

CHAPTER 56

I was dragging the next day when I met Colleen at the hair salon, and it didn't take long for her frustration at my lack of enthusiasm for upsweeps, French braids and/or a side something or other, to begin boiling over.

"Good God, what is it today? Would it kill you to be present just once?" she asked.

"No, of course not. I'm sorry, I'm just feeling bad for Corky," I sighed.

"What for? And which is my best side?" she asked, staring at her face in the mirror as her stylist brushed her bangs over to the left.

"That definitely. Your left has always been best. Certainly you know that from photos, and Corky is miserable," I answered.

"Because you are making money and she's not?"

"Of course not. She and Scott had a huge fight over their future."

"Oh great," she said, rolling her eyes.

"What's that supposed to mean?"

"That they need to get it together before the wedding. I don't want a bunch of drama overshadowing my day. Is that really so awful? They are both invited, you know?"

I groaned as Dee Dee rushed in apologizing for being late. She ran over to Colleen, kissed her cheek and excitedly told her she was feeling nauseous.

"Now?" Colleen shrieked, before quickly adding more supportively, "Really, you think this is it?"

"I don't know. I don't want to jinx it. Maybe I just have the flu."

"I'll keep my fingers crossed."

"That I have the flu?" Dee Dee laughed.

"No, of course not," Colleen smiled, but I could see that there was at least a part of her that was thinking exactly that.

"You've been pregnant a thousand times," Dee Dee said to me, "what do you think?"

"I have not, and how should I know? I can't just look at someone and know if they are pregnant," I said.

"She's in a mood," Colleen told her.

"Too much pressure?" Dee Dee asked me.

"Sure, why not?" I said, desperately wanting to leave.

We were at the salon for nearly three hours, but it was finally decided Colleen would wear her hair up with a few wispy strands left down to frame her face, while Dee Dee and I would both have soft curls. Dee Dee was anxious to go home, claiming to be exhausted, but Colleen wanted us to go to lunch. When Dee Dee refused, I felt obligated to go. After all, I wanted her to get to feel indulged, even if she was driving me up the wall.

"Let's go to Victoria's Secret after," she proposed as we left the salon.

"Gavin is going to kill me. I'm sure he thought I'd only be gone for an hour or two," I cringed.

"I need to get something sexy for our honeymoon. Did you see the tacky stuff I got at my shower? I can't wear a lace and mesh bustier! Christ, it should have come with a whip! And instructions!" she added.

"Okay, let's just get something to eat at the mall then," I suggested.

"Fine," she sighed. "I'll meet you at the Grove," she said walking off to her car.

The Grove was not our local mall. The Grove was over the hill, through the canyon and all the way down on Fairfax. I debated calling Gavin to warn him that I was never coming home but knowing he wouldn't be pleased, I called Corky instead.

"Hey," she answered, still sounding down.

"I'm checking in with you because I'm too chicken to do so with Gavin. What does that say about equality and women's rights?"

"That Colleen is bossing you around, I'm guessing."

"Pretty much. So have you guys talked?"

"Nope. I haven't heard from him at all."

"Well, maybe that's good. Maybe it's best to take a few days to think so that you don't end up saying things you aren't sure about," I suggested.

"Sure," she sighed.

"Corky," I whined.

"I know, I'm going to pull myself together," she said, taking a deep breath. "It is what it is and we'll figure it out. You shouldn't be worrying about this."

"I just want you to be happy," I told her. "I want everybody to be happy, and now Dee Dee might be pregnant so she's kind of bailed on Colleen, and I feel as though I have to step up because she deserves to be pampered right now, but then Gavin is going to be stuck in toddler land all day, and I don't know, he kind of deserves to be pampered a little too. I just can't win."

"I need to get out for a while, so I'll walk over to your house and warn him, and maybe then I'll take Jack and Meg to the park for a little while," she offered.

"That would be incredibly helpful! Thank you. Tell him I'll ditch her as soon as I can."

"Will do," she promised.

So I headed off with every intention of having a good time, but it was a definite challenge.

CHAPTER 57

As suspected, Gavin was not thrilled to be left alone all afternoon and kept texting me to ask where I had put things, as well as when I would be returning. Colleen wanted me to relax and have some fun, constantly telling me I should be ecstatic instead of stressed out.

"I'm trying, but come on," I said, as we looked through lingerie. "I have to write now, don't I? And as much as I want to, what if I can't? What if it's shit, or I just go blank and can't finish it?"

"That's not going to happen," she said. "I mean realistically, okay, it could, but that is the risk every writer takes when accepting a contract. And sure, I guess it happens occasionally but this is in your blood. This is what we do, and worst case scenario, if you really, really choked, you have me, Keith, Dev, Dad, and Scott, and even Corky you could get to help you. You'll be fine."

"Is that what you would do if you went blank?"

"Oh, hell yes," she said, pulling out a short black lacy nightgown. "What do you think?" she asked.

"I think black seems dark for a honeymoon."

"Why?"

"Because it represents the rest of your life together while at the same time being a new beginning. I don't know that you want to jump into the dark side right away."

"The dark side?" she laughed. "It's not as if he thinks I'm a virgin. What are you talking about, or do I even want to know?"

"I just think it should be lighter."

"Fine," she said, putting it back, but still laughing.

She eventually settled on an icy blue silk gown that she joked reminded her of Elsa from *Frozen*. She asked if fantasies were allowed on honeymoons and I told her if she needed them then she might want to reconsider getting married at all, but to each their own. We left Victoria's Secret and fell into a few more stores before agreeing I would meet her on Monday at the caterer's to go over the final details of her menu.

I arrived home to find Gavin, Meg, and Jack all sitting out on the front step. Both kids were climbing on his back, but ran over to greet me as soon as they saw me.

"What are you doing?" I asked, curious as to why they were in the front yard instead of the back, not to mention where Nick was.

"We has to give them some privacy," Meg informed me.

"Who?"

"Scott and Corky."

"Where's Nick?" I asked, looking to Gavin.

"He's sleeping in Corky's arms," he informed me.

"And the rest of you have been put outside?"

"It would appear that way, wouldn't it?"

"How long have you been out here?" I asked, sitting next to him.

"I'm not sure. I wasn't allowed to grab my phone. It feels like a long time and yet I suspect it's been less than fifteen minutes."

"You weren't allowed to?" I laughed.

"Scott just told us to go."

"And he's the boss of you?" I teased.

"For a moment, I suppose."

"Okay," I agreed, even though I knew I'd soon be needing the bathroom.

Scott walked out a few minutes later, and hitting Gavin on the back asked him to go get a beer with him. I took the kids inside where Corky sat in the living room cuddling a sleeping Nick.

"What's up?" I inquired.

"He wants to live together again because I'm the one with commitment issues, at least according to him."

"Okay, and you are going for this or no?"

"I'm sitting with it and letting it sink in," she smiled wearily.

"Where would you live?"

"I just signed a lease, so I think it would have to be my place. I mean it's more convenient. I like being close to the shops and restaurants, and I love being able to just walk over here."

"I'm loving that, too."

"Of course, he'll want to move half his crap over, along with his stupid 80 inch TV that will block out the sun."

"True, and he'll get in my way when I want to use your place to write."

"He'll get in my way all of the time," she laughed.

"Right, but he is good at fixing things," I joked.

"He makes for a good pillow sometimes too."

"Yeah, that's nice."

"I guess I'm going to agree to this, aren't I?"

"I suspect you are."

"Am I crazy?"

"I suspect you are," I laughed.

"But so is he, right?"

"It is the tie that binds you."

"I figured," she said.

CHAPTER 58

I signed the contract on Monday, but due to paperwork and such, that didn't instantly put money into my pocket. As happy as I was to tell Estelle of our good fortune, I still couldn't afford to pay her. I promised it was coming, though. Then we discussed my panic attack that was also set to arrive any time now.

"It's all about balance," she told me. "The trick is to be honest with yourself while not allowing emotion to overtake you. It would be silly to say that there is no pressure that comes with this, but at the same time you must remember that this is what you do, and you are good at it. You would not have been given this opportunity strictly based on the reputations of others in your family. You have proven yourself with your writing in the past."

"That was then and this is now," I said, only half kidding.

"True, and granted you'll have different challenges this time, but then that's just life. It's always changing and you have to acknowledge that to keep from getting stuck. I'm sure you can do this, and once you have the wedding out of the way, you may even get to enjoy it."

"I am looking forward to that cottage at the Chateau Marmont."

"I should think so," she laughed.

"I could probably just sleep the entire month."

"Well," she teased, "at least wake up long enough to order their chicken and avocado sandwich. I hear it's to die for."

Colleen had asked that I come out to her new house the next day to help her and Dee Dee decide how things should be set up for the wedding, and of course, for the reception after. Due to the renovations, they weren't planning to move in until after their honeymoon, so she said it would be empty. When I arrived, it was anything but. There were workers everywhere. Not only were they re-landscaping, but there was full-on construction happening, and that was just the outside.

Inside there were painters on scaffolding, and cabinets being replaced in the kitchen. Not one, but two of the bathrooms had no floor and another was being retiled. Still, I was re-impressed by the endless natural light and the views.

"It really is going to be beautiful," I assured Colleen.

"Do you think? Come look at what we are doing out back above the pool," she said pulling me outside.

Where before there had been a couple of small brick patios interspersed with woodchips and roses, there was now only one midsized patio surrounded by fresh grass and some beautiful ceramic flower pots yet to be planted, set against the fence that overlooked the pool. It made the entire expanse look inviting and far more relaxing.

"We are going to put a play structure right over there in the corner for the kids too," Colleen said proudly, "plus we'll have a couch out here and of course a table for dining outside."

"It's fabulous. Oh, my God, Colleen," I exclaimed, "it changes the whole feel of the house. It's so much better."

"Right? But how are we going to get everything together in time for the wedding and where the hell is Dee Dee?" she complained looking at her phone. "She was supposed to be here twenty minutes ago!"

"Maybe the freeway is screwed up," I offered.

"You got here and so did I," she pointed out.

"Sure, but there could be an accident or something. You know how bad traffic is."

"She's totally going to flake on me," she sighed. "She's going to be pregnant and completely flake."

"Don't panic, I've got your back. Everything is going to be fine. So what do we need to decide?" I asked.

"Okay, come with me," she said heading back inside.

She took me back into the foyer with the grand staircase, and asked if I thought they could make everyone stand for the ten minute ceremony, saying she wanted it to take place in the living room to the right of the steps.

"Because why? I mean where are you having the reception, in the same room?" I asked.

"No, here is what we are thinking. We have the ceremony in here in front of this gorgeous picture window, and then the guests move into the family/great room where there will be a bar and dancing. And while they are there and no doubt spilling out onto the patio as well, the caterers can set up tables back in the living room where we had the ceremony to serve dinner and cake."

"Maybe," I considered, as her phone rang and she took a call from Keith.

I was trying to determine how complicated it would be to set the room, while the reception was in full swing. Not only would you have to bring in tables and chairs, but there would be linens and place settings, not to mention centerpieces and placement cards. There were beautiful French doors to close off the room however, and it's being at the front of the house while the great room was towards the back, would give it enough separation that the guests wouldn't have to be aware of the transformation as it took place.

Colleen hung up with Keith and looked at me with a sad smile.

"And it's official, she's not only pregnant and flaking, but she didn't even tell me first. She went to Keith because she thought I'd kill her. What kind of a bitch am I that my best friend would do that?" she cried. "Am I really that awful that she wouldn't tell me?"

"No, of course not," I said hugging her. "She's probably just freaking out and knew you'd be a trigger. You know, because you are her best friend."

"I'm happy for them, really I am."

"Of course you are. My shrink told me just yesterday that life is constantly changing and that's all this is. Let's figure this reception stuff out and then we'll go buy Dee Dee something to let her know you are being supportive."

"What would that be?" she sniffled.

"Well, um, I have no idea," I admitted, "but we'll come up with something."

"Promise?"

"Absolutely!"

I was suddenly feeling very protective of Colleen. Sure, I knew how overwhelming it was to be pregnant, especially for the first time, and I could only imagine that would be magnified when you had struggled to get there. However, this was Colleen's wedding and I wanted it to be perfect. Dee Dee, I concluded was going to have to suck it up.

CHAPTER 59

The entire week flew by and I had absolutely no time to even think about the book, let alone write it. By Friday, I had spent so much time trying to play mediator to Colleen and Dee Dee's relationship that my head was about to explode. They were both being hyper-sensitive and feeling misunderstood. They each acted as if they were the first to ever plan a wedding or have a baby, and I spent all of my time defending their right to be overwhelmed by all that was happening to them. Add to that Corky's vacillating between moving in with Scott or running away again, and I wanted to run away myself.

When just as we were going to bed, Gavin announced that he didn't wish to be left with the kids all weekend again, I was tempted to slug him. Instead, I simply glared.

"I've every right to let you know," he defended in response.

"Oh, do you? Really? "

"You are wound way too tight," he muttered, climbing into bed.

"Oh no, am I? Gosh, I wonder why."

"The point is, you needn't take it out on me, and all I am saying is that the children and I could use a little of your attention as well. We've been completely ignored this week, now haven't we? You as well."

"What does that even mean?" I groaned.

He slid his hand under the t-shirt I had paired with my flannel pajama pants.

"It means we miss you," he whispered, moving closer.

"You, the kids and myself?" I questioned sarcastically, and as he kissed my neck, I added, "That's really creepy"

"What?" he asked.

"If you are horny, why not just say so, instead of bringing the kids into it and trying to guilt me besides?"

"I'm doing no such thing!" he objected.

"Of course you are."

"Do shut up, Kelly," he sighed, moving his mouth to mine, while his hand caressed my breast.

I turned my face away and objected to his telling me to shut up, but the reality was that I kind of wished I'd shut up, too. After all, everything he was doing felt good, and I had a chance at enjoying myself if I could just let go of the past week. Why I was fighting him, I had no idea.

"Relax," he instructed, gently turning my face back towards his.

Again he kissed me, at first tentatively, but then more deeply, and I chose to surrender completely. For the next twenty minutes the rest of the world melted away and there was just the two of us, just like there always had been in our best moments. We were just finishing up when the phone rang.

"It's Scott," Gavin informed me as he answered.

He listened for a few seconds, said sure, and then hung up.

"Bloody hell, he wants me to help him move that monstrosity of his tomorrow," he sighed.

"The TV?'

"Precisely."

"So they are going for it, huh?"

"Apparently so."

"Well," I considered, "that's good, right?"

"Yes and no."

"In what ways?" I asked.

"It's good in that he loves her and very much wants to make this work. However, if it does, then they'll soon want a bigger place and he'll expect me to help him move that thing again."

"I have to write this book and it has to be really good," I announced.

"Off topic, but alright," he said.

"Not really, because if I do this and it sells well enough, then I'll be able to hire movers for them, and you won't have to lift a finger."

"Ahh yes, quite right. I like the way you are thinking. Get on that, won't you?"

"I'd like to."

He kissed me goodnight and went right to sleep as if he no longer had anything to worry about. I envied his ability to do so. I stayed awake worrying about Corky and Scott, the wedding, the book, and whether or not the kids really were feeling abandoned. It was nearly three in the morning before I finally drifted off.

CHAPTER 60

The weekend was swallowed up by chores, errands, moving Scott into Corky's, and another visit out to Colleen and Keith's new house. That was Gavin's first time to see it, as well as the kids, and Gavin and Meg in particular, were very impressed. Keith suggested we go to Toys R Us and let Meg and Jack pick out the play structure of their choice, and they were more than happy to do so. They chose one that included a fort, slide, swings and a rock climbing wall, and Keith promised them that he would have it set up in time for the wedding.

On our way home, Gavin asked if I'd like a home of equal size.

"I don't think so," I said.

"It's awfully nice though, isn't it?"

"Sure, but it's going to be a pain to keep clean. The dust alone will be staggering."

"Well yes, but certainly with a house that size you'd hire a maid."

"And then there would be some stranger in my house, moving my things and getting under foot," I frowned.

"Are you mad?" he laughed. "That place is bloody huge! They wouldn't be underfoot, you'd be lucky if you could find them."

"I like our house. All I need is to get the gardener back and we'll be fine."

"You don't want a pool?"

"No, not at all. Not until the kids are older, we've been through this, remember? We can use the pool at Corky and Scott's this summer though."

"Have they a pool? I didn't realize."

"They do."

"Fantastic!" he said.

I was hopeful that it would be. I dreamt of things settling down once the wedding was over, and prayed we could enjoy a calmer and more peaceful summer.

The following day I received a call from someone named Anthea. She said she would be my editor, and asked that I send her what I had of the book so far, inquiring as to when I thought I would have it completed. That ushered in my panic attack with ease.

I choked and stumbled over my words, no doubt leaving her to believe that a horrible mistake had been made in giving me a contract, let alone such a generous one. Nick wailed in the background, and Jack ran in to demand Cheerios as I frantically tried to come up with an answer.

"I see here that we have given you all of June at a very nice hotel, certainly you should be able to complete the first draft during that time, don't you agree?" she asked.

"Well, uh, I can't promise. I'll certainly do my best, but it's not as though I'll be spending all of my time there. I mean I do have three very young children."

"Which I can only assume would motivate you further. The quicker you finish, the quicker you can devote more of your time to them. I'll tell you what, I've meetings in Los Angeles later this week. Lets meet and I'll help you to set up a schedule."

"This week is crazy for me. My sister is getting married on Saturday and..."

"Love a good wedding," she interrupted. "No worries. I won't take too much of your time. I'll have my assistant make the arrangements. I do apologize for the short notice but it's unavoidable. Be sure to send me what you have, and I'll read it on my flight over. Tata for now," she said, sounding like a character out of the Winnie the Pooh series.

Before I could object, she had hung up and I was left trying to catch my breath. I got Jack his Cheerios, took Nick from Hilary and asked him what his problem was. Hilary said she thought he might have a slight fever and sure enough when I checked, he did. I told her I was going to get him down and then go talk to Corky because I was freaking out. She pointed out that I had an appointment with Estelle and I said better yet!

In this instance, however, it turned out not to be better because she threw logic at me, and the truth was, I wasn't ready to deal with that. I needed to freak out and I couldn't do that with her, in the way that I could with Corky. Estelle said all of the right things, but as soon as our hour was up, I ran over to Corky's and shrieked about what a nightmare this was.

"Why did I let Gavin do this? I should never have sat there like a stupid mute while he waxed on about what a brilliant novel I'm writing. Why didn't I stop him?" I demanded.

"Because you were desperate."

"Exactly and now I'm screwed." I cried.

"Maybe, but we'll figure it out somehow. I mean worst case scenario, you stall."

"How?"

"I'm not sure. I mean you could get sick. That would be good for a few days anyway, and then your computer could delete some pages, by which time the kids could catch what you'd had, something," she offered. "we'll figure out something. And who knows, maybe you will be able to finish it."

"In a month? It's practically June already!"

"Yeah, that's kind of unfortunate, but look at how fast I wrote my script. Maybe it'll just flow."

"And when it doesn't?"

"We'll get you drunk and free your mind," she joked.

"I need some coffee," I sighed, wiping my eyes and feeling exhausted as my phone rang and Hilary told me she thought

Nick might have an ear infection. "Oh crap," I groaned, promising I'd call the doctor and be home in a few minutes.

"See there? Nick is helping out already," Corky teased.

CHAPTER 61

Sure enough Nick had an ear infection, and as I walked the floor with him in the middle of the night, I did my best to convince myself that it was better he got it now, than later in the week when he'd have been inclined to cry all through the wedding. Colleen was a nervous wreck however, and called at the crack of dawn the next morning to tell me the upstairs bathroom was never going to be ready in time for Saturday.

"So what? Why does it have to be?" I grumbled, not ready to be awake.

"Because that is where we are supposed to be getting dressed. It's the best light for having our makeup done."

"There will be plenty of light in another bathroom. That whole house has nothing but light."

"We need to ask Maggie to come look and let us know what to do," she said, referring to the makeup artist she had hired.

"She's already given you your consultation. She is not going to have time to go out there, and even if she did, she would charge you a fortune."

"Who cares?"

"Colleen, let it go. You are making yourself crazy."

"With good reason."

"With no reason," I said, as Nick began wailing. "Look, Nick has an ear infection, I have to go."

"What? No!" she groaned, as Gavin did the same and went to get him.

"He'll be fine in another day or two," I reasoned.

"But I need you. We are going over locations with the photographer at two, remember?"

"I know. Hopefully Nick and Jack will both be down for a nap then. I'm going to bring Corky with me though, because she's really visual and will be able to help us choose where the photos should be taken, not that the photographer can't do the same."

"Yeah, sure, that's great, and Dee Dee swears she'll be there, too."

"Just breathe," I told her. "You are in the home stretch, but things are going to come up and you have to go with it."

"I want it to be perfect," she sulked.

"And it will be," I promised as Gavin came in carrying Nick at an arms distance and headed straight to the tub.

"We've a situation here, Kelly, I need your help," he said.

"Got it. Diarrhea calls, Colleen. Later," I said hanging up.

Once in the tub, Nick was happy as could be and would have been content to splash all morning. He was clearly feeling better even if his diaper indicated otherwise. In fact, he was so content that as the morning continued to go smoothly, I decided I would drop Meg at school, get some coffee, and then try writing at the coffee shop, since I didn't want to disturb Corky and Scott.

My coffee was exceptionally good that morning, but there were so many customers coming and going that it was distracting. I decided to drive up into the hills, park on a quiet street, and try writing in my car for a while. I wanted to explore the idea of Callie's being jealous of Anna even though Anna wasn't doing anything to provoke it. I found a pretty, tree lined street, turned off the engine and immediately realized that I should have used the bathroom before leaving the Coffee Bean. Doing my best to ignore that fact, I placed my laptop on the passenger's seat, pulled up what I had, and read over the last chapter.

I was both pleased and relieved by how good it was, but concluded I really had to go to the bathroom. There was going to be no concentrating on anything until I had taken care of that. I closed my laptop and drove to the nearest mall, where I took my laptop in with me because I was too paranoid to leave it in the car. Choosing to use the facilities in Bloomingdales because they were the nicest, I couldn't help but notice how quiet it was. They had a lovely waiting area before you entered the actual bathroom, complete with comfy chairs and a table to hold my coffee. I sat down, took a breath and began thinking back to that summer in Italy when my mother had been so consumed by what my father was or wasn't doing.

I wished I could just ask my Dad if she'd had reason for concern, but I knew I didn't really want to know. Instead I concentrated on my characters, imagining another party Ben would need to attend in order to get closer to his targets. He says without Anna he has no reason to be there, and therefore he can't take Callie with him. He has to pretend to be involved with Anna, and Callie clearly doesn't like it. I began writing and lost all track of time. Before I knew it, Corky was calling to see why I hadn't shown up to take her out to Colleen's.

"Oh shit," I cursed. "She's going to kill me. I'm on my way right now," I promised.

I saved what I had written, gathered my things and made a mad dash through the mall and back out to my car. I drove over to Corky's like a bat out of hell and then rushed onto the freeway only to have it come to a complete stop. It was two twenty and my phone was ringing.

"We're on our way, but the freeway is stopped," I yelled to Colleen as Corky picked up for me.

"She knows, she's right behind us ," Corky laughed.

I turned to look and sure enough there she was in her beautiful Porsche, looking less than pleased. Dee Dee was sitting next to her and opening the door, leaned out and threw up all over the asphalt.

CHAPTER 62

Hilary took a message from my editor's office while I was out dealing with Colleen, informing me that Anthea would meet me at her hotel, The Beverly Wilshire, on Thursday afternoon at three p.m. sharp. She neglected to get a number where I could confirm, or as I'd have preferred, refuse, so I was left with no choice but to keep the appointment. Gavin insisted I was being silly to want to put her off until after the wedding, seeing right through my desire to stall.

"You mustn't think of her as the enemy, but as an ally. She is simply here to assist you," he told me.

When Thursday afternoon rolled around I was nervous, because I had sent Anthea the opening chapters of the book and she had not yet responded. I didn't know if that meant she had hated them, or if as again Gavin insisted, she was simply waiting to discuss them in person.

By the time I got to the hotel I was so nervous that I was breaking out in hives. I anxiously scratched my wrist as I rode the elevator up to her room, not knowing what to expect. I was sure I had the wrong room when a girl in her late twenties at best, opened the door in her bathrobe, holding a tissue to her nose. Before I could finish backing away and apologizing, she grabbed my arm and pulled me inside, saying she was Anthea.

"Please forgive me for not being prepared. I have this bloody miserable cold and I'm afraid I'm still quite jetlagged. I fell asleep unexpectedly and only just woke when the desk called up to announce your arrival. I've ordered us some tea and biscuits. Make yourself at home," she said, leaving me in the sitting room as she rushed into the bedroom, not bothering to close the door between us. "I have to say, I was intrigued by the chapters you sent. I'm very much looking forward to working together," she called back.

"I'm so glad," I said, thinking there was no way this was the same woman I had spoken to earlier in the week.

I had been certain that I would be met by a woman far older than me, probably by at least ten years or more, and I never would have guessed that she would be so informal. She remerged a few minutes later in a casual black wrap around skirt, a bright pink blouse and pink and silver dangling earrings. She had gathered her shoulder length golden hair up into a ponytail, and she remained barefoot. She all but bounced down on the sofa across from me, putting her feet up on the glass coffee table between us.

"So," she smiled, "tell me, Ben and Callie, will they end up together, or will Anna come between them?"

"I think they will definitely end up together, but Anna is unintentionally causing trouble."

"Do you think? You know how we girls can be. I suspect she has a massive crush on Ben," she speculated as there was a knock at the door. "Ooh, our tea and biscuits!"

I was stunned the entire time we were together. There was no sign of the bossy woman I had spoken to earlier. Even when she brought up scheduling my time and the need to have a completed first draft by the end of June, she was all smiles. She asked if I had pictures of my kids and then went on and on about how cute they were. She could not have been more pleasant.

I swore I would do my best to have the first draft done on time, but was sure to tell her that I couldn't guarantee it. We discussed Colleen's wedding and how I hoped to get more writing in once that was over, and she wished me all the best. I returned home and told Gavin I was certain I had met with an imposter.

"What did I tell you?" he asked smugly.

"Doesn't matter what you told me because I'm telling you the real Anthea Whiticker has been kidnapped or worse, and we should really be reporting her missing."

"I'm glad it went well," was all he had to say.

I called Corky and she told me to be relieved and not to look a gift horse in the mouth. I wanted to be grateful and yet I couldn't help but feel the real Anthea would reappear. Especially if I didn't get her that first draft on time.

CHAPTER 63

Gavin attended Keith's bachelor party and came home declaring himself to be old. It was held at a so called trendy LA strip club, and he reported to me that it had been ridiculous. He said half of the guests were so drunk they couldn't stand, and the other half were just crass and boring. He told me they threw money like a bunch of prep-boy, white wannabe rappers, and the strippers all looked disingenuous. I loved that. He said he was sure I could give him a far greater lap dance than any of them, and therefore he had chosen to leave early.

"But Keith was going for it?" I asked.

"No comment."

"What? What did he do?"

"Nothing, I'm just playing Switzerland," he insisted.

The next day was the rehearsal, after which there would be a dinner at a nearby restaurant someone had told Colleen was

358

good. The fun began with Colleen calling me at nine that morning to say the living room had been painted the wrong color and that Keith was threatening to repaint it himself because he was so angry about it.

"What color did they paint it?" I asked.

"The pale pink I had chosen for one of the guest bedrooms."

"I see," I said trying not to laugh, as I could tell she wasn't finding it as amusing as I was. "Just make the painters re-do it," I suggested.

"We can't get them to pick up their phone! Just come over here."

"And do what?"

"Keith won't act as stupid in front of you," she hissed into the phone. "He's hung over and crazy. Just hurry up," she insisted.

I said I'd get there as soon as I could, hung up, and called Dee Dee, asking if she couldn't scare up a painter to fix this. She said she was too sick to do anything.

"I think I'm having twins or worse! I've got to go," she wretched.

That was sobering because I realized she was going to be of no help what so ever. Gavin insisted that if it were truly a pale pink, no one would notice and said he'd come with me and tell Keith to get over it. I was delighted to have the company, even if we did have to take separate cars so that he could go to work once things settled down.

We arrived to find Keith pacing back and forth in the driveway, yelling obscenities into his phone. It seemed he'd finally managed to get his painter on the line, but he was not taking responsibility for the mistaken paint. He hung up and encouraged us to follow him inside to see for ourselves how hideous it was.

It was not great, but I tried to play it down.

"In the afternoon light it might be subtler," I told Keith. "Morning light really emphasizes color."

"Sure it does. I'm not getting married in a little girl's bedroom and that's what this looks like," he insisted, as Gavin tried unsuccessfully to suppress his laughter.

Colleen came in from another room and announced that Dee Dee was so sick that Roman wouldn't even let her talk to her. I confessed that I had already called her and said we'd figure this out on our own.

"How?" she demanded.

"By going to the paint store," Keith said.

"This is a huge room. How are you going to even reach the ceiling?" she asked.

"I'm buying a ladder! Are you with me?" he asked Gavin.

"In so much as I'll call Scott for you," he laughed. "This is far more his thing than mine."

"Fine, but I'm buying us all paintbrushes," Keith said, heading out.

"Go with him!" Colleen hissed at Gavin.

360

"You'll need big rollers," I called after him, as Gavin told Colleen he was not a painter.

"Just go for moral support," she insisted.

"I have to work," he grumbled, yelling, "Hold up there, Keith."

Gavin followed him out to his car and Colleen buried her head in her hands, releasing a strangled scream.

"It's going to be fine. Scott will know how to fix this. We should have thought to call him from the get go."

"It's a huge room!" she repeated.

"I know, but panicking isn't going to help, so take a deep breath. In fact, let's go get some coffee and organize what else has to be done today."

"We have to paint a huge room!" she shrieked.

"Let's get you some valium, too," I teased.

"We can't leave because everything is being delivered today. My dress, the tables, chairs, linens, dishes, everything!"

"Okay, okay, so you go get the coffees and I'll stay here."

"No you go," she insisted.

So I did. I drove down to the nearest Starbucks that I discovered was not as near as you would expect, and who should I find in there, but Devon, looking hung over and arguing with a girl I had never seen before.

CHAPTER 64

The girl was introduced as Ashley, and I was told she was an old friend whom he had called when his rental car had died right outside, and he'd been left waiting for a replacement car. They were arguing about him not having called her as soon as he'd arrived in town, as apparently they had hooked up the last time he was in town and, she thought, were carrying on a bicoastal affair. She had just assumed she would be his date for the wedding, but he said he had never invited her to the wedding because he was trying to spare her our family. She looked to me as if I should tell him how awful he was to do so.

"I'd thank him, and enjoy my Saturday if I were you," I advised.

"Why?" she demanded.

"Because I've just recently had a nervous breakdown, my sister is getting married and her best friend is pregnant and throwing up on everything in sight, while she herself is in crisis with renovations gone wrong, and pre-wedding jitters. And then there are my parents who are, and always have been, certifiable, not to mention a whole assortment of strange aunts, uncles, and cousins. Run before Dev here starts clinging to you like a drowning swimmer and pulls you to death's door with him, because believe me, it's just a matter of time," I warned.

"I don't scare that easy," she said.

"How are you at painting?" I asked.

"I painted my dorm in college."

"How'd that go over?"

"Not great," she admitted, and I decided I liked her.

"Cool, so go put on some crap clothing and meet us up at the house," I shrugged, as Devon pushed me. "Oh what, you know you like her if you have been carrying on an affair," I teased.

"Yeah, you know you do," Ashley smiled.

"Fine, but remember, we tried to spare you," he told her.

I got our coffee while Dev congratulated me on my book deal, saying he had a gift he'd give me later that night.

"What is it?"

"You'll see when I give it to you," he said, refusing to give a clue.

We agreed we'd meet up at the house once he had a new car and I left him to return to Colleen. I found her standing in the garage, looking at the linens that had since been delivered.

Again, she had issue with their color, insisting we had chosen the cream, not the ivory.

"What's the difference?" I asked.

"This is darker, and not what I ordered," she said.

"So we can call and see if we can exchange them, or you can let it go, because seriously in the grand scheme of things, is one shade lighter or darker really going to make a difference?"

"I guess not, but open up those boxes over there and let's make sure all of the place settings are the same, and hopefully what I ordered."

Fortunately they were.

Next to arrive were our dresses, and those, too, looked to be fine. Keith, Gavin and two non-English speaking painters arrived, complete with ladders, paint, tarps, rollers and brushes. When Colleen squawked at having what she could only assume were undocumented workers in the house, Keith and Gavin both told her to relax. Gavin reasoned that Scott would be there at any moment to supervise and he was fluent in Spanish, while Keith reminded her that the house was empty, so there was nothing for them to steal.

"Now!" Colleen said, " but what is to stop them from coming back when there is?"

"The security gate. Don't be so paranoid, we don't have time for it," Keith told her.

Devon arrived and while he and Keith compared hangovers, Ashley drove up the driveway, followed by Dee Dee.

"Who is that?" Colleen asked referring to Ashley.

"Dev's girlfriend, don't ask. She's going to help paint," I said, as poor Dee Dee nearly fell out of her car looking green. "Maybe she is pregnant and has the flu," I suggested.

"Maybe she's carrying a litter. They put four eggs back," Colleen muttered.

"I'm here, what's all this?" Dee Dee asked, referring to the ladders being carried inside.

"Come look," Colleen told her, dragging her into the house.

They made it as far as the entry when Dee Dee veered off to the left making a bee line for one of the bathrooms.

CHAPTER 65

Dee Dee was a mess, but determined to oversee the set up of the great room where the reception was to take place. Couches and tables were delivered, while the bar was stocked, and a small platform was constructed for the band. Fortunately, after an hour or so, Dee Dee began to feel a little better, and while the painting began in the living room, she organized where everything should be placed.

Ashley not only helped paint for a while, but she also went out and bought lunch for everyone. A lunch that Dee Dee all but inhaled, making it clear that she was not suffering from the flu as I had feared. Gavin had long since left for work, and after lunch I had to go home to get the kids ready for the rehearsal and dinner. I promised Colleen I would be back no later than four, and began what turned out to be a very long, very warm drive home.

As luck would have it, Meg had refused to nap for Hilary, so she was cranky and unreasonable as I did my best to get her dressed in the outfit I wanted her to wear, and attempted to tame her hair that was going in several directions at once. In contrast, Jack was dead asleep and refused to wake up, while Nick kept fussing and wanting me to hold him. Hilary did her best to distract him, but it was anything but smooth sailing.

Later, when Hilary waved goodbye as I drove off, Meg was yawning, Nick was wailing, and Jack was whining that he was hungry. Although the freeway was moving in the beginning, about six exits from Colleen's it slowed considerably. Looking at the clock, I watched as the minutes ticked away and we became later and later. When we drove up to the house it was four twenty, Meg was asleep, Jack was crying for his daddy, and as usual, Nick had clearly messed his diaper.

Looking at the cars parked in the courtyard styled driveway, I could see that the only one later than me was Gavin. Meg now refused to wake up, and I was sweating as I pulled both Jack and Nick from their car seats. Thankfully, Devon came out to help.

"Hurry," he told me, "Mom is in there planning the next wedding with Ashley."

"I have to admit I liked her, too," I said, handing him Nick.

"Oh, Dude!" he objected, as he took him. "What have you done?"

"You know what, hand him back. I'll take him and you get Meg," I suggested, deciding she might behave better for him and knowing I was going to have to change Nick anyway.

Inside, everyone was gathered in the entry and it reeked of the wet paint to the right. Dee Dee and Colleen were sitting on the steps, while Keith was talking to the priest and his parents. My mom was indeed talking to Ashley. My dad was talking to Dee Dee's boyfriend, Roman.

"It's about time," Colleen said, standing up. "Is Gavin with you? Where is Meg?"

"No, and Dev is getting her," I said, as my dad turned to greet me.

"There's my girl," he smiled, hugging Nick and I both before backing away frowning. "What have you done, little man?" he asked.

Nick smiled and babbled proudly as if he were trying to explain. I took him into the bathroom to change him, but Jack was nervous and refused to let go of me, making it challenging to say the least. While I was dealing with the two of them I heard Meg come inside and snarl at Colleen that she was tired.

We waited another few minutes both to give Meg time to wake up, and for Gavin to arrive. Keith managed to talk Meg and Jack into going outside to check out the play structure they had picked out, but Colleen thought it was a bad idea and she was right. Neither one of them wanted to come back inside.

Gavin continued to be a no show, and when I tried calling him I got no answer, so we decided to start without him. It was getting late and his only role in the wedding was to make sure Meg cooperated while holding onto the boys. Once we had talked Meg and Jack back inside, I forced my mom to hold Nick while we girls all ran upstairs. Jack wanted to come with us, but again Keith stepped up and was able to talk him into staying put. Because we didn't yet have the flower pedals for Meg's basket, Colleen filled her basket with tissues and we said she should wait until she got downstairs to start tossing them. We both quickly decided she should hold onto the railing too when she nearly stumbled on the second step.

I was the next one down, but as I was descending, Meg stomped out of the living room, claiming that it stunk, which in fact it did. Gavin arrived as I was hissing at her to behave and to get back in there, so she fell dramatically into his arms, weeping that it was making her tummy feel sick. He apologized for being late, picked her up, and told her to suck it up for a few minutes at the very least.

Once the rehearsal was over, Meg and Jack wanted to go outside again, so we promised them they could play for a little while before heading over to the restaurant.

"Where were you?" I asked Gavin, as we stood around outside passing Nick back and forth.

"I was reading Sirri Bingingham's outline and the first couple of chapters she's sent me for this new book of hers. I'm sorry, I just got caught up in it."

"Because it's good?"

"We'd hope, wouldn't we? It's actually light years ahead of that last piece of rubbish, but I have to say, it's not as good as I'd like. Certainly more marketable, though."

"Perhaps you've become a literary snob," I suggested.

"Perhaps, but then it's important to have some standards. Hopefully, with some creative editing, this will become another of her bestsellers."

"Hopefully. I'm dreading this dinner. Are you dreading this dinner?" I asked.

"Oh, no," he laughed, sarcastically. "Three small children in a restaurant with a lot of adults is always a treat."

It was anything but, just as we'd both suspected. Jack couldn't sit still to save his life, and Nick was tired of being passed around and needed to be put down. My dad made a toast to Colleen and Keith, and then surprised me by making a toast to me as well for my new contract. A toast that with the help of all that he'd had to drink, went on a little too long, and that I could see was making Colleen bristle. Admittedly, he made it seem as though I was the only one of his children to ever write a book, and his pride, as appreciated as it was, felt a little over the top. I tried reminding him that this was Colleen's dinner and not mine, but he couldn't praise me enough. It became increasingly uncomfortable.

When as we were later leaving Devon pulled me aside to give me his promised gift, I prayed Colleen wouldn't notice. I was thrilled and touched when he presented me with an old fashioned typewriter, much like the one that sat in my dad's den. As kids we had all snuck in to play with it at one time or another. It was the symbol of writing we all loved most.

CHAPTER 66

As crazy as my mother drove me when I was preparing to marry Gavin, the one thing she got right was my wakeup call on the day of the wedding. She and Colleen had snuck into my room, climbed into my bed and hugging me, sang "I'm Getting Married in the Morning!" Then we all squealed and cried, no doubt for a million different reasons, but I'd never felt so connected and loved in my life. It was a shared moment like no other, so when my mother had come over to me at the restaurant and asked me to pick her up the next morning to take Colleen breakfast and our best wishes for a happy marriage, I was all in.

Because Colleen was spending the night at Dee Dee and Roman's house while Keith was staying at their house, I'd warned Dee Dee that we would be arriving around nine. She gave me her spare key, speculating that they would all still be sleeping, and if not, she would probably be throwing up. I asked where Roman's killer dog would be and she promised me she'd keep him in their bedroom and that we would be safe.

The next morning, the kids were up long before nine, but as soon as I had them fed, I told Gavin I was leaving.

"You're jumping the gun a little, don't you think? It's only eight and your mum is staying right down the road."

"I want to stop and get some croissants and fruit, and champagne and orange juice first," I explained.

"Ahh, so you are really just going to get drunk?" he asked.

"Only if necessary. Do you have any money?"

"Yes, in my wallet but don't take it all," he requested.

I was relieved, because I hadn't been sure how I was going to pay for all of that if he hadn't. I grabbed a few twenties, thanked him, and split with him pleading with me not to be gone all day. As I assured him, I couldn't be, because we had a wedding to attend.

On the way to Dee Dee's, my mother said she couldn't believe how lucky she was to be getting another great son in-law.

"And that Ashley," she exclaimed, "she is absolutely perfect for Devon."

"How can you tell?"

"Call it a mother's sixth sense."

"Really? So when my kids meet the right guy or girl, I'll just know it?"

"Well, only if my ability has been passed down to you," she smiled.

"He's only known her since the last time he was home. That's less than two months," I pointed out.

"Time doesn't count. If it's right, it's right and she feels right."

"Well, right or wrong, I guess only time will tell," I speculated.

I was nervous as I put the key to the lock of Dee Dee's front door. I didn't trust her to have kept the dog in her room. As soon as we walked in I heard loud barking and although it was muffled, I only prayed the dog wouldn't break through their door. Colleen came stumbling down the hallway looking sleepy and disturbed as we reached the top of the stairs.

"Get back in bed!" I scolded

"You've come to join me?" she asked, her face lighting up.

"Yes, hurry up before we are all eaten," I said pushing ahead of her to run into the room she'd come from.

"What have you brought?" she asked, as she locked arms with our mom and followed.

"Breakfast in bed, but first we must get into bed," I insisted.

We all hopped in and as I pulled things out of the bag we realized we had no glasses to mix up our mimosas in.

"No problem," my mom insisted, "we'll simply have breakfast first, drink a little orange juice, and then toss some champagne down on top of it."

"Now that sounds like a recipe for disaster," I laughed.

"As is marriage," my mom laughed, "but if you are lucky it will all workout just fine."

"What?" Colleen jolted.

"What, what?" Mom asked.

"What do you mean marriage is a recipe for disaster? I recall Kelly got "I'm Gettin' Married in the Morning" and you are so lucky to be in love, and I get marriage is a recipe for disaster?"

"Oh right, we have to sing!" Mom told me, immediately bursting into song.

"No, stop!" Colleen insisted. "Why is it a disaster?"

"It's not. Not yours. I was merely speaking to the concept. I mean it's rather preposterous, the idea that you'll never love another for the rest of your life, but you and Keith are fine."

"Fine? We're fine?" Colleen balked, looking to me as if wanting me to validate that she was getting a completely different story than I had gotten.

"Marriage is wonderful," I promised. "She didn't mean anything by it."

"Of course I didn't," Mom said, falling back into song. "Ding dong the bells are gonna ring!"

Colleen buried her head in her hands and groaned. Somehow it really wasn't the same feeling of warmth that I had experienced. When we were leaving an hour or so later, Colleen pulled me back and asked if I thought our mother was in love with someone else.

"What?" I choked

"Well why else would she say that about it being absurd to love one person?"

"It was just an observation, relax."

"Based on what though?"

"Who knows, the amount of people who get divorced, but you are fine, remember? Stop worrying."

"Does she know what your book is about? Maybe she meant Dad."

"Colleen, go back inside, get dressed and go to your manicurist. I'll see you out at the house at one. Everything is good. It's a beautiful day, and you love Keith and he loves you. You are going to have a beautiful wedding and a happy life."

"Okay, alright, go so you won't be late," she urged.

"No worries," I smiled.

Then I got in the car and asked my mother why in hell she would have said that.

CHAPTER 67

I returned home to another recipe for disaster in the making.
Gavin had the kids out in the backyard, and while Jack was
attempting to lift a watering can half his size, overflowing with
water, Gavin was on the phone, absentmindedly pushing Meg
on the swing as she did her best to hold onto a squirming Nick.
She let go of the swing to get a better grip and lost her balance,
starting to fall backwards as I screamed at Gavin to grab her.
She wound up dropping Nick, but luckily it was in such a way
that he didn't land too hard and wasn't hurt. Of course he was
plenty upset, as was Meg herself.

Gavin had dropped his phone to try and stop her from falling
and before he could pick it up again Jack had dragged the
watering can over to ask for help, and was splashing water all
over it. Gavin yelled for him to stop while trying to retrieve it,
and Jack threw himself on the ground, kicking and screaming
with frustration that no one would help him. Gavin cursed,
Meg wept and both boys wailed. I wanted to go drown myself in
a nice relaxing bath.

As I had suspected, my mother had claimed not to be thinking anything when she had blurted out that marriage was a recipe for disaster. Then she had gone on to say that she still believed it and that I would be naive not to think the same.

"Should you be blessed to have an enduring marriage, there will be times when it's not all peaches and cream," she told me.

"Sure, but that doesn't mean you don't still love each other."

"There will be moments when you won't," she insisted.

"Okay, fine, but it doesn't mean you will love someone else," I said.

"In a long marriage? It might not be absolute, but men in particular have a tendency to stray."

"Has this got to do with that trip we all took to Italy?" I asked.

"What trip to Italy?" she asked, and I looked at her dumbfounded that she would pretend not to know. "Oh, that trip. Yes, of course, if you must know. That was not a very happy time for us."

"Gee, you don't say. But Dad wasn't in love with that woman, was he?"

"To hear him tell it, he wouldn't know what I was talking about, but of course he was."

"How do you know? I mean, if he denies it," I said.

"It was obvious at the time, and you might as well know, there have been other infatuations and temptations over the years for both of us. It just isn't a perfect science, so to speak, which is not to say that I haven't always loved your father, well, except in some occasional painful moments."

"Okay," I said, not certain how I was supposed to respond.

"So you should be aware of that, because after all you and Gavin have been through, it would be easy, and understandable that he might be feeling taken for granted. You might want to spice things up for a while."

"What?" I laughed.

"Are you having sex on a regular basis, Kelly?" she asked.

"Mom!"

"What? You know what a desirable man he is, and with that yummy accent of his, he could have any girl he wants, any time he wants."

"Ew! Stop it."

"I'm only trying to spare you some of the stress that I have experienced."

"Thanks, now stop talking," I told her.

She hadn't of course. She had continued to go on about how she worries that both Gavin and Keith have many opportunities to cheat on us. Just the sort of thing every girl wants to hear, especially on their wedding day. I pleaded with her not to share anymore with Colleen.

"Well Honey, if I don't warn you girls, who will?" she had defended.

When the kids had settled down, Gavin had determined that his phone still worked, and he'd concluded his call, he informed me it had been Sirri Bingington he'd been talking to.

"She is a lot of work," he sighed. "How was your morning?"

"Oh my God Gavin, my mother is the one who is a lot of work!" I moaned.

"Uh oh, that can't be good," he smiled, rubbing my back. "What's she done now?"

"Besides assure us that marriage is a recipe for disaster?"

"Is it?" he laughed.

I explained all that she'd had to say and he just shook his head, telling me not to let her rattle me because we were fine, and Colleen and Keith would be as well. Knowing that Colleen was understandably nervous, I called Dee Dee and suggested we do our best to serve as buffers between her and my mom, at least until the wedding was over. She promised she would do her best.

CHAPTER 68

Colleen looked more beautiful than I had ever seen her, as she prepared to pose for pictures with her bridesmaids, and of course the most adorable flower girl in the world. Dee Dee and I had so far done a good job of keeping my mother busy and away from Colleen, but now Colleen wanted her to be in a couple of pictures as well. We were in the master bedroom, which featured another gorgeous picture window. The photographer had us all angled so that Colleen was bathed in natural light, but my mother was certain that she would come off looking washed out. We all cringed as she told the photographer how to do her job, and then questioned whether or not Colleen had on more makeup than necessary.

"Gee, I don't know, Mom, have you brought the guidelines with you?" Colleen asked, clearly irritated.

"I'm only trying to protect you. These pictures will haunt you if they aren't as nice as possible."

"I think she looks amazing," I offered.

"The camera loves her," the photographer chimed in.

"Suit yourself, they are your pictures," Mom shrugged.

Once Colleen had posed with each of us individually and in a variety of groups, Mom said she wanted to talk to Colleen in private. Dee Dee and I held our breath as she pulled her deep into the walk-in closet. They emerged five minutes later, just as Keith's mother came in to ask if we were all ready. Colleen said she was extremely ready, and as both mothers left the room, she looked at me and rolled her eyes.

"What did she say?"I asked.

"She was explaining her comment from this morning, and letting me know that Dad has never loved her as much as she has loved him, but that doesn't mean that he isn't the one for her."

"What?"

"Yeah, who is she?"

"Who does that?" Dee Dee asked.

"Our mother," Colleen said.

"You know what," I sighed, "she's crazy, but maybe she is just trying to tell you not to have unrealistic expectations once the honeymoon is over."

"She loves us, right?" Colleen said.

"In her own warped way, she does," I confirmed, as my Dad knocked on the door and came in to walk Colleen to her future.

"You love Mom, right?" she asked him, as he picked up Meg and asked if she was ready to get married.

"Not me silly," Meg giggled. "Colleen."

"The one asking if I love her mother?"

"Yes," Meg nodded.

"She's clearly nuts. Of course I love your mother. Has she told you otherwise?"

"Sort of," Colleen answered.

"She's having some difficulty accepting the passage of time at the moment. I think working on my memoir has brought up some old wounds. Don't worry about it. We're good."

"You might want to tell her that," Colleen suggested.

"I will, but first I have to hand you off to Keith," he smiled, putting Meg down.

From that point on, the wedding went off without a hitch. Meg walked down the stairs like an angelic cherub, sprinkled her rose pedals, and then took her place next to Gavin. Dee Dee and I followed, and not only did neither of us trip, but Dee Dee didn't even throw up. Colleen made the grand entrance of her dreams, and all of her guests oohed and ahhed in response.

I was both relieved, and thrilled that Nick slept through it, and Jack and Meg behaved. Once the priest pronounced them husband and wife, everyone broke out into applause as Keith kissed and dipped Colleen in what could only be described as a cinematic embrace.

There were more photos to be taken before we could ever get to enjoy the reception, and those did not go as smoothly. Meg, who had been so perfect beforehand was suddenly in need of a nap, as was Jack. They both required a lot of prodding and multiple bribes in order to get them to cooperate. Keith as always was the one to get Meg to behave by promising her she and he would cheat and stick their fingers in the cake as soon as the pictures were done. True to his word, and amongst Colleen's objections, they did it too.

Between Corky and Scott, and Devon and Ashley, who did turn out to be Dev's date for the wedding, Gavin and I were given occasional breaks from the kids, and able to dance and enjoy ourselves. Once the cake had been cut, however, it was time to go. The kids were exhausted and so were we. Colleen started out saying that we couldn't leave, but seeing Nick raging, she gave in and thanked me for having stuck it out as long as I had.

It was agreed that Dev was going to have brunch with our parents in the morning and would then come over to our house to hang out for a while after, and then we left. Once in the car, Gavin and I both let out a sigh of relief. Smiling at me, he squeezed my knee.

"Now we can get our lives back, can't we?"

"I certainly hope so."

"This next year is going to be massive, just you wait," he beamed. "It's all going to come together now."

We drove away and I couldn't help but wonder if that was true. I knew we had been through a lot, as my mother had been so quick to point out, and that the ground had nearly been pulled out from under us, and I knew what I needed to do next. I just hoped I could make the book everything that I imagined it could be.

CHAPTER 69

The Chateau Marmont was fabulous. During the first few days that I spent there it was difficult not to be distracted by the ambiance and history of the place. As I sat in my perfect cottage, with it's beautiful furnishings and enticing bedding, I imagined all of the people who'd stayed there before me. The cottages were grouped around a lovely courtyard and accessible by a private entrance. I could only imagine the number of illicit affairs that had taken place among Hollywood's elite. I even enticed Gavin into coming down one afternoon to indulge my fantasy of a passionate rendezvous.

Before I knew it I had squandered the first week with lunches with Corky, rendezvous' with Gavin, and "think" time out by the pool. Although my color was improving, Ben and Callie were still debating his attending that party with Anna. Doing my best to suppress my growing fear that I'd never have this book finished, I vowed to get serious during that second week. I dropped Meg at school, stopped for coffee and drove down to the Marmont, not allowing myself to leave until I had written the next chapter.

As with most things, it didn't go quite as smoothly as I'd hoped, but by five that evening I had finally managed to get Ben to the party, and he was even making the connections he needed to make in order to expose the corruption he had long since suspected. The following day I took up where I had left off, but much to my surprise, Anna began making subtle overtures to Ben that left not only Callie confused, but me as well. I spent the rest of the afternoon out by the pool, replaying every encounter I had ever had with my dad's "assistant" on that family trip to Italy. I was dying to ask my Dad if he'd developed feelings for her, or had felt she'd had feelings for him, but I just couldn't bring myself to go there.

Gavin reasoned that I didn't really want to know and I suspected he was right, but that left me not knowing how to proceed.

"You're pressing," he insisted. "Just let it come to you and don't question it."

"But it's not coming to me," I objected.

"Because you are stopping to question everything your characters are doing. Let them be. If at the end you don't like what they've done, then you go back and rewrite, but this isn't about your dad. This is about three fictional characters."

Gavin's pointing that out changed everything. I realized that I was desperately trying to rewrite the past, and that I had to let it go. Whatever my Dad had or hadn't done was none of my business. Both of my parents had made whatever choices they had made, and those belonged to them. That was in the past and I needed to focus on the present.

Over the next two weeks I wrote all day, every day, and not only did Anna turn out to be falling for Ben, but she withheld information in an effort to get him to remain in Italy longer. As for Ben's father, it turned out he had been dealing with the Italian government not as a coconspirator, but in an effort to expose the same corruption that Ben had uncovered. Lastly, Callie returned home when Ben refused to accept that Anna's motives were anything other than noble. When he eventually discovered that Callie had been right all along he begged her forgiveness.

I agonized over how the book should end. I could go for the fairytale ending, or I could say that in real life you don't always get those. That life is messy and not being believed by the one you love could destroy your trust, thus making it impossible to be together. Again it was Gavin who dictated the ending by reminding me that forgiveness was a choice. I decided that in this instance, since Ben hadn't partaken in what Anna had offered, it could have been as simple as love being blind. At least that was the story he gave Callie. He told her that his love for her had made it impossible to see Anna as anything other than a fellow journalist helping him with his investigation, and she chose to believe him. I ended the book on an up note, held my breath, and allowed both Corky and Gavin to read it before sending it off to Anthea.

Gavin finished it first, and other than a few notes on the relationship between Ben and his father, said it was everything that he had hoped it would be. Corky read it and said love isn't blind, and that Callie and Ben shouldn't get back together.

"You and Scott got back together," I pointed out.

"Sure, but that doesn't make it right," she laughed.

We were at the Chateau cottage, enjoying the pool, just me, Gavin, Corky and Scott when she made this pronouncement.

"Are you kidding me?" Scott demanded.

"Well, you don't know what the future holds," she insisted.

"Because no one knows what the future holds," he told her.

"Maybe, but at the very least Callie shouldn't just take him back. She should take some time to think about it."

"To torture him?" Scott asked.

"Whatever is necessary," she laughed.

At that moment Scott got up, and walked back to the cottage, while Corky and I debated whether or not he was now mad at her. He returned a minute later with a small velvet box in his hand and knelt down before her.

"I was going to wait until tonight, but although I might not know what the future holds, I know that I want to spend it with you, so please, say you'll be my wife," he proposed.

"Oh my God," Corky cried.

"Oh my God, yes?" he encouraged.

"Oh my God, are you sure?" she asked.

"Yes," he laughed, "I'm down here on my knee, holding a diamond ring."

"Yes," she cried.

Scott put the ring on her finger and Gavin leaned over and whispered in my ear that he hadn't seen that coming. Corky and Scott kissed and then Corky asked if I was ready to plan another wedding.

"Not even close," I laughed.

"We'll have to have a long engagement," she told Scott.

Now the book is in the hands of my editor and I am left wondering what the future will bring. I look at the success Colleen has had and wonder if I could handle the same. I think back on the past several months, and I am happy just to have survived. Gavin and I are good, the kids are good, and Corky and Scott are good. Keith and Colleen are back from their honeymoon and good. My parents are good and Devon is good. I have managed to regain my balance and for all of this I am extremely grateful. Here's hoping I can keep it!

This is Bridget Straub's fifth published novel.

Also available in paperback and Kindle:

Searching For My Wand

On a Hot August Afternoon

The Salacious Marny Ottwiler

Crashing Into Us

www.ingramcontent.com/pod-product-compliance
Lightning Source LLC
Chambersburg PA
CBHW061302170626
46817CB00001B/17